Days of the High Morning Moon

Howard Johnson

To order additional copies of this book, contact:

Senesis Word

904-687-1865 - 579-265-3386 Cell

Website: www.HJwriter.com (Not yet active)

Email: Senesisword@yahoo.com

DHMM-txtAll-17707N   90,950 words Acrit OK

The cover:

In the folklore of some native American Algonkians, there is a belief that the five days when the moon is high in the sky near mid morning, are days of big troubles. This moon is called **Wakiapah Tibik-kìzis** in the local Algonquian dialect. This translates roughly into **High Morning Moon**. The danger rises with the gibbous moon, two days before the half moon of the third quarter and continues for the two days after. During this period, the worst day is the middle one when the half moon stands at the zenith at sunrise. Many researchers think this belief originated around women's menstrual period. During these days, believers will not plant any crops, hunt, fight wars, or conduct any business. They will, however, defend themselves if attacked.

The story begins around labor day in modern times during these days when the morning moon rides high. Its locale is in an area of Indiana rich in the lore and history of the Algonquian tribes, mainly Miami and Potawatomi. These tribes were among those driven out of the east shortly after Europeans began arriving. They were not driven out by Europeans, but rather by the Iroquois nations who saw them as competitors for trade with the Europeans as well as food and game.

It was much later, almost two hundred years, that the Americans plundered the Algonkians of their lands in violation of promises made in many treaties often abrogated soon after the ink was dry. The Americans drove them out of Ohio, Indiana, Michigan and Illinois. Many died of European diseases or starvation during these forced marches. Much of this happened soon after the war of 1812 when many tribes had joined with the British to fight the Americans. Long after the forced transfer to reservations, many of the Miami, Wea, Plankeshaw, Potawatomi, Wyandot, and even the Delaware and Kickapoo returned to their ancestral homes in those states. Some have also reestablished tribal organizations.

The photo of the moon was taken by Howard Johnson on October 16, 2011, the first of the five days of the high morning moon. The photo was taken from the lanai of the room he and his beautiful lady Daphne enjoyed at the Hale Koa hotel on Waikiki. The story was started while they were in Hawaii on one of their many trips together.

Books by Howard Johnson - year of publication

Blue Shift - 2002 - An Armageddon type novel about people dealing with a rapidly moving star that will pass through our solar system in thirty years. The star's passing and possible annihilation of life on Earth is a menace man can do nothing to prevent or change. The main characters battle with government agents and others to ensure the danger is portrayed accurately when the information is released to the public.

Energy, Convenient Solutions - 2010 - A non fiction book on energy, its history, sources, uses, and possible future technologies. It is written for average Americans, not skilled technicians and scientists. It looks at everything related to energy production, transport, and use. It gives attention to the real effects of increased atmospheric CO_2.

Starring - 2012 - An anthology of the author's short work, mostly Science Fiction written between 2002 and 2012 offer a variety of fiction stories that take place on Earth, and other planets near and far. Some even involve other universes. Many describe and interact with strange alien life forms.

The Crystal Feather - 2012 - The author's second SciFi novel is different from the first and won first place in the FWA Lighthouse novel contest in 2008. Dr. Draxel Syl has a wild, off-Earth adventure with a drop-dead gorgeous lady named Leura Clauson. He wonders about trying to learn what happened, who Leura actually is, and what these strange happenings can be. He ends up involved with two different related human species from two universes.

Climate and Much Worse Dangers We Ignore - 2014 - This publication is a collection of Howard Johnson's commentary on Global warming/climate change from 2005 to the present. It includes some commentary from other individuals and remarks about other possible menaces to our planet. Mr. Johnson, says about this book: "This controversial book is quite the opposite of Al Gore's *An Inconvenient Truth*. Al's book had little truth of any kind in its pages."

Memoirs from the Lakeside II - 2015 - This is a collection of memoirs from a long and varied life that replaces several earlier editions. This large book contains more than 90 memoirs, stories from the author's experiences from the early 1930s to the present and a number of essays, letters, poetry and commentary from varied sources of general interest. There are quotes, mostly one liners, from 270 famous and not so famous individuals dating as far back as before the Christian era, favorites saved over a lifetime. It's a terrific coffee table book.

Sahm' Allah (the Arrow of Allah) in St. Augustine - 2016 - This is an action adventure thriller that involves three protagonists in three different and seemingly unconnected adventures that only come together in the last chapters. The lead characters include, Calder Voss, a geothermal engineer, Brooks McKibben, a child prodigy/computer genius, and Carol Mitchell, a Florida business woman who takes on an unusual role. Each of the three protagonists experiences their own different adventures in their conflict with the same mysterious group of antagonists. There are some unusual romances for several of the main characters, some great dangers and exciting adventures.

Double Jeopardy - 2016 - The second book of the *Blue Shift* trilogy, starts several months before the end of the first book, with a slightly different cast of characters. Dr. Charlie Botkin, from Cal Tech, one of the world's top authorities on high energy physics is asked for help in determining what the effects of the star's passing so close to the Earth might be. Working with the original group from Gemini, Crazy Charlie helps in their effort to keep the public calm. Armed with increasingly accurate projections of the path and possible effects of the ghost star, Charlie predicts there is a good chance it will pass with little or no effect on the Earth. In the midst of this, a new menace appears as a large asteroid is on a collision course with Earth. International cooperation on an unprecedented scale is organized to try to solve this unexpected new cataclysmic danger. The book ends right after the Ghost passes Bernard's Star, four years before it passes Earth.

DEDICATION

I dedicate this book to the memory of my dear friend, Frances Stelling.

During the last few years, Frances frequently sat next to me in meetings of the COA writers group where she often read interesting memoirs she had written. She urged and inspired me to put together a book about the relationships with the fantastic ladies who were so important in my life.

When I completed the first version of *Days of the High Morning Moon*, she offered to critique it for me. The result was a comprehensive, in depth and most valuable document which I used to greatly improve the quality of my writing of the book. She also carefully marked the book itself with corrections and suggestions. I agreed with and made many of the changes she suggested in a careful rewrite mixing her suggestions with my own ideas. I wrote a long letter of thanks and appreciation for her thoughtful effort. Sadly, she passed away before seeing the letter. She will be sorely missed.

CONTENTS

Prologue - A Serious Happening
✳ Labor Day, September 3, 2012, 5:05am ✳

Deputy Gordon Genoa of the Kosciusko County Sheriff's Department was headed north on State Road 15 toward Milford when the call came in from his dispatcher, Ellen Cross.

"What? . . . A badly injured woman. . . . On the beach at the Tippy Dance Hall. . . . I should be there in less than eight minutes."

He flipped on his flashers, took a right at the funeral home on 900 N and headed for the dance hall some eight miles away. The early morning of Labor Day was cool and clear. Dawn would come with a waning moon rising high in the eastern sky. Ellen reported an EMS vehicle was also en route but he would be there first. The Indiana State Police had been notified, but their nearest available unit was nearly half an hour away. She continued giving him the information she had. Early in the morning, two young boys found her near their boat as they were going out fishing.

East on E 900 N, a hard right turn on 300 E, a run due south on the curvy road through the woods past Lake Oswego, a sharp left over the Tippecanoe River onto Armstrong Road and through the sleepy little town of Oswego, another left through the old brick gateway that used to be called Cripplegate, down the short narrow road to the dance hall parking lot, and he was there. Driving as fast as was safe, he made the trip in a bit more than six minutes.

There was a small group of people and one car with headlights turned on at the edge of the lake at the far northwest corner of the parking lot. He drove right up to the shore with headlights illuminating the scene, stepped out and trotted over to the group surrounding the woman. She was lying on a blanket and covered with another someone had provided. A woman was kneeling, holding a bloody compress against her head and trying to comfort the injured woman. The victim's face was a bloody mess. She had been badly beaten and cut up some. His quick examination determined all the blood was coming from her face. Most came from a nasty slice extending from the right side of her chin, up in front of her ear and clear across her head. The cut across her head was quite deep and bleeding profusely. He found no other deep wounds or heavy bleeding elsewhere. He contacted Ellen and reported his findings.

"What's your name?" he asked the woman kneeling by the injured woman.

"Annabel, Annabel Rheem. I'm the mother of the boys who found her. They were frightened to death but ran right home and got us. My husband immediately called 911."

"You all certainly did the right thing. They are good boys. Did they tell you what they saw when they found her?"

"They were headed out fishing. That's our boat right there on the beach. She was crawling up the beach on her hands and knees. Stark naked she was and so bloody. Both boys were crying and terribly frightened. I called the neighbors here and we brought some blankets for her to lie on and to cover her up and keep her warm. Lois, our neighbor brought us this compress we used to try to stop the bleeding."

"You did good. An EMS is coming within the next few minutes. Since we cannot find any other serious wounds, we'll try to stop the bleeding as much as we can until EMS is here. Did she say anything? Anything at all?"

"The poor thing mumbled something we couldn't understand when we moved her onto the blanket and covered her up. She was shivering so terribly, shaking so hard we could hardly keep the blanket on her. Harold went in to fix something warm for her to drink. She's so young. Will she be okay?"

The siren of the ambulance announced the emergency medical team would soon be on the scene.

"That's the EMS now. They can possibly answer your question," Deputy Genoa said.

The deputy marked off the crime scene and shooed everyone away. He let Annabel stay with the injured woman. "Everyone move back please. Could someone move that car so EMS has room to do their work?"

He had parked his cruiser so there was plenty of room. Someone moved the car almost immediately, and the EMS arrived. Within a few minutes the medics were doing their thing. Once they determined she could be moved, two of them brought out the Gurney, fastened her on board, and put her into the ambulance. The medics would do what they could to stabilize her on the way to Kosciusko Community Hospital twelve miles away. A deputy would be at the hospital to question her when the doctors would allow him.

As Deputy Genoa finished securing the area around where she was found, he turned to the group of seven neighbors. "Did any of you hear or see anything?"

One man stepped forward. "I heard the motor of a powerboat, a loud, powerful V8 motor. Woke me up. Hearing that kind of boat so early in the day is unusual, and taking off fast too. No one is supposed to go fast at this time of day before sunup. Without the moon rising, you can't see nothin' on the lake."

"I heard the same boat," Annabel said. "About the time I was waking the boys up to go fishing. They do love to fish. I hope this doesn't make them afraid to go fishing. I need to tend to them. May I go, officer?"

"Go ahead. I will talk with you and your boys later. Please try to remember what she mumbled to you. It could be important."

Deputy Genoa talked to the rest of the neighbors, but other than the motor, no one heard or saw anything. They were all asleep. He examined and photographed the area. The only thing he found was the path in the sand and gravel where the young lady had crawled out of the lake, up the beach and onto the parking lot. There was a lot of blood. Once he had marked off the area with yellow, crime-scene tape, he headed over to the Rheem house.

"Mr. Rheem? I'm Kosciusko Sheriff's Deputy, Gordon Genoa. May I come in?"

"Certainly, deputy, we've been expecting you. That poor girl. Is she going to be all right? She was so badly beaten, and that cut was terrible. Who could do such a thing?"

"I hope she will be okay. That's in the good hands of the doctors at KCH now. My job is to find out what happened and who might be responsible."

"We'll help any way we can," Harold Rheem offered.

"I'm going to want to talk to your boys soon. How are they doing?"

"They're still frightened and upset. I'll try to get them to talk to you."

"Before you do, I want you to tell me everything they said to you—everything—every word. I'll be asking your wife the same thing. What you remember and tell me could be significant."

"I'll do my best, but Annabel heard a lot more than I did. She was awake when they came in. I was sound asleep. All I remember was Donnie screaming, 'There's a hurt lady on the beach. She's got no clothes on.' over and over. That woke me up. Timmie, the older boy was so scared he couldn't talk, just pointed to the beach. I grabbed my robe as did Annabel, and we ran out to the beach and found her. Annabel wrapped her in a blanket she grabbed off our bed as we ran out. That's when I ran back in the house and called 911. On the way I saw our neighbor and asked her to take out something to try to stop all the bleeding. One of the neighbors moved his car so his head lights let us see. Annabel was trying to talk to her while I ran in to fix something hot for her. She was shivering, shaking terribly, even after we put that heavy blanket on her, and so much blood. I was afraid she'd bleed to death. While I was fixing cocoa, you drove up, that's all."

"Did you hear her say anything?"

"No. I wasn't there long before I ran inside to fix the cocoa. She never got a chance to drink my cocoa."

Annabel could add little to what she told him earlier. She thought what she heard her mumble sounded like "wall" or "mall" and she repeated the same word several times.

Deputy Genoa was gentle with the boys. His own son was six and he was a good father, a gentle man. Timmie was so traumatized by the event he couldn't speak of it. He seemed to be in shock. Donnie was another story. He had lots to say, mostly about all the blood and that she was "Totally naked."

Donnie also said. "She kept saying 'Water, water.' and never even looked at me when I asked her what was wrong. She kept crawling up the beach saying, 'Water, water.' Then I ran to get Mom."

After Deputy Genoa learned all he thought he was going to learn and had recorded the names, addresses, and phone numbers of all the people who had gathered, he prepared to leave. His radio stopped him. Eric Blanding, the deputy at the hospital, was trying to contact him.

"Gordy, I've called Captain Yoder. He lives close by."

"I'll hold down the fort until he's here," He knew why immediately. "She's that bad?"

"She's in bad shape and has not regained consciousness. The doctors found she lost a lot of blood. That was definitely a knife inflicted wound. Doc says someone tried to cut her throat, but missed, possibly because she tried to escape. The cut is deep enough that she has lost a lot of blood. The examining physicians discovered she is pregnant, about six weeks. Why she has not aborted because of the beating is nothing short of a miracle. Of course, she still could. They also found she had sex recently. Her assailant obviously raped her. She is in critical condition in the intensive care section of the hospital. The doctor in charge told me she might not live. If that happens, it's a murder case."

"That's why they called Ragan. They want him on the case as early as possible."

"As soon as I reported the doctors didn't expect her to live, they asked me to call Ragan. He said he would be at the scene in fifteen minutes. If the doctors decide Jane Doe might make it, they will consider an air transfer to a hospital in Indianapolis where she could receive more specific treatment. Otherwise she will probably go to the coroner as a homicide victim. Oh yes, she is still a Jane Doe."

"Thanks Eric. I expect you'll contact me if anything changes. I hope she comes through okay. She's so young, no more than seventeen or eighteen is my guess. I especially hate when we deal with young kids like her."

He walked back to the Rheem's house and spoke to them. "Our homicide investigator, Captain Ragan Yoder will be here shortly. He will examine the crime scene and probably ask you some of the same questions I did. Ragan is a retired Chicago homicide detective who moved back here where he grew up after he retired from the Chicago police. He helps us out on especially tough cases, loves a challenge. This one's right up his alley. I'll be in my car till Ragan is here in case you think of anything you forgot to mention to me. While we're waiting, please rethink about what happened. Try to remember anything you think of but forgot to mention, even the smallest thing could be important."

ONE

I was about to head out on the lake with my fly rod for a couple of hours of relaxation when the damned phone rang. At this time of day a call couldn't be social so I anticipated a problem when I answered the phone.

"That you, Ragan?" a familiar male voice asked.

"Yes, Eric. I don't suppose this is a social call. You will probably take me away from my bass fishing which will now be out for the morning."

"Only if you decide to follow up."

"And what would I be following up?

"A young woman crawled up on the beach at the Tippy dance hall about an hour ago. She was stark naked and had been beaten and cut badly. She's at KCH and the doctors think she might not live. She is comatose and had no ID of any kind, so she's a Jane Doe."

"Damn. I was going to try out a new bass fly I tied this morning. Today is perfect, quiet and bright. Oh well, I suppose I can amble over to the dance hall. I assume an officer is there now?"

"Gordy's waiting for you. I told him I was going to call you since you will probably end up being called anyway. I'm sure you would rather start early."

"Tell him I'll be there in fifteen minutes. Give me all your info about the girl."

"Okay, Ragan."

When Eric finished giving me all he knew about the girl, I checked the clock. The hands were at six-thirty. I replaced my bass rod on the hooks above the door, and dropped my fly box with my new bass flies into the pocket of my fishing jacket. Taking one last regret-filled glance at the glassy surface of the lake, I saw several circles where my finny adversaries were chasing minnows at the surface. *You guys must wait till I return,* I said under my breath as I gazed longingly at the mirror reflection of the opposite shore. I turned, grabbed my camera, my netbook, my case of forensic magic, and headed for

6

my old pickup. I knew the sun wouldn't be peeking through the trees on the eastern horizon for the next half hour. Still, the early light was enough to see by. The high morning moon was almost at the zenith as I rolled my little, red pickup out to Kalorama Road. My Algonkian ancestors believed the moon indicated an evil time for five days. This time their belief was right on the mark.

My pickup was not an ordinary Chevy S10. The original engine, transmission, rear end, and suspension are long gone along with several other items. In their place is a state-of-the-art, LS1 V8 from a 1996 Z28 Camaro. This engine was coupled with a five speed manual transmission, a sturdier rear end, a GM S-truck Extreme Sport Suspension, and all the necessary cooling and exhaust additions. This nearly triples the horsepower and makes this S10 a completely different vehicle—a fire breathing little monster in disguise. Another Chicago cop, a good friend, joined his brother in a hot rod shop in Hammond Indiana after he retired. They did the swap for me. Their shop specializes in engine swaps and is among the tops in the business. Later, when I started working with the local police and sheriff, they installed a hidden interceptor light bar with the usual red and blue flashing lights, "In case you ever need it," my friends told me. Except for the power, the handling, the light bar, and the sound you would take my little truck to be an ordinary S10.

I revel driving this machine as I head north on Kalorama Road, climb the hill and traverse the usually busy space between the country club building and the pro shop. The winding road takes me right through the golf course where I caddied as a kid. In the dim first light of dawn, a few early birds are already heading for the first tee.

At the top of the hill between the 18th and the 13th tee, I turn left onto 750 N where I can finally loosen the reigns a bit on my frisky truck. A left onto 300 E, a drive through the woods past Oswego Lake, and I follow the same route Gordy took a bit earlier. He's waiting as I pull up next to his car.

"Hello, you old fart," he says holding out his hand. I've known Gordy since he was a baby, literally. Many years ago his dad and I played on the same Warsaw high basketball team that made the state finals.

I took his hand and grinned as we headed down to the beach. "That's not a professional greeting for an officer of the law, kid."

"And when did you become a stickler on protocol between us?"

"Touché. What about her? Do we have anything at all that Eric didn't fill me in on?"

"Probably nothing. She had no ID of any kind. No clothing, not even panty hose. No jewelry. She crawled out of the lake carrying just what she came into the world with. It's far too early for a missing person report to be prepared. She's a real Jane Doe. I talked with everyone I saw here including the boys who found her. None of them recognized her."

"Eric told me the doctors put her age as between seventeen and twenty. Also, she's about two months pregnant and was probably sexually assaulted by the same man or men who beat and cut her. They found fresh semen in her vagina. A sample will go to the lab for DNA testing."

"Yeah, Eric gave me the same report."

"I've seen some nasty murders over the years, but something about teen age girls being savaged boils my blood. I hope we can catch the slob who did this."

"I'll certainly a-men that."

"After I check out the spot where she crawled ashore I'd like to speak to the people who found and helped her."

"I told them you would be talking with them and asked them to try and remember anything they could, no matter how trivial. The boys that found her are special cases. The older boy, Timmie is ten. He was so traumatized he can't even talk, or couldn't at the time. Donnie, eight, will talk your arm off. I think those are simply their individual ways of dealing with the situation."

"I'm sure. . . . I can tell where she crawled up on the shore. Look at the trail of blood. She certainly lost a lot considering she probably lost the most blood in the water. I wonder how long she was swimming?"

Although there wasn't much to photograph, I took several photos of her path out of the water and of the bloody spot where she stopped. I wondered and asked, "Has anyone gone into the water where she came out?"

"No. We'll need a diver for that. The bottom drops off steeply about twenty feet from shore. Should I call Skip?"

"Might as well, in case she dropped something. It's not likely, but you never know."

While Gordy was calling Skip, I tried to put together a scenario from the few bits of information we had. Obviously, the man who had sex with her raped her. He beat her badly before raping her. Probably the rape took place out in the lake on a power boat with a big V8 engine, the one those people heard. At first the strange injury made no sense. I couldn't figure how the cut was inflicted, a shallow cut on her chin and up past her ear, and a deeper cut clear across her skull. Inflicting such a wound would be extremely difficult. In one of those wonderful *aha* moments, I knew how it happened, why the cut was so strange.

"Skip's over on Chapman Lake searching for a lost outboard motor. He says he can be here in about an hour," Gordy reported.

"Good. Let's go talk to the folks you spoke to. They may remember something they didn't earlier. I'm not questioning your interviews. A new face, a slightly different approach, might trigger a new memory."

"Come on, Ragan, you surely remember I've been a law officer for the last ten years? I understand that."

"Yes, I should, shouldn't I? Consider that a senior moment."

Gordy guided us to the porch of a nearby white cottage and knocked on the door to the Rheem's house.

Harold came to the door. "Come in officers. I'm Harold and this is Annabel. I assume you are Captain Yoder. Deputy Genoa explained you would be coming here."

Ragan was good at putting people at ease in tense situations. He carefully observed their place. "Your home is quite lovely here, much more than a summer place."

Annabel smiled with pride. "Yes, this was a summer cottage my parents built many years ago. When the boys were babies, Harold took a job with Da-Lite in Warsaw. Three years ago we bought their cottage and converted it into a year round home. We love living on the lake."

"I do as well. All my years in Chicago I visited Tippy when I could and took many vacations here. When I retired, I bought a place across the lake on Kalorama Road about a mile from the country club. That was about the same time as when you moved in here. . . . Why don't we all sit, if that's okay with you folks."

We men were soon seated around an old, well preserved table in the front room. Annabel stood by the doorway to the back of the house and instantly became a hostess. "I'm sorry. I should offer you seats. Would you like a cup of coffee, or something else to drink?"

I looked at Annabel. "A cup of coffee would be wonderful. I like mine black."

After everyone expressed their preferences, she disappeared into the kitchen.

"Harold, are you a fisherman?" I asked.

"Used to be, but I've been so busy at work and with taking care of the place, I didn't fish much for several years. My boys fish a lot though. They were heading out fishing when they found the poor girl."

"That may be something I could use to reach the older boy. Officer Gordon briefed me on all you told him. After we are through with our initial talk, I'd like to try talking to your boys. I understand Timmie is terribly upset about what he saw. That's certainly understandable. I'd like to try getting through to him. Being in civilian clothes, especially in my fishin' clothes, may make me a bit less intimidating than those in uniforms, especially sheriff's uniforms."

"I'll call him for you."

"Not yet. I must ask the two of you a few questions to confirm what Deputy Genoa told me. Incidentally, Deputy Genoa has known me all of his life. His dad and I were friends from high school. We never lost touch over the years."

Harold was relaxing as Annabel brought our coffee. We talked for about fifteen minutes, confirming what Gordy told me. I didn't learn anything new.

"Where are your boys now?"

Annabel stiffened in her chair. "They're back in their room playing computer games. I thought it would be a good idea to try taking their minds away from that terrible scene."

TWO

✳ Labor Day, September 3, 2012, 7:00 am ✳

I sat back in the chair and tried being as relaxed as possible. "I'd like to speak to them in their rooms, a more relaxing place. I would like you not to mention I am a policeman. Tell them I'm a fisherman who lives on the lake and wants to talk to them, fisherman to fisherman, and show them something, something they will like. That is true, you know," I drew the box of bass flies out of my jacket pocket and set them on the table. "Tied these myself, mostly out of deer hair. Do either of the boys use a fly rod?"

"We bought Timmie one for last Christmas, but he hasn't learned how to use it yet. Not as far as I know. I never learned how so I couldn't teach him."

"Well now, that could provide the opening I need to reach him."

I turned to Gordon. "Do you suppose you and your cruiser could disappear for a while? I'd like to lower the level of tension on the boys."

Gordy grinned broadly. "Sure, Captain. I will leave the scene in your capable hands and resume my usual duties."

"Come on, Gordy. Aren't you being a bit over dramatic? Don't take him too seriously, folks. He's been poking fun at me since he was a kid."

As Gordy drove off, I turned to the Rheems. "I'd like to talk to your boys now. As I said, introduce me as a fisherman from the lake."

Annabel stood up. "That may seem a bit strange to them right now. They might be suspicious."

"Let me handle that, Mrs. Rheem. I can dispel their suspicions quite easily, as long as they think I'm a civilian."

"If you're sure. Right this way."

As I entered the room with their mother, both boys stood. "This is Mr. Yoder, boys. He's been fishing Tippy for many years and wants to talk with you."

11

I sat down on the bed, mainly so I would be closer to their eye level. "What do you boys usually fish for? Also, which one of you is the best fisherman?"

That brought a couple of guarded giggles from the boys, but no conversation.

"Timmie, I understand from your Dad that you own a new fly rod. Tried it out yet?"

Donnie answered for him. "He hasn't, not once. He's afraid he'll break it and upset Dad."

"I am not afraid and I won't break it," Timmie said sharply to his brother. He turned to me. "He's upset because he didn't get one."

"I am not."

"How old are you, Donnie?"

"Eight."

"And, how old is Timmie?"

"Ten."

"It's usual for parents to give a gift to an older child first. Gifts like fly rods require levels of skill and training. I'll bet your folks will give you a fly rod if your brother starts using his, and becomes a fly fisherman. I'll also bet they won't if Timmie never uses his. That rod will stay stored in the case. By the way, where is your fly rod?"

"In a tube on the porch with the other fishing rods," Timmie said. "The reel and line are still in the box they came in along with an assortment of flies. Dad told me he would try to find someone to teach me how to fly fish. Is that you, Mr. Yoder?"

"You bet. Timmie. Let me show you something," I reached into my jacket pocket and took out my box of bass flies. "Take a gander at these bass flies. Tied every one of them my self. Tying flies is one of my hobbies. I've been tying flies since I was about your age."

"Wow, you made those? How'd you learn to do that?"

I went through the flies with both boys showing them the difference between *wet* and *dry* flies, and explaining the different techniques of fishing them. In a short time we were fishing buddies.

"Now, how about we put your fly rod together, load the line, and go out and fish?"

Both boys jumped up, smiling and enthusiastic. "Lets go," they said.

Half an hour later, we were all out on their pier. I held Timmie's fly rod, now with reel, line and tiny dry fly in my right hand. Several overhead swings of the rod and the tiny fly dropped lightly on the surface fifty feet out.

"You try, Timmie," I said.

Fly fishing is quite easy once you learn the knack of lifting the rod sharply, smoothly rolling the line back over your head, guiding the line swiftly forward, and dropping it softly on the surface in front of you. In less than an hour of practice with instructions, Timmie was laying the fly quite smoothly onto the surface. I even let Donnie try, but the two-year difference in their ages showed in Donnie's impatience. Some time would pass before he could be ready.

I sent Timmie out near the end of the pier. "Now, let's try to catch some fish."

I explained and demonstrated how to make the dry fly move in the surface like a real insect. I had Timmie drop the fly near some lilly pads. Two small flicks of the tip, a swirl of the surface, and the fly disappeared. Instinctively Timmie set the hook. After a short furious battle, a beautiful sunfish was taken, unhooked, and released. Timmie's face told me a new fly fisherman was being born. Timmie was hooked.

By eight o'clock we were back on the porch and I was finishing teaching a few more of the basics of fly fishing. I promised I would introduce Timmie to fly fishing for bass when he had mastered catching pan fish. I also promised Donnie I would do the same for him when he was ready if he would be patient. The boys were both relaxed and talking freely with me. I decided to try to speak with them about the incident with the young lady.

"Boys, I would like for you to help me out with a problem I am working on. Would you do that, help me?"

They looked at each other. Timmie spoke. "Sure, Mr. Yoder, how can we help?"

Donnie agreed. "What can we do?"

"First of all, I'm a fisherman. I fished Tippy and other lakes for more than fifty years. Fly fishing is my favorite hobby. I also have a job. Are you clear about the difference between a hobby and a job?"

"You are paid for a job," Timmie answered. "A hobby is something you do for fun, right?"

"Very good. Donnie, do you understand the difference?"

"My Dad works for Da-Lite Screen. That's his job. My mom makes quilts. That's her hobby. She doesn't get a pay check."

I had to laugh at that. "Well, my job, my real job for the last forty years has been to search out and find bad people, some of them are really bad. I've been an investigator. Do you understand what the word means?"

"Yeah, I've seen investigators on some of those TV programs. Aren't they policemen?"

"Not always, and not like ordinary policemen. Investigators try to solve crimes, major crimes, and put bad people in jail. They are part of many teams who work hard to protect people like you and your parents. Protect them from those few bad people, criminals who do terrible things. Do you understand that?"

I realized Timmie was beginning to tense up. "Timmie, if I asked you to help me find a bad person if all you had to do was answer some questions, would you answer my questions?"

I could tell he was fidgeting and getting apprehensive. "I don't know. Are you talking about what happened this morning?"

"Yes. Can we talk about what happened this morning? I need your help. Someone did terrible things to the lady, they hurt her seriously. Did you realize she is just a few years older than you are? Would you talk to me about what you saw and heard? One little word could help me find those people who hurt her. We could talk in a closed room with no one else present if you want."

I waited as Timmie wrestled with his fears. Finally, he spoke. "Didn't Donnie tell you everything? We were together."

"Timmie, over years of experience, I learned that different people usually see the same event differently, even those in the same family. Yes, Donnie told us what he saw and heard. I would certainly appreciate hearing what you saw and heard, in your words. Your description could be helpful."

"I don't want to talk about it."

"I tell you man to man, one thing I learned through the years deals with exactly how you are feeling. Those who are most troubled by any experience, as you are, often feel much better, are much relieved, once they open up and talk. Talking won't bother you nearly as much when you've shared with someone you trust, that I can guarantee."

"One thing."

"What's that?"

"Donnie's wrong about what she was saying. It wasn't *water*, it was a name, *Walter*. I heard her say *Walter* several times, clear as a bell. I also heard her say *help me* a couple of times."

"Timmie, that's a huge help. I now have a name, a man's name."

Once Timmie started, his fears seemed to subside. I talked with him for nearly an hour, but didn't learn much else.

When we were finished and I was about to leave, Timmie took hold of my hand and looked up at me. "Mr. Yoder?"

"Yes, Timmie."

"You were right. I feel much better since we talked. I saw terrible things, but now I can think about them without being so scared. I hope that poor lady recovers."

"Thanks, Timmie. I too hope she recovers. Don't forget, when you learn more how to use your fly rod, we'll go bass fishing. I'll take you in my boat." The smile I received was worth all the effort and more.

I was quite certain I had learned all I was going to from the Rheems. I had a few more words with them and headed outside. Skip Miller and his crew were examining the marked off location. He was still in his wet suit

"Mornin', Captain Yoder."

"Good morning, Skip. You're all ready."

"I had suited up and was checking my gear when Gordy called. I hadn't entered the water because it was still too dark to work. I can go back to search for the motor later. The search here is a much higher priority."

"Are you familiar with this part of Tippy?"

"The last time I dived here was a number of years ago, but things don't change much under water. The water here is quite deep, about sixty feet between this bank and the point on the other side of the channel."

"She came ashore right there." I said, pointing. "My guess is she swam to the nearest shore so you should probably concentrate your search straight out from this spot."

"Anything in particular I should hunt for? I'll bet there's lots of junk on the bottom. This is a busy part of the lake."

"Anything, anything even a little out of the ordinary. What you pick up must also be fresh—dropped early this morning."

"That makes things easy. Anything that recent would not be even lightly covered with dirt settled out. By the way, this will take some time. I'm guessing a couple of hours so I'll need to come up for another air bottle once, maybe twice."

"I think I'll head over to KCH and find out if anything has been missed. I'll be back here around eleven."

"We should be finished by then. Oh yes. I will photograph everything that might be relevant before I pick it up."

"Sounds like you've done this before," I said with a broad grin.

Skip chuckled. "Naw! This is my first try. . . . I should be finished no later than eleven, unless we run into a problem.

THREE

Ray Walters and Al Jonas were seated at the table in Al's trailer in a trailer park east of Indianapolis. It was early evening on Saturday before Labor Day. Several boxes containing the remains of their Chinese dinner were on the sink. A map of Kosciusko County a hundred and twenty miles north of their location was spread out on the table.

Ray had been in trouble most of his life, from getting into fights with other boys to petty thefts and muggings. As an adult he grew into strong arm robberies, mostly of women. He spent three years of jail time for beating and robbing a fifty-six-year-old woman in a shopping center parking lot. He was drunk at the time and claims he remembered none of what he was charged with. All the woman had was $36. Ray was not a nice person, especially when he was drunk, which was often

Al was in many ways the opposite of Ray. He was a smaller, skinnier, much less physically violent man than Ray. A conniver, he used wits rather than brawn to escape difficult situations. He was the balancing brains of the pair to Ray's often unthinking brawn. Al had rescued Ray from difficulty several times by smoothly talking him into backing off from a potential conflict. Once he talked a cop into releasing him when he was being arrested.

Al was pointing out the route to their destination.

"We leave tomorrow afternoon about two and end up taking SR 13 from Wabash to past US 30 and Pierceton. Then we go about eight miles further and turn left here at the second traffic signal after US 30. That's Armstrong Road. We drive west about eight miles and, well, then we make lots of money. I used the Internet to check out the place we're gonna hit, a huge brick house, the biggest and only white brick house on the southwest side of the lake."

"How can you be sure they'll be gone?"

"That's easy. I am connected with an old buddy who works for an international travel company. For a price, he gives me tips on which wealthy people are going on long trips and leaving their homes empty. That's how I knew when and how to hit those two small jobs we did recently. The folks who own this house will be in Spain for three weeks. The place will be deserted."

"No guests or house sitters?"

"He says not."

"How about the alarm system?"

"I'll take care of that first off when we are there. That's my specialty. I got a job with an alarm company for six months. I learned all the ways to disable alarms. Piece of cake if you learn the ropes."

"Maybe, but I heard there are all kinds of new security technologies, motion detectors, heat sensors, things like that, hi tech stuff."

"I can shut off or avoid all that stuff. Besides, my friends in the security business tell me the system in this house is old, unreliable, and easy to shut down."

"How the hell did you find all that information?"

"My friend, I worked on just such a project, actually a whole lot of projects, for years. I got jobs that would give me access to people and information I could use later on. I'm a long range planner. This one came up months ago when I learned the owners would be out of the country over Labor Day. That's an ideal time for a job like this. We'll blend in with lots of people moving around on the lake. We can break in, clean the place out, and leave without anyone noticing us."

"You make it sound so easy. I'll bet it won't work out so easy."

"Every job like this has risks. I plan for almost any unexpected problem that could arise, and develop two plans for every problem we are sure of. No, my plan's not fool proof, but nothing in life ever is."

"Isn't Labor Day a risky time to be doing this? There will be lots of people around."

"My contact told me to hit the house the week after, but I think he's wrong. Labor Day weekend, gobs of people will be on the lake and around the place. Those people make my plan ideal since we'll be unnoticed, invisible in all the confusion among all those people. Trust me, Labor Day weekend will be the ideal time."

"I hope you're right."

"It's part of my planning. Let me give you an example. Their security system is powered primarily from their main circuit. Should that be cut or the main switch thrown, a battery operated system cuts in. At the same time, an alarm signal is sent out to the security people telling them a breach has occurred. The police and private security people are notified immediately, and will be on their way."

"If you throw the main switch to shut down the system we'll be screwed."

Al picked up a small metal box with five wires tipped with alligator clips. "This little beauty is the key. When I attach these wires to the correct posts in the main circuit box, I can open the main switch without the system sending that signal. The rest of the security system will be without power, and nothing will happen. The box simulates the load from the house circuits and the security system. The system thinks everything is okay. No warning signal is sent. Next, I switch off all the circuit breakers except for the outlet we'll need for the cutter."

"How in hell can you tell which one?"

"If they're not marked, and I'll bet they are, I will test them one at a time. That will take a few minutes, but no problem. Afterward, we can go about our business in complete safety. Should we trip any other sensor, the lights and alarm that would normally turn on, won't for lack of power. In their system, those lights include dozens of bright floodlights all over the property. They would light up the entire place, inside and out."

"How in hell are we going to be able to find anything in the dark and in a strange house?"

"First of all, I'm bringing two pair of night vision goggles we can use in the dark," Al reached over and rolled out a set of plans on the table. "Here's a complete floor plan of the house. You can examine and memorize the plan while we're on the way."

"How the crap did you ever get hold of that?"

"I told you I began researching this job as soon as I learned the owners would be gone. I found out the guy built the house using plans for another house. Those plans were in an architectural magazine. I bought this set of plans directly from the magazine. Pretty slick, eh?"

"Even with all that, how can you be sure there are things we can turn into cash, and will those things be in the house while they're gone? They surely wouldn't go away and leave cash and jewelry laying about."

"I doubt there will be any cash and jewelry at all, other than a few items they forgot about. What we will go after is the stuff they can't take with them or put in a safe. Big things worth lots of moolah, things difficult to haul away and almost impossible to fence."

"If they are so hard to steal and fence, why bother?"

"Because I figured a way to haul them off and sell them, stupid. The harder things are to steal and fence, the less protections the owners place around them."

"Like what for instance?"

"Like a solid silver fountain on his patio, for instance. He paid nearly half a million twenty years ago when he brought it from Greece. The silver in the fountain is worth twice that much at today's prices. The fountain sits right here," he said pointing to a spot on the plans. "We take the thing, melt it down and sell the silver. Melted and recast, it would be untraceable. If we sell a bar at a time to different buyers, we'll be millionaires in a few weeks and no one would be suspicious."

"I'll bet the fountain is heavy. How will we be able to carry the damned thing out?"

"Hell, you're the metal worker. Can't you think of a way it could be carted away in pieces small enough for us to carry easily?"

"Of course. Cut the damned thing up. That's what you wanted the portable diamond disk cutter for."

"Right. That's the single main piece, but there are expensive paintings and other stuff all over the place, including sterling silverware. Once we sell the silver, we'll be able to buy our way into the secret sales channels for stolen art. From what I've learned, the art could net us as much as another million."

"We'll need a truck to haul all that stuff. How in hell can we load up a truck in his driveway? Someone's bound to see us and call the cops."

"A boat."

"A what?"

"A big open fishing boat, a twenty footer with an eight foot beam, the biggest boat I could find that will fit through a culvert we must go through to go into the lake. In fact, that's how we go to the house without being seen. I rented this boat, trailer, and a tow truck for the whole time. The rig is sitting out back, already hitched up and ready to go. We load our tools in the boat, launch it from the trailer on a public boat ramp up a river called Grassy Creek. While it's still light out and before dark, we negotiate this creek all the way to the lake. We take the boat down the lake, spot the house, and stay out in the lake with all the other boats until it is completely dark. Next we go in and tie up at his pier. Then we clean the place out and dump all the stuff from the house into the boat. We take the boat back to the boat ramp, pull it out, cover the stuff with the boat cover so no one will see, and be on our way home. Weeks will go by before anyone discovers the house has been robbed. By then we will be long gone. Neat, eh?"

"I gotta hand it to ya, that sounds like a plan. I hope nothing goes wrong. What will we do if they come home early, or if some friend comes by to check on the house for them?"

"That's why I planned for Labor Day Sunday, and at night. We can wait in the boat out in the lake. We'll be one boat among lots of others on the water. After dark, we tie up at their pier and wait, to make sure no one's around. When we're sure the coast is clear, we break in. Those sliding glass doors in the front are easy to break open. We put on those night vision goggles I bought and be able to do everything without any lights. The entire front of the house is glass so anyone on the lake in front of the house would see any lights we use.

I figure four hours to strip the place, load the boat, and be on our way. That should give us plenty of time to find our way back to the boat ramp before daylight. Those goggles will help us there too, if the batteries last long enough."

"What about the batteries?"

"They are rechargeable but last only about four hours on a charge. We will bring two fully charged batteries and a charger with us. Should either one of them run down, we will switch and drop it into the charger. We'll only need one for the trip back to the boat ramp."

"I don't know, Al. It sounds complicated to me. Lots of things could go wrong. I don't know nothin' about the area."

"Damn it Ray, I've spent months of planning on this job. If I had any suspicion you would develop cold feet, I'd bring along another partner. You can't back out now."

"I'm not backing out. I'm nervous, that's all."

"Well, get over it. This job will be a piece of cake."

FOUR

Early Saturday evening Walter and Warren were lounging next to their pool and nursing drinks while waiting for friends to arrive. They had on matching gray trousers, blue blazers, and the correct accessories, also matching. They were dressed for going out, not for the pool.

"Where the hell are those two babes?" Walter commented. "If they aren't here soon, Our plans for the evening will be all screwed up,"

"Damn! They're always late. What time did you tell them to be here?"

"Five-thirty. If we're to be there by eight we must leave before seven."

"It's after six already, almost six-thirty. Those damned bitches may not be coming."

"I predict they'll be here at six-thirty-five. They are almost always a bit more than an hour late. Tell me more about this place. I've heard about it, but isn't Tippy a kids' dance hall? We'll stick out like clothes horses at a nudist colony."

"You'll love their clientele. Lots of young girls, teenagers, most of them horny as hell."

"Who told you that?"

"Jake Ramsey. You remember Jake. He's the guy we met on our Carribean cruise, the one who owns a small orthopedic company in Warsaw."

"Yeah, I remember him. He's the one with the two hundred buck hairdo who thought every babe on the cruise ship wanted to go to bed with him."

"That's the guy. He's got a spectacular place on Tippy, cost him several million. Remember, he invited us to come and visit him any time. His place is within a quarter mile of the dance hall. He told me he has picked up some choice young stuff there, choice, willing and appreciative."

"That's a switch if true. Methinks he exaggerates quite a bit. I never saw him with anything hot on our cruise."

"I think the place is worth checking out. The girls will too."

"I still wouldn't believe him."

The girls walked in. "Hi, you old farts. Ready to go?" Blaze asked.

"Warren, please note the time, six-thirty-five. Did I call it or did I call it? I'm sorry I didn't bet on them."

Brandy says, "What's that all about?"

"Warren and I were discussing your habits of tardiness. I predicted you would be one hour and five minutes late and I hit right on the money. You two are so damned predictable."

Warren headed for the side door. "Let's stop wasting time and head out right away. Incidently, girls, I'm driving the beemer tonight. It's parked right by the side door. Everything we will need is in the trunk, except those overnight cases of yours."

"Why not the limo? Wouldn't the trip be easier with a driver?" Brandy asked.

Walter lead the girls toward the side door. "With what we are planning, we don't want anyone but the four of us to learn what we're doing, understand?"

Blaze said, "sometimes you guys scare me with your weird ideas. What kind of naughtiness are you planning?"

"A weekend of wild debauchery is all. Check these out," Walter dangled a set of keys. "These are the keys to a big place on Lake Tippecanoe. I had lunch with our friend, Jake, last week when he was in town—his invitation. Anyway, he will be away for two or three weeks and said we were welcome to use his place, as long as we promised not to do any damage, even gave us the keys to his boat."

"I'll bet that cost you a pretty penny," Brandy said as she stepped into the car.

Walter grinned as he got behind the wheel. "We had a little negotiation about a piece of art from our collection. I think we made a good deal."

Blaze was curious. "How'd you manage that? I thought you were forbidden to sell any of the art in the house."

"Who said anything about selling?" Warren said. "The painting is merely on loan."

Walter added, "Besides, there is an perfect copy now hanging on the wall, a copy only an expert could tell from the real thing. It only cost us about $150. We used a guy who is good at copying old art."

"And how many copies has he made for you since he started?" Blaze asked.

"I consider that privileged information. You certainly don't need to know."

Not trusting her memory, Blaze made a note on her iphone. That info might come in handy at a later date.

✳   ✳   ✳

Slightly less than an hour after leaving the mansion, the four of them pulled up behind a huge house nestled into the steep hillside on the southwest side of Lake Tippecanoe, a quarter of a mile from the dance hall. Walter entered first.

"I must punch in the code on their alarm system within a minute of opening the door or the alarm will go off, the security company will be notified and the police will be on their way here pronto. . . . Okay, that worked. The green light went off and the red came on. The alarm is turned off. We won't need to reset the alarm till we leave on Monday."

"Wow! What a lovely place," Brandy said as they carried in their luggage including one large case the twins brought, their portable bar with a number of extra special items. "The lake is right down there. Look at all the boats."

"Right now pick out one of the bedrooms and move in," Warren announced. "There will be plenty of time to walk around when we come back. Freshen yourselves so we can be on the dance floor early and troll for some young stuff."

Brandy squealed, "Sure sounds like fun. Let's go."

✳   ✳   ✳

Amid whistles and hoots at Brandy and Blaze from the young men around the entrance, they walked in and hunted for a table on the edge of the dance floor. They seemed out of place among all the teens. It was after eight and there were no tables left. Walter walked over to one table with two jeans clad young girls. A fifty-dollar bill changed hands and the girls got up and walked away. That was always the way the twins got what they wanted.

"Jake told me we might not find a table unless we got here early. A little moolah and here we are. What do you think?"

The girls checked out the prospects. "Nothing but pimply faced kids so far," Brandy remarked. "I sure hope something decent shows up."

Warren grinned. "I thought you liked young stuff."

Brandy scowled. "Yeah, but not those in their bad skin days. Wait a sec . . . over there by the column. Those two are pretty sexy. No pimples on their faces."

Blaze turned to see. "Not bad. Not bad for starters. We'll keep checking, but if nothing better shows up we'll work on them. Walter, what was wrong with the two girls at this table?"

"Too young, too scrawny. I saw a couple of good ones when we walked in, but they were with guys. Our targets must be unattached, otherwise, no dice. So far there are no prospects, but it's early. With all of these kids, there should be a few good ones."

When the first set ended the girls went outside to the car for some refreshment. Promoted as a pure teen club, the owners allowed no booze inside. All soft drinks were served in clear plastic cups. Security confiscated any container of any kind being carried inside. Bringing any booze inside was so difficult those who wanted to drink went out to their cars. Even in the parking lot security cops patrolled ejecting anyone caught with intoxicants of any kind. Still, many managed to imbibe without being caught after the mass exodus to the parking lot during every break. The twins chose to sit this break out at their table so they could look for prospects, going and coming. They did see one girl who fit the bill, a tallish brunette who seemed to be alone. They flipped coins and Walter won. He was the one who approached her.

"Excuse me, young lady, are you waiting for someone? I saw you standing there alone for some time."

"Actually, I'm waiting for my brother. He was planning to come here to meet me as soon as he got off work."

"My brother and I noticed you standing here all alone. That's why I came to talk to you. Why don't you come and join us at our table?"

"Oh, I couldn't do that."

"Why not? I'm sure your brother would find you sitting there. We're sitting right by the dance floor, at the table with the guy dressed like me?"

"Well . . . gosh . . . you must be twins."

"And the lovely lady wins a coke. Come on over and join us. I'm buying. Your brother will be welcome to join us too, when he's here, honest." Walter could be quite charming when he wanted to, usually when he wanted something.

"You're sure it's okay? I wouldn't want to be a bother."

"No bother at all. There will be a party of eight or nine with your brother. The more the merrier. I'm Walter and my brother is Warren. What's your name?"

"Charlotte."

"A lovely name, lovely indeed. And where are you from?"

"Goshen, about twenty miles north of here. I live there with my two brothers when I'm not away at school."

"Where do you go to school?"

"IU. I'm at the Bloomington campus. We start classes next week."

Shortly after Charlotte joined the twins, Blaze and Brandy showed up with two teenage boys.

"We found these two over by the door," Brandy announced. "This is Fred and Randy. I latched onto Randy since our names go together, Randy and Brandy, you know. Blaze will be Fred's *tour guide* on our little trip."

"Trip? What kind of a trip? Are you going somewhere?" Charlotte's fear response was kicking in slightly, but was only mild apprehension at people who were still strangers.

"Only a figure of speech my dear," Brandy said as Walter gave her a searing glance. "I meant . . ."

Walter interrupted, silencing Brandy. "We're having a small party after the dance at the lake house of a friend of ours right up the road, walking distance from here. That's what Brandy meant when she said, trip. I'd like you to came along, your brother too."

Charlotte was still a bit fearful. "I don't think I should, not unless Stan is here."

Walter turned on his soothing brotherly charm and calmed Charlotte. Soon they were all seated and introductions made. Clearly the boys were in awe of the two buxom beauties who were overly attentive to them. Charlotte had no idea what to make of the new arrivals. Young boys in jeans and mature women in high-heeled boots who seemed to be getting high on something didn't belong together in her mind. They made her feel a bit uncomfortable. She hoped her brother, Stan, would come soon. She took her cell phone out of her purse to call him.

"Excuse me. I'm going to call my brother. He should be here by now."

When he didn't answer, she left him a message, "Stan, call me as soon as you can. It's almost nine and I'm wondering where you are."

"He didn't answer?" Brandy asked. "Don't worry honey. His phone battery may need charging. That happens to mine all the time."

With both twins using their considerable charm, Charlotte's apprehension was finally dispelled. With everyone but Warren out on the dance floor, he set about trying to find an unattached young woman. Blaze and Brandy were attracting lots of male admirers as they gyrated among the throng on the crowded dance floor. The two young boys ate up all the attention they were drawing dancing with such sexy exhibitionists. The ladies were in their element—the object of all eyes. So went events through the next two hours. Stan never showed, nor did he return Charlotte's call. She lost all of her fears thanks to the influence of Walter's efforts and became one with the group, small talk, jokes, laughter and all. Warren's efforts to latch on to another young woman were unsuccessful.

"Let's head for Jake's place, now," Walter suggested as things came to a lull. "We seven would be a tight fit in the beemer so Charlotte and I can walk."

Charlotte immediately pointed to a car in the lot. "There's no need to walk. I can drive us in my car."

"Great," Warren said. "Would you mind driving us a few miles into town? We need a case of Coke and some chips. We brought lots of dip but need coke and some chips."

"Not at all," Charlotte replied. By this time she was a willing part of the group.

Warren handed the BMW keys to Blaze. "Think you could manage to drive to the place without hitting anything?"

Blaze snatched the keys from Warren's hands. "I'm less likely to hit anything than you are. You're the one with all the car accidents, remember?"

"You'll need to enter the security code to start the engine. Do you remember?"

"Of course. 0777."

"You can turn on the lights, fire up the sound system and bring out the snacks."

FIVE

Jerome Wells lived in Warsaw where he struggled to make passing grades all of his young life. School was not his thing, However, sit him down at a piano or keyboard and he was pure poetry.

His musical charm won him admiration and Susan Germain, a bright, pretty young lady and an unlikely companion to the surly piano player.

Jerome had few friends. He was a loner. He also carried a rather fragile chip on his shoulder, snapping back verbally at almost any real or imagined slight. Fortunately for Jerome, he was a rather large, muscular young man. Those subjected to his occasional verbal abuse usually took it, In spite of this, he was never physically abusive or even threatening. He was particularly angered by slights administered by young women, and responded with much verbal abuse, with all but Susan.

Jerome seemed to almost worship the girl. In his eyes she could do no wrong. Strangely enough, Susan seemed to treat him in a similar fashion. They were certainly an unusual couple, so extremely different in so many ways, yet they seemed devoted to each other. All of Susan's friends thought them a bad mismatch. Once they started going together as high school sophomores, they stayed together.

Saturday night, Labor Day weekend at the Tippy Dance Hall on Tippecanoe Lake in Indiana is the last summer weekend the band will be playing. First band break, Jerome, who plays the keyboard, drifts down to the table where Susan is sitting.

"How'd things go? Are we on tonight? I didn't feel like I was so maybe I wasn't."

Susan smiled sweetly. "Jerome, you're always on. You're the best. How about all those ladies standing by the stage drooling? They all want your bod because of the sound you make with your keyboard. Your music even makes my juices flow."

"Come on, Susan. You're talkin' to me. Anything in pants makes your juices flow."

"That's not true. Why are you so damned nasty tonight? it's the last weekend of the summer for God's sake. I turned down a big payday to be with you so be nice. And besides, I paid you a huge compliment, and meant it."

"I'm sorry, Babe. I guess I'm off because tonight's the last weekend here. I like playin' in this place. I'm gonna miss it. Especially with you goin' off to college and all. What will I do while you're away?"

✳   ✳   ✳

Susan had a dark secret, one none of her friends knew about or would ever suspect. Susan was addicted to sex, big time. She never had sex with anyone in her school or any local men. As a result, her reputation was unsullied. She was deemed one of those nice girls who *didn't do it*. In actuality, Susan was more of a private call girl with a few well-heeled clients. First, there were three in Toledo and later, two in Fort Wayne as well. She would visit these five on an individual appointment basis quite regularly.

The two in Fort Wayne were identical twin brothers. She visited them together, at a luxury spa they owned on the outskirts of town. She never visited their huge mansion, as this was against her self-imposed rules. Those rules were quite simple. She only entertained clients at her uncle's home or in a public place like a hotel or, with the twins, the spa.

Susan made lots of money. Jerome knew all of this, but didn't seem to bothered by her activities. Susan's regular income paid for his clothes and car. This could be the reason.

Susan broke into the business in an unusual way. When she was fourteen, she was a fully developed, mature young woman who could easily pass for 21 if she dressed the part and wore the right makeup. After her parents moved to Warsaw, Indiana from Toledo, Ohio, she remained in Toledo, staying with a wealthy uncle, her mother's brother, Adrian. This enabled her to finish the last four months of the school year in the school she had been attending. The third night she was in his house he crawled into her bed and had sex with her. Not only did she not object, she enjoyed the experience, big time. As a result, Adrian became her first lover.

She quickly became so turned on she was demanding more sex than Adrian could supply. This led to several of her uncle's wealthy friends helping out. At Adrian's suggestion, they would leave a couple of hundred dollar bills on the night stand by her bed. He told them her name was *Samantha*, and that she worked for his successful travel business, Adrian's Business and Adventure Travels. He also told them she was twenty-one.

Susan went along with all this. She was bright enough to recognize a good profitable business and soon had half a dozen wealthy and regular clients. All of them were her uncle's rich friends. They held their trysts in her uncle's house regularly. She was particular about those she let into her bed. They had to be wealthy, well known in the community, and she had to like them personally. She made no exceptions.

By the time the school year ended and she was about to move back with her parents in Warsaw, forty miles from Fort Wayne, Susan had worked out travel arrangements with her uncle. He would arrange flights and limo service between Warsaw, Fort Wayne, and Toledo and make occasional hotel accommodations as well, all first class. Her clients would visit her in a hotel when Adrian's house was not available. Her cover for her parents was her job working for Adrian's travel company, checking out hotels and vacation places. They were thrilled she had such a good job and was being so well paid. Susan often wondered what would happen if they ever found out what she was actually doing to earn her money.

When school started in the fall, *Samantha* had to cut out all but weekend trips. As a result she gave up all but three of her clients. The ones she kept, were the three wealthiest of her uncle's friends. These three raised the amount of their *gifts* all on their own in hopes she would continue serving them. They were now paying four times what they paid before, willingly. She was making lots of money and kept half as cash—unreported income. This was Samantha Gowan's bankroll. The money came in as cash, was kept as cash, and was spent as cash, no records. The other half she banked as Susan Germain. She reported this half and paid income taxes as a business, a travel consultant. Susan was sharp about money even at her tender age.

In the middle of her sophomore year in Warsaw, she met and hooked up with Jerome.

For the last two summers, Jerome played keyboard in a band at the Tippy Dance Hall on nearby Tippecanoe Lake. For some reason he was not as surly at the dance hall and even gathered a few friends among the band members and patrons. Sometimes Susan would be sitting at a table near the performers while Jerome was playing. Often she would be absent for one of her *trips*. Jerome always offered the same reason for her absence. "She's visiting friends."

✳   ✳   ✳

Susan said, "Why don't you do what I told you? You could move down to Bloomington and we'd be together. Jobs aren't any harder to find than here, probably easier."

"And, be away from home?"

"What home? You haven't gotten along with your parents since I've known you and most of your friends are right here, freakin' lakers, from all over the place: Indy, Fort Wayne, South Bend, Chicago. How many of your friends are from Warsaw? Tell me."

"Come on Susan. What I mean is I've never even been to Bloomington. Where will I stay and how will I find a job?"

"With me, Jerome, and I'm sure you could find a job in Bloomington even easier than around here."

Susan stood up and turned around, her face blanched with shock. "Oh my God, Jerome, the twins from Fort Wayne are here. They're right across the floor at that front table. I can't believe me eyes. What are they doing here? Take me out before they see me."

"Okay, stay next to me and I'll walk you to the door. Keep in the crowd as far as we can go. Which ones are they?"

"The two wearing identical gray slacks and blue blazers. The overdressed ones. I must get out of here, **NOW**! I've never been seen by a client here and I don't want to now. Go! Go!"

"They're two of your clients?"

"Yes, damn it. I told you about them. They live in a huge mansion north of Fort Wayne. They're the ones who always want me to do them together. I told you about that, I know."

"I remember now. Did you ever tell them about Tippy?"

"Never! I never tell any of them where I'm from or who I really am. My life is much safer that way. Hurry! The sooner I'm out of here the better I'll feel."

Susan didn't relax until they were outside and she was in his car. "Wow, that was close. I hope they missed seeing me. They did for sure or they would come right over."

"What are you going to do now?"

"Stay here in the car and wait for you until you finish, I guess— until they leave."

"It's Saturday night. That won't be for four hours."

"Well, I sure as hell can't go back inside."

"I'll come out during every break. You want anything?"

"For them to go back to Fort Wayne, that's all."

"Okay, break time is about over so I must go back in. I'll tell you if they leave."

"Thanks, Jer. I'll probably crawl in the back seat and try to sleep."

Jerome came in barely in time for the next set. He saw the twins had a table at the edge of the dance floor. Two thin but buxom babes were with them, both dressed in the latest bimbo chic, black thigh-high boots with spike heels and big boobs almost falling out of tops almost open to the waist. They were not at the table when Susan first spotted the twins. Jerome thought, *I wonder how much those jokers paid for those babes. It must be nice to be rich.*

✴ Saturday, September 1, 2012, 11:00 pm ✴

Jerome took a bottle of ginger ale to Susan during the next break. "Thanks, sweetheart," she said.

"Your twins are at a table with two real flashy bimbos. They're sitting and drinking. They probably brought hidden flasks because the bimbos act like they are getting high."

"Skinny, lots of blonde hair, black high-heeled boots, and big boobs mostly exposed?"

"Yep. That's them."

"Wigs, silicone, and liposuction make the new woman. They must be Brandy and Blaze, two regulars with the twins, Walter says they are lousy in bed but make for good eye candy—decorations when they go out. Blaze even has a masters in psychology so she's no dummy. I wonder how they found Tippy, and even more, why they came here. It's not their usual upscale place to be seen."

"They could be visiting some of their rich buddies who own huge mansions on the lake. A lot more super rich own places over on Wawasee, lots more than on Tippy even."

"If that were the case, they'd be at the Country Club, not here. They are so out of place among these kids. I wonder what mischief brings them here. This is so unlike them."

"What the hell is the difference and why should we give a shit?"

"Curiosity. Aren't you curious? I certainly am when people do things far from their norm, especially people with too much money and way too much time on their hands."

"I'd best go back inside. Old Duggan gets pissed when any of the band isn't back on time. I may not be able to come out next break. I've been late now twice and Duggan's usual punishment is making us stay inside during the break."

"I may take a walk down the road. I am bored as hell sitting here."

Jerome got a nasty scowl thrown at him from Duggan, the band leader, as he slid into place. He knew he would receive a tongue lashing next break. The twins and their bimbos were still at the table engrossed in conversation, but now three others were at their table, two boys and a girl, all attractive teens. The Bimbos were getting high on something and talking louder and louder.

✳ Saturday, September 1, 2012, midnight ✳

Next break, true to form, Duggan made Jerome stay inside. At the next and last break at midnight, and after swallowing more of Duggan's vitriol, Jerome headed outside. Susan was gone. He walked up the sloping lot and glanced down the road both ways. No Susan, so he headed back inside.

During their first number, Jerome noticed the twins and their friends were gone. They never came back to their table. This was the last set and would finish about one o'clock.

After finishing, Jerome locked his keyboard and left it in place. They would be playing a full evening program tomorrow, the last one of the season. He pulled the memory card, completely disabling the keyboard, and stuck the card in his pocket as he left.

He was upset when he discovered Susan was not in his car. He last saw her during his break two hours ago. He found an empty ginger ale bottle on the floor of the back seat. Susan's purse was on the floor of the front seat. She probably didn't want to carry it with her while she walked around so she locked it in the car. He decided to drive around the neighborhood to find her.

Half an hour later, he finished driving slowly down the road both ways and up every lane to every group of cottages within half mile of Tippy. He was growing more worried and upset, almost panicky. She would never leave without telling him, especially without her purse. He parked in the western corner of the Tippy parking lot right by the beach and walked rapidly west on the concrete walk running along in front of about thirty closely packed cottages built in the nineteen-twenties. He called her name several times near places where she might sit down and go to sleep. Nothing! No Susan. By this time Jerome was worrying big time. This was not like Susan, not something she would ever do. He had no idea what to do next.

SIX

Susan was still unnerved by the presence of the twins. She turned on the car radio and listened to a night time talk show until Jerome appeared with a bottle of ginger ale.

"Thanks sweetheart," she said. "How are my *friends* doing inside?"

"They are talking and drinking cokes. They probably added a kick to their drinks. The women get up every once in awhile and meander through the crowd. They seem to be searching for someone. Every male eye in the place follows them wherever they go."

"I'll bet they are trolling for males. That's strange with the twins present."

They talked about the four until Jerome had to head back.

"I may take a walk down the road. I get terribly bored sitting here," she told Jerome before he left.

She sat and drank the ginger ale while listening to the radio for the next half hour. When the eleven o'clock news was over, she locked the car and walked down the road that entered the parking lot from the east. The road provided access to many lake homes and cottages skirting the shoreline at the rear of those lakeside homes for more than a mile. She took a leisurely stroll down to the curve at Silver Point and half a mile south before she turned to retrace her steps. She was almost back to the parking lot when a pair of headlights blinded her as a car turned onto the road from the lot then slid to an abrupt stop on the gravel-covered road.

✳ Sunday, September 2, 2012, 12:30 am ✳

Half an hour after they left the parking lot, Charlotte and the twins returned. They drove through the lot and turned onto the road to Jake's, the car lights almost blinded a young woman walking toward them.

"Holy shit. Do you see what I do?" Walter asked Warren. "Charlotte, stop the car—now."

"I don't believe it," Warren said in amazement. "That's Samantha. What the hell is she doing here?"

Susan heard a voice from the inky blackness. "Samantha? Is that you?"

Recognizing the voice, she knew the twins had found her. In an instant of panic she started to run but realized they would certainly catch her in the unsure footing of the gravel parking lot. She played dumb. "Who is that? I can't tell. Those headlights are blinding."

"It's Warren, honey. You know. What in the name of heaven are you doing way out here, anyway? You're a long way from home."

Samantha's mind was frantically searching for what to say. "I could ask you the same thing," she said stalling. "Is your brother with you?"

"Right here in the car," Walter said as he stepped out and into the light from the headlights. "I can't believe you're way out here in the sticks. It's a miracle we saw you. What are you doing so far from Toledo?"

The story she was quickly conjuring must work. "I came here to visit a cousin who spends summers nearby. I was walking to his car to go to his place. His mom is one of my favorite aunts."

"What's his name and where does he live," Warren asked as Walter joined them.

"You remember our deal, no connections, no names, no questions. Otherwise our deal is off, permanently. Remember?"

"Okay, Samantha. I was so surprised, seeing you in the headlights, way out in the middle of nowhere. You'll admit this situation would arouse anyone's curiosity."

"Well, squelch that curiosity right now. And if you will continue on with your business, I can go on with mine—alone."

"I'm afraid we can't do that, Sam. You see, we need a young lady, especially one with your talents, for a little party up the street."

"Sorry, my cousin is waiting for me. I must go," She said starting to back out of the light from the headlights.

As she did so, Walter stepped over and grabbed her wrist. "We can't let you go, Sam. We are a party of seven and you will make an even four couples.

Don't make a scene. A young lady is driving the car, and we wouldn't want to upset her."

"Let go of me or I'll scream," She said through clenched teeth.

"Okay," Walter said, holding her for a minute and then letting her go. She stepped out of the headlights into the darkness and ran for the parking lot. From the darkness behind the car where he had moved, Warren grabbed her as she passed, putting his hand over her mouth and her neck in a stranglehold.

Warren whispered in her ear. "Keep your mouth shut and climb in the back seat of the car or I'll break your goddamn neck. Once in the car, don't make any problems for us or you will be sorry. Understand?"

Susan was terrified. She had never seen the twins even hint at violence before. They had always treated her kindly. She decided to play along and wait for a chance to escape later.

"You're kidding, Warren, and that's not one bit funny. Let me go and I'll cooperate, but please let me call my cousin and leave a message, okay?"

Warren relaxed his stranglehold, but held on to her wrist. "No phone calls, but I'll let you text him. I'll check what you write before I let you send it."

"What's with you two anyway? I've never seen you act like this before."

"Sometimes drastic circumstances call for drastic steps."

"That's a bunch of bull. Now give me your cell phone."

"Yours is not with you?"

"No, I left it in my purse at my cousin's."

"That was stupid wasn't it?"

"I didn't expect to be hijacked."

Warren took out his cell phone. "What's the number?"

"Give me the phone. I'll text him."

He watched her dial Adrian's number. "That's a Toledo number."

"He happens to live in Toledo so that's the area code for his cell phone."

"Don't hit the send button. Let me read your message."

GOT WAYLAID. MAY NOT BE WITH YOU UNTIL TOMORROW. SAM.

"What kind of a message is that?"

"It's the truth, plain and simple."

"Okay. Into the car, the back seat."

As they got into the back seat, Warren was all charm and pleasantries. "Charlotte, This is Samantha, an old friend of ours from Toledo. She's joining us for our party."

The two young women eyed each other and went through the standard meeting formalities. The tension was even more than with the usual reservations associated with two attractive young ladies, completely unknown to each other and meeting for the first time. They each faced the total unknown of what was going to happen in the next few hours. Both were apprehensive for different reasons.

"Pull in right next to the beemer. That's our car and this is the place," Walter said. "I'll grab the stuff while Walter takes you in the house and shows you around."

When they walked into the main living room the other four were lounging around listening to music. Blaze stood up as soon as she recognized Samantha. She was not happy

"Where in God's name did you find her?" she asked disdainfully.

"Now behave yourself, Blaze," Walter said sharply. "Believe it or not we ran into her walking down the road on the way here. We were even more surprised than you were. We had no idea she was anywhere around, or had ever even been here."

"Yeah, I'll bet. You expect me to believe that?"

"Come on, Blaze. That's a fact. Neither of us had any idea," Warren added. "So calm down. Let's all be friends and go on with our partying."

"They're telling the truth, Blaze," Samantha said. "I could hardly believe when they jumped out of the car. My cousin has a place on the lake and I came down for a visit. I was walking to his car when these two saw me."

Eyeing the two boys she added, "Aren't those boys a bit young for you two?"

Brandy flashed her a superior gaze. "Aren't you a bit young for Warren and Walter? Two can play that game."

Walter was getting pissed. "Will you please stop the damned cat fighting? Let's all calm down and enjoy the evening. Why argue about totally meaningless things when we can delight in far more enjoyable things. I for one am going back to mix drinks for everyone from my portable bar. Warren, will you give me a hand?"

"Sure Walter. Let's go. The rest of you relax and enjoy the music while we fix rum and Cokes for everyone. We'll be back in a few minutes."

They immediately headed for Walter's room and the bar in the large case they set up. As soon as they reached the room and closed the door they smiled at each other and burst into laughter.

Walter opened the bar. "This may be going better even than we planned. Those two boys are perfect. I wonder if they ever snorted coke before. Blaze and Brandy will teach them how."

"Yeah, drink a little, smoke a little dope, snort a few, surprising things will happen."

"I wonder about Charlotte. She may not be into any of this stuff. She seems to me she could be a hard sell. Sam won't take anything. She always avoids drugs. Says they make her feel like she's losing control. You remember what a control freak she is. The sisters will do whatever we provide."

Warren laughed. "It will be interesting watching what happens when they are all high. Any bets on what's going to happen?"

"Not on your life. That's the fun. Not knowing what will happen. Sam is something else though. She may resent being pulled into this. She and the Phillips don't get along too well as I remember. Anyway, we should get some interesting movies. I assume you're going to set up the cameras while I serve the drinks."

"Yeah. It won't take long. These tiny little cameras will clip right to the top of the drapes. Being wireless, they will be virtually impossible to see. The computer in the bar will capture everything, right in this room where no one will know but you and me."

"You're not going to tell the girls"

"Hell no. That way they'll act more naturally. If they knew, they would probably ham it up for the cameras. That would ruin everything."

Walter grabbed the tray of drinks and headed down the hall. "Don't take too long or someone might be suspicious. We wouldn't want anyone seeing you mounting those cameras."

"Don't worry about me. Tell them I had to go potty or something."

Warren came in soon after Walter passed out the drinks and sat next to Charlotte. Thus began an effort to lure her to his bedroom that was to take a long time. About twenty minutes later, all but Charlotte and Samantha were getting a bit high. Neither of them wanted anything to do with drugs. By one o'clock, Charlotte, Samantha and the twins were the only ones left in the main room. Brandy and Blaze had disappeared upstairs with the two boys.

Warren turned to Samantha and whispered quietly, "How about we two sneak up to my room?"

Samantha smiled. "Not on your life. I want to wait until Walter heads upstairs with Charlotte. I can sense she's not too keen on going upstairs. I want to watch him in action, right here. I'll bet he doesn't score? You want to bet against me?"

"I don't know. They're getting quite friendly right now. They may be clear across the room, but you especially should look at what's going on."

"A little kissy face is not the same as a trip to the bedroom."

"Maybe he'll drag her. I might do the same with you."

"Warren, under the right circumstances you could hurt a woman, even beat her, but rape is not for you or your brother. You both are too much into the pleasures of sexual cooperation to rape any woman, even one you can't buy. I'm guessing that if he can't convince her to go willingly, nothing will happen. That goes for me as well."

"Don't be too sure about that. Some guys get off on sex with unwilling partners."

"Some guys, yes, but not the Simmons twins. I know you quite well, especially how to please you. Rape, even slightly forced sex is not part of who you are. You want the full cooperation of any sex partner, right?"

"You're probably right. I could drag you back into bed and find out I couldn't manage sex without you being a willing partner."

"Exactly. That's why your brother will never score with the young lady. He'd need to rape her and he'll never do so. Trust my intuition. You guys are quite predictable."

"What about those boys? Any thoughts about them?"

Sam knew who they were from being around Tippy. She also heard they had a rather unsavory reputation. She had never spoken with them, only knowing about them from remarks made by other kids at Tippy. "Thoughts, yes. Concrete knowledge or even suspicions, no. Still, they appear to be earthy, almost animal like. I would guess they would forcibly rape a girl if they thought they could get away with it and not be caught. Unlike you, they would not give a damn if the girl cooperated or not."

"Where did you find all those ideas . . . learn all this crap?"

"I'm planning on majoring in psychology in college, so I've read a number of books on the subject. I found most to be good old common sense applied to people and situations, a lot I learned from personal observation and experience."

"You know, Sam, you're certainly sharp for a high school senior."

"College freshman," she corrected. "I'm already registered at Indiana."

"Whatever, you're sure a lot sharper than those four up in the bedrooms screwing."

"Wrong. Blaze has a masters in psychology. That takes a lot of smarts."

"Yeah, but what has it gotten her?"

"Look who's talking."

"I don't believe it. Check out who's heading for the bedroom. My brother apparently convinced her. I'd love to watch the results," he said, all the time realizing the camera in their room would enable him to do that.

"I guess I misread her. I don't do that often."

"Okay. They've gone to bed. How about us?"

"Same price. Same way. Same routine."

"Sam, you sure drive a hard bargain."

"Gotta pay for college somehow."

SEVEN

It was 2:30 Sunday morning when Jerome finally called 911 on his cell phone.

"Emergency operator, how can I help you?"

"My girlfriend has disappeared. I've been searching for her for almost two hours."

"What is your name, sir?"

"Jerome, Jerome Wells. I'm by the Tippy dance hall."

"Thank you, Jerome. What is your girlfriend's name?"

"Susan Germain. We just graduated from Warsaw High. She's never done anything like this before. She's reliable."

"Did you contact her parents?"

"At this time of night?"

"Perhaps she went home."

"Impossible. She left her purse in our car. She wouldn't go anywhere without her purse. Something terrible has happened to her. Could be someone abducted her, grabbed her and took her away."

"Now don't go imagining things. When were you last with her?"

"Around ten. I brought her a bottle of ginger ale. She was waiting in our car in the parking lot while I was playing with the band. I played keyboard here at Tippy all summer."

"Why wasn't she inside while you were playing?"

"What's that got to do with anything? She's gone and she doesn't do things like that. Something bad has happened to her. Can't you do anything? Send someone, a cop or sheriff's officer?" Jerome's frustration and fears were obvious in his voice.

44

"Try to calm down, Jerome. I will need more information in order to decide if and when to send someone. Why don't you drive to the sheriff's. You're only a few miles away."

"What if she came back and saw our car gone. She would be confused, stranded, and wondering where I went. Also her cell phone is in her purse with me. Impossible."

"You said you had been searching for her. Where did you search and for how long?"

"I went to our car to leave as soon as we finished. That was about one-thirty. She was gone and our car was locked. I got in the car and found her purse on the floor. She told me earlier she might go for a walk so I drove all over the place, even down every cottage lane, but no Susan. I've searched ever since. That was more than an hour ago."

"You say the car was locked?"

"Yes. We each carry a set of keys. She probably locked the door when she left for her walk."

"What if she accidentally locked herself out and couldn't get back in the car?"

"No way. She would come inside for my keys. Wait a minute while I check her purse for her keys. . . . No, they're not here. She obviously took them with her."

"Could she go some place to try to phone you, a filling station or other business?"

"She had her cell phone in her purse for Christ's sake. Besides, there's no place open within miles. She wouldn't walk clear to Leesburg, and I doubt anything is open at this time of night."

"If she ran into some friends, someone she knew, she could be with them. Quite a few Warsaw teens go to Tippy, don't they? Possibly she lost track of time. It happens."

"Not Susan. If that had happened, she would leave me a note or come in and tell me. We've been going together for more than two years. I know her. She would call me on their phone, or send a message to me somehow. She's good about things like that. I'm sure something has happened to her."

"No one is available I can send out for a call like yours. It is considered a non emergency. Why don't you drive to the sheriff's, or even the Warsaw police station? They are each less than ten minutes away from where you are. You can fill out a report and give them a description of what she is wearing. That's the best I can provide. I'll notify both of them you're coming so you can head for either place. Can you get to where they are?"

"The police station is closest so I'll go make a report."

Jerome spent an hour at the police station talking to Wilma Foster, the officer on duty. He filled out a long report. Among the helpful information was Susan's drivers license with her photo in her billfold they found in her purse.

Wilma explained, "We can't do much right now. She will not be considered a missing person until tomorrow at this time. I checked with EMS and the hospital and learned no young women were admitted or treated so far this evening. The next sheriff's car to go by the area will do so in about half an hour. The deputy will use his spotlight to search the ditches on both sides of the highway. If she was hit by a car while walking, they'll find her. That's about all we can do at the present."

"I never thought about her getting hit by a car. That's possible. Damn, I hope she's okay."

Wilma was empathetic and good at calming upset or aggravated individuals. "Why don't you go home and try to sleep? I've entered all your information as well as Susan's into our computer. We'll be on the lookout for her and call you and her parents as soon as we hear anything."

"Please don't call her parents, not now. They think Susan's out of town for the weekend. I'm sure you understand."

Wilma smiled. "Okay. We won't call them until we must. When a missing person report is filed they will of course be notified and given all the details. That won't happen for twenty-three hours. You should probably speak to them before then."

"Don't worry, I will."

✳ 3:30 am ✳

Jerome headed back for Tippy, not home. As soon as he turned into the old gate he parked at the side of the road and dug out the big flashlight from his tool box in the trunk. He started down the road, shining the light along the side of the road. He would find Susan if she had fallen victim to a hit and run. He prayed he wouldn't find her.

He hadn't walked far when a car turned in the road and stopped where he parked his car. The deputy sheriff had arrived. Seeing Jerome's flashlight, the deputy drove to where he was.

"Are you Jerome?" the deputy said as he stepped out of the car.

"Yes. How did you know?"

"The dispatcher said you might be here. I'm Deputy Paul Noonan. I am concerned about your girl friend too. Would you like to ride along with me and help search?"

"I sure would."

"It would be a help to me. While I drive, you can search with the light. If you see anything or any spot where you can't see clearly with the light, let me know. We can step out and take a closer look."

Jerome felt better now that he was doing something. They searched up and down both sides of all of the roads in the area for almost two hours without seeing anything but several racoons.

"Well, Jerome, I think in this case no news is good news. We're fairly sure she wasn't hit by a car, not around here. I'm quite sure she couldn't be beyond our search area in the time since you last saw her, not on foot anyway. I'll leave you here at your car. I think you had better go home and go to sleep. I promise I'll call you if I hear anything, anything at all."

"Thanks, officer, and thanks for taking me with you just now. I'm not ordinarily friendly with authorities, but you sure changed my mind, about the sheriff's office."

"We're just people like you. I'm glad I could help. Good luck with your girl friend."

Jerome climbed into his car and headed for home. He was tired, but still sure he wouldn't be able to sleep much. The first light of a new day was beginning to show in the east. He was not looking forward to the program he would play during the last dance of the summer that evening.

The deputy headed east on Armstrong Road to continue his night patrol.

EIGHT

Sunday morning early, Samantha got up and began searching the far reaches of the house for a window or other place to get out without tripping the alarm. She was also searching for a possible place to hide so the others would think she had escaped. A circular stairway to the roof went to a possible place to hide. She climbed to the top but found the door to the roof locked with a dead bolt requiring a key. Dead end. She retraced her steps to the entrance of the stairway and walked down the hall to a maid's closet at the end. Opening the large closet she saw a jumble of mops, buckets, brooms and a commercial vacuum cleaner. On the wall to the right a large slop sink was mounted. On the left ceiling-to-floor storage cabinets covered the wall. The back wall was featureless except for a vertical crease or deep line in the wall about two feet from the right end. She pushed several mops aside to examine the crease more carefully. She found the crease was a carefully disguised piano hinge. Somehow the wall opened up. No way to open the wall was apparent, no knob, ring or projection of any kind. That section of the wall was completely smooth from ceiling to floor and from the corner to the hidden hinge.

After walking around for about ten minutes, she pushed against the wall in frustration. A loud click and the right section of the wall swung out. It was held shut by a touch latch. Behind the wall was a narrow passageway and steps leading down somewhere. Samantha decided to find out where the steps led. When she turned on the light switch in the wall to her right, a light illuminated a long staircase. She turned around and examined the back side of the door. When she pulled the door shut with the handle, the touch latch clicked and held the door closed. Another pull on the handle, another click and the door again opened. A person would need to be aware of the door and how to open it or it would remain a flat wall. She found no way to lock it. The purpose of the door and the passageway were a mystery.

She went down more than fifty narrow steps to a plain door that latched exactly the same way as the door in the wall in the maid's closet. The door opened to a narrow passageway that led directly to the boathouse and pier at the lake's edge. *A way out,* she thought. This door, however, had a dead bolt requiring a key from the outside, but could be unlocked with a simple lever inside. Samantha started to run south beyond the place next door, stopped, and retraced her steps to the broom closet, latching both doors after she passed through them.

I can take Charlotte with me, she thought. *I could go this way almost any time I want. The twins quite obviously knew nothing about this stairway. But why so well hidden? A secret passageway perhaps from upstairs to the boat dock, a mystery.*

She closed the door of the maid's room and walked downstairs and into the main room with all the glass facing the lake and turned on some soft music. At seven-thirty she took a book on astronomy out of the book case and curled up on the couch to read.

About nine-thirty she heard someone coming down the stairs from the bedrooms. Charlotte was dressed, but not moving steadily.

"What's wrong, Charlotte? You don't look too well. Are you sick?"

"I lost everything that was in my stomach. I don't feel good."

"I'll check in the kitchen to find anything that might help."

Samantha soon came back. "I found tea and cocoa," would you like any of either or should I find something else?"

"Some tea sounds good, with a little bit of sugar."

"Comin' right up as soon the water's hot. I'll make your tea in the microwave. That's the fastest."

When she came back with the tea, Samantha sat down next to Charlotte. "Here's your tea. Now, why don't you tell me what's wrong. I realize you're not feeling well, but that's not all."

Charlotte immediately burst into tears. She leaned against Samantha and couldn't speak for the tears. Something was definitely wrong. When she finally regained her composure, Charlotte spoke slowly and deliberately. "Walter was kind to me last night. He wanted to have sex with me and I was going to, but when I told him I was two months pregnant it turned him off.

I was amazed. He became almost fatherly and protective. I told him my boyfriend, the father of my child, broke off with me and went off with another girl before I could tell him I was pregnant. He became angry. Oh, not at me, but at my exboyfriend."

"That's surprising to me. The Simmons twins could be mellowing out. I don't know. I didn't think they had a whole heart between the two of them."

"After he got over being so angry, he offered to help, even to pay my hospital expenses, for an abortion or otherwise. That was so kind of him."

"Are you going to abort the baby?"

"I couldn't. I could give the baby up for adoption, but I couldn't abort my own baby. He's part of me, my own flesh and blood."

"That's a noble attitude. I doubt I could ever be that way. Those things shouldn't happen to decent girls like you."

The twins walked down the stairs together. "Are you girls ready to go into town for breakfast? I doubt those other four will be out of bed before noon. No point in waiting for them," Warren said.

Samantha said, "I'll stay right here with Charlotte. She's not feeling well. Would you please bring us something."

Walter immediately became quite concerned. "Anything we can do for you, Charlotte? I'll check for some Pepto-Bismol in the medicine chest"

In no more than a minute he returned with a pink bottle in his hands. "I found this the first place I searched. Take some of this. It's the best thing for an upset tummy."

"Samantha? Do you think Pepto-Bismol is safe for me to take?"

"Here. Let me read the label."

After reading the label thoroughly Samantha said, "No comments or warnings for pregnant women so I guess you can take some."

"Pregnant? Who's pregnant?" Warren had a pained look on his face as he asked.

"Charlotte is," Walter said. "She told me last night. That sure puts a different slant on our little weekend party for Charlotte and me."

"I can't believe it. My brother concerned about a pregnant female. Will wonders never cease?"

"Shut up Warren," Walter said emphatically. "The young lady deserves a better hand than she has been dealt, and I intend to change what I can of that for the better, for her anyway."

Samantha was surprised. "Walter, I'm so pleased to find out you might own a heart after all. You're right about Charlotte. She does deserve a break."

Warren stood. "I tell you what, folks. Before I am caught up in all these niceties, I'll run into town and pick up some sweet rolls or doughnuts. If you all can fix some coffee, hot chocolate, tea, champagne or whatever else you want to drink, we can eat our breakfast right here. I'll buy enough so even those still upstairs can eat—if they ever come down that is."

"Thanks Warren," Samantha said. "Everything will be ready by the time you return."

NINE

Randy Wellman and Fred Fuzario were two troubled teens who grew up in Huntington, about forty miles southeast of Lake Tippecanoe. They had been in trouble with police jointly since they were twelve. Both boys had an appearance of youthful innocense about them that belied their behavior and frequently helped them get away with serious mischief. Now seventeen and inseparable, they seemed destined for a life filled with anti social behavior at the least. A few broken windows, some minor shop lifting, mugging of a few younger kids and taking their lunch money, and a few two-on-one fights had built their reputations with both police and parents of other young men.

Raised by working mothers and without fathers, they had been undisciplined from an early age. Living next to each other since age nine, they quickly bonded and became a nasty team. One sixteen year old neighbor girl claimed the two dragged her into a private garage, closed the door, and both raped her. The boys were fifteen at the time. Unfortunately, months went by before she reported it so no evidence was available. Several other girls reported being harassed, but no indications of rape were mentioned.

A local policeman reported, "Don't let those innocent looks and 'who, me?' responses fool anyone. Their actions progressed from mischief to petty theft to more serious offenses. Though they were arrested several times, nothing yet has been pinned on them. In time those two will drift into a life of crime. I hope they soon are caught and convicted for some of their activities and locked up before they commit a major crime or kill someone."

✳ Sunday, September 2, 2012, 11:30 am ✳

Randy almost collided with Fred as he burst out of the bedroom in a rush for the bathroom. "Wow, man, I've gotta go so bad my back teeth are floatin'."

"Hey, me too. Are my eyes turning yellow? Race you to the pot."

Randy won. "Can you believe those women? I had more pussy last night than I've ever had in a month. How about you, Freddie boy?"

"I wondered why my old peter never gave out. We did it over and over until I finally fell asleep. She woke me up and we did it some more. We sure fell into some fancy stuff old buddy. Blaze taught me things and did things to me I never dreamed of. She sure knows a lot about sex. . . . Hurry up. Damn it Randy, can't you shut it off. I'm in pain. I gotta to go too."

"Hell, use the sink or the shower. I'm going as fast as I can."

Fred peed in the sink. "What a relief. I didn't think I would survive. . . . Hey, Blaze told me her boobs are implants. cost several thousand bucks, Brandy's too."

"They sure felt real to me. Those two sure show a lot of skin they're not afraid to show. After Brandy paraded around the room in the nude I told her she would sure be gorgeous in a bikini. She howled laughing."

"Why do you suppose they latched onto us?"

"Because they knew we could screw all night. Older guys don't last."

"Yeah. Women can do it over and over again, but guys run out of steam after a few times, even us young bucks."

"I don't know, Randy. I never ran out of steam. We did it more than a dozen times. I never lasted so long or did it so much before."

"Do you suppose they spiked our drinks with something? If they did, I'd sure like to own a bottle of whatever they used."

"I heard some of the guys at school talking about taking several Viagra pills. They said that made them last forever. Maybe they gave us some Viagra. Let's ask them."

"Do you suppose they'll want to spend all afternoon in bed? I don't think I can after last night."

"Am I hearing the great lover doesn't want to be laid any more?"

"Not right this minute anyway. I bet I can't right now."

"I hate to admit old buddy I'm feeling the same way. I'm all screwed out. Let's dress and go down stairs before they wake up and ask for more."

"Sounds like a plan. Lets go."

When they went down stairs the twins and the two young girls were out on the pier. "How about them?" Fred said, pointing. They're all in bathing suits, relaxing in the sun."

"What the hell is Susan doin' here? Miss snooty sure seems out of place."

"Yeah, she and the other girl, Charlotte, don't fit with the rest of them. Could be she's related to those guys. They both might be related, somehow. They sure are sexy chicks."

"So? Let's join them. I'd like a swim myself. It might feel pretty good."

"Yeah? Can't you see something a whole lot more inviting."

"What?"

"Check around you, dummy. Look at all the expensive stuff waiting for us to snatch."

"Yeah. You're right, but how would we snatch anything without them knowing it was gone?"

"First of all, Brandy told me this isn't their place."

"No? Whose is it?"

"It belongs to some rich friend of the twins. They borrowed the place for the weekend. This is the first time they were ever here. We could carry off half of those paintings on the walls and they would never realize they were gone. I'll bet those cabinets hold all kinds of silver things in them. We could take them and no one would suspect, no one here anyhow. By the time the owners are back we'll be ancient history. No one would think about us. We're just a couple of kids from the sticks. Hell, none of them even ask for our last names. I didn't tell them. Did you?"

"Now that I think, no I didn't. . . . How would we turn any of those paintings into cash? Stuff like that is impossible to sell unless you're in the business. I don't know anything about art. I wouldn't be able to come up with the slightest idea what to do with paintings. And anyway, how we gonna take the stuff out of here without them finding out?"

"That's easy. Ill show you. Yell if one of those babes starts down the stairs."

Fred reached over and took a small painting from a shelf on a book case, walked to the far left end of the main room and stepped out a side door. In less than a minute he returned without the painting.

"Well? See how easy?"

"What did you do? How will we get it from wherever you put it?"

"I was going to hide it in the shrubbery in the side yard, but I ran across an even better place."

"Oh, where?"

"The light from the doorway showed me a rickety old tool shed outside, right on the edge of the neighbor's yard When I pried open the shed door, I saw a few old garden tools inside. The shed obviously hasn't been used for years, a perfect place. Once we put the stuff inside, no one will find it except for us when we come back on Monday night. Perfect!"

"Yeah, we could cart the stuff out without being seen. Let's grab what we can find in those cabinets."

During the next hour, a number of platters and serving dishes marked *sterling* found their way into the old shed along with one small painting, and a chess set Fred decided was valuable. He closed the side door and hurried in and sat down when he heard the Phillips sisters descending the stairs. They put an end to the boy's thievery for the time being. They were wearing matching yellow bikinis beneath net cover ups leaving little to the imagination.

Blaze showed surprise. "Why aren't you boys in your bathing suits? Water activities are the order of the day, and you won't be able to participate in those clothes."

Randy quickly put down the silver ash tray he was holding. "We don't have bathing suits."

"You boys are not observant. If you checked the tops of your dressers in our rooms, you would find bathing suits about your size. Brandy, should we go upstairs and help them into their suits? That might be fun."

"I don't think the boys are into any more fun right now. You guys think you could handle getting into your bathing suits without our assistance?"

Randy replied immediately. "We'll put our suits on and be outside in a minute. Come on Fred. Let's go."

TEN

The twins took the big power boat out, but couldn't interest anyone in skiing or tubing. They ended up cruising slowly around the lake for several hours. While they were cruising, they pulled in at a marina on the south side of the lake and found Pie Eyed Petey's restaurant and bar. While the twins, Brandy and Blaze took a table in the bar, the four youngsters had to stay out on the patio or in the family room, no alcoholic drinks allowed since they were obviously underage.

"Why don't we come back here for dinner?" Blaze asked. "It's handy and a couple of locals I talked to said the food's not bad and their bar is also outstanding."

"What about us?" Fred asked. "Will we sit around pickin' our noses while you all are getting high? That's no fun."

Brandy spoke up. "We brought stuff better than booze in the boat. You guys can try it in a little bit.

"Wow!" Fred said. "That sounds like fun. What do you say, partner?"

"Sounds like a good time to me."

✳ Sunday, September 2, 2012, 8:00 pm ✳

Later, after they had cleaned up and dressed to go to the restaurant, both Walter and Samantha were concerned about Charlotte. Samantha abandoned any ideas she had about escaping. She would stay with the group to protect her new friend.

"Charlotte, are you sure you don't want to stay here while the rest go out for dinner?" Samantha asked. "I could stay here with you if you want."

"No, I'm fine. I'll be okay."

56

"Are you sure?" Walter asked. "I'd be glad to stay here and keep you company. I don't need to go."

"No, really, I'm fine now. I must be careful what I eat. If I do, I will be okay. Anyway, mornings are when my problems show up."

They were piling into the boat when Blaze stopped. "It's still light now, but how in the hell will you find your way back here in the dark, Warren? I would be totally lost out on the lake once it's dark."

"Walter, flip the switch and show the worry warts our guiding light," Warren ordered.

Atop the flagpole at the end of the pier a blue light appeared when Walter flipped a switch mounted on one of the pier poles. "No other blue lights are showing anywhere on the lake. That's what Jake told me," Warren said. "Turn on the light and you can see it from almost every part of the lake. Head for the blue light and you will find the place for sure. Jake told me he navigated home to the blue light several times when he was drunk as hell out on the lake. Besides, we can use the spotlight mounted on the front deck of the boat when we come back after dark."

By the time they pulled up to the dock at Pie Eyed Petey's, the sun was going down. The light in the west would slowly diminish for the next hour before finally being overcome by the blackness of a moonless night. The meal proved surprisingly good and with jokes and small talk. At ten-thirty they finished their meal. Warren and the Phillips girls headed for the bar. The two boys headed for the boat and were soon deep in marijuana induced fogs. Walter, Charlotte and Samantha took seats at a round table out under the stars, ordered soft drinks, and got into a long, complicated discussion of what Charlotte was going to do about the new life inside her. After one they all got into the boat and headed slowly back down the lake.

Halfway down toward the west end of the lake Warren shut off the boat's engine, doused the lights and said, "Listen to how quiet . . . and . . . all those stars. Amazing."

Blaze laid her head back against the seat cushion and looked up. "I can't remember ever seeing so many stars. Overhead—the Milky Way. I've never seen it so clearly."

They drifted slowly for half an hour when Samantha asked, "Where's your blue light, Warren? I don't see one anywhere. It should be over on shore somewhere," she said pointing. "We moved out to the middle of the lake and didn't pass it. No way did we go past it. I never saw it, anywhere."

"Damn," Walter said emphatically. "You don't suppose it burned out do you? it was an incandescent bulb. I bet it burned out. Now we're in a fix. I for one can't tell where the place could be or how we can find it."

Samantha spoke up among loud murmurs from the others. "My sense of direction is quite good. If we head for the shore on our left and use the spotlight I'm sure we'll find it even if it takes awhile."

Warren turned the boat toward the shore on the left. Lights from the many cottages crowding the shore made it easy for them to get close to the lakeshore. "If no one objects I'll follow Samantha's suggestion. She makes sense to me. As soon as we are near those cottages on shore, I'll turn on the spotlight and we can start searching. I don't think we could miss the pier and boathouse."

About fifteen minutes of searching and Warren finally trained the spotlight on the boat house. "There we go! But what is that big outboard boat doing next to the pier?"

Blaze added, "It wasn't there when we left. The lights along the stairs and down the walk to the pier are also out. When we left for dinner, I turned them all on so we could find our way back when we returned. Do you suppose something electrical blew in the house?"

Warren said, "A circuit breaker probably blew. Walter, do you remember where the main electrical box is?"

"Exactly where. It's right behind the closet door, the closet beside the back door."

"Do you think you could find your way to the main electric box in the dark and check those circuit breakers?"

"It would be easier if I had a flashlight. Try to find one in the boat. Search while we guide the boat into the lift so we can climb out."

As Warren maneuvered the boat into the boat lift everyone was searching for a flashlight.

"Found one," Samantha called out. "And it works."

She handed the light to Walter who stepped onto the pier and headed for the glass doors at the front of the house. Everyone got out of the boat and followed Walter's flashlight toward the house except Warren and Charlotte. They stayed to put the boat on the lift as soon as the power was back on. Warren aimed the spotlight through the huge windows and lit up the entire interior of the house.

"That should help you to see where you're going," Warren shouted after them. "Charlotte, a pair of stout ropes are fastened to the pier in front of the boat. If you'll hand them to me, I'll hook up the front. We will need to fasten the stern ropes, one on each side. They will hold the boat in place while we operate the lift if Walter ever turns the power on."

"What about those stern lines?" Charlotte asked while looking out at the pier. "I can't find them."

"They're attached to eyes in the back of the boat. They should be stuffed down behind the back cushions. If you can step in the boat and toss them to me, I'll fasten them to the lift. That will hold the boat in place so we can operate the lift when the power is turned on. I wonder why the power went off?"

ELEVEN

Ray and Al climbed into Ray's rented pickup for their trip at about two on Sunday afternoon. With no need to hurry, they avoided Interstate 69 and drove north on State Route 3. Neither said much until after they passed through Wabash and were on State Route 13, headed north.

"That boat and trailer will be a lot heavier on our way back home. Will that be a problem?" Ray asked.

"Hell no old buddy. That's why I rented such a big, heavy boat. The trailer will handle twice the load we'll be carrying."

"You're sure?"

"Damn it Ray, quit being such a worry wart. I planned this job for months. Don't you think I covered all those things when I planned? I am thorough. You saw the results of my planning, and all the stuff I put together."

"Yeah, I guess you're right. Those two little jobs we did together went smooth as clockwork, thanks to your careful plans. But they were small ones and local. This is a big job far away in unknown territory, unknown to me anyway. I can't help being nervous."

"Think of it as a pleasure jaunt. We'll be out on the lake in our boat among all those millionaires who won't have a clue as to what we're about. We can smile and wave to them like nothing's going down. It will be fun. Think of all the money we'll make."

"Yeah . . . That part sounds real good to me. Maybe we could buy an island in the Carribean. I can see us now, laying on the beach with a couple of broads, having a great time, or in the South Pacific, Tahiti for instance."

"Not for me. No damned desert island for this guy. I want action and lots of it. Buenos Aires or Sao Paulo in Brazil. I hear those Latin chicks are real hot. That's more my style. Besides, it would take a whole lot more than we get to buy any island. I hate to disappoint you, Ray, but at best our take will be something less than a million bucks apiece. We can invest in something and live quite comfortably on the proceeds, some commercial real estate for example. What I'd really like is to buy a bar in Buenos Aires. I'd hire some flashy chicks as bartenders and waitresses. Make a high class place for wealthy guys. Bars like that make lots of money. I would take a different one of those chicks to bed with me every night. Now that would be the life."

"When you describe that, it sounds pretty good to me. We could run the bar together, you know, partners. With one of us watching the cash drawer and the bartenders all the time we could keep them from ripping us off. I heard lots of bars go bust because the owners aren't around and the help steal them blind "

"Hang on Ray. I think we're comin' up on the place we turn. On the right should be an old wooden restaurant on the southeast corner at the light. . . . Yep, right as rain. We will put the boat in the water in half an hour and be out on the lake long before dark. The boat ramp should be about six miles down this road."

The boat ramp was on the south side of Armstrong Road where it crossed Grassy Creek. Parked in the lot were several empty boat trailers attached to tow vehicles. About twenty minutes later, the truck and trailer were parked with the others and the boat was in the water. Al carefully steered the boat through the culvert under Armstrong road, and they were on their way down Grassy Creek to the lake.

"Shouldn't we wait for dark to do this? In the broad daylight everyone can see us."

"Ray, don't be such a damned pain. We'll be one of many fisherman on the lake. We'll be invisible right out in the open with hundreds of boats and those little PWCs running around. If we act like fishermen going out to fish, no one will pay any attention to us. Besides, going down this narrow creek in daylight is a helluva lot easier. Also, we'll remember how to come back in the dark with our flashlight."

"Suppose something goes wrong. Maybe a game warden will ask us for our fishing license, or the motor quits before we go back to the ramp?"

"God damn it, Ray, shut up with all the crap. Nothing like that is going to happen. When it's completely dark, after nine o'clock, we tie up to the pier, clean the place out. Then we climb in the boat and head up Grassy Creek. I figure we will be on our way back to the launch ramp by no more than one in the morning. We pull the boat out on the trailer and cover it with the boat cover. We should be back in Indy in three hours, before it's daylight."

"The whole job seems so simple when you talk. My experience is those simple projects never turn out to be simple. Problems always come up, unexpected problems."

"If that happens, and I doubt it will, we'll deal with it. Our biggest problem will be getting the silver melted and cast into bars we can sell easily. That's all arranged with a guy who has access to a small foundry. I told him we picked up a bunch of scrap silver at bargain prices from some guy who thought the metal was lead. He agreed to melt the scrap and cast bars for us for a price, one bar of silver."

✳ Sunday, September 2, 2012, 8:10 pm ✳

The sun was setting as they pulled out into the lake from Grassy Creek. Al took the boat out into the middle of the lake. He ran slowly down the lake until they were out in the middle, directly in front of their target. Many boats of all kinds passed them going both ways.

"Ray, check out the blue light," Al said, pointing.

"Yeah. What about it?"

"That's the pier for the place."

"What's the blue light doing on now. . . . And what about all those lights going up to the house? I thought you said they would be gone."

"Hell, Ray, those are lights they leave on all the time. Lots of people turn lights on to make people like us think they are home when they're not. I'll turn them off though. Otherwise people will see us. We don't want that. I'll take care of those lights when I go in and disable the alarm system."

"I don't like it Al. Already several things are different from what you said."

"Son of a bitch. Will you shut up with all the worries? You want I should dump you on the opposite shore, do the whole job myself and keep all the money?"

"I'm sorry. I'll shut up. We had some problems with the other two jobs we did together and they turned out all right."

"That's better, old buddy. It'll be pitch black in less than an hour. Then we'll motor over to the blue light, tie up, do our business and high tail it out. No one will be suspicious until they come back in two weeks. By that time the silver will all be turned into cash. We can put the paintings and other stuff in one of those storage lockers and leave them until the heat dies down and I find the best way to turn them into cash. That could be several years from now."

When they tied their boat up to the pier, Ray climbed out onto the pier and didn't like what he saw. He whispered, "Damn it Al, where's the boat that should be in the boat lift?"

"Hell, I don't know. They might be having it worked on while they're away. Who cares anyway? Come on, give me a hand with this heavy cutter. I don't want to drop it in the lake. Put it over on the table. Do so quietly and come back for this extension cord."

"Damn, it's quiet. Someone might hear the cutter and come over and check on things," Ray said as he handed Al the extension cord and the bag with the rest of their tools.

"Shit, Ray, the entire Indiana State Police force may be waiting for us when we break in. . . . Don't be such a chicken-livered coward. This one will go smooth like those last two."

"Okay, Okay, I hear ya. Let's cut the sliding door out so you can disable the alarm."

Ray took a hammer and chisel and cut away the bottom and side of the fixed part of the sliding door. As soon as that was done, they lifted the double pane glass out of the frame without disturbing the alarm sensor.

Al immediately grabbed his box with the five wires and headed up the stairs as quickly as he could. When he reached the top of the back stairs, he saw the red light on the alarm control box he was perplexed. *Had they actually gone off to Spain without setting the alarm,* he wondered? No matter.

To be sure, he attached the box to the alarm within a minute so the motion sensors did not send out an alarm. He decided not to tell Ray, but hollered down instead, "The alarm's off. I'm gonna douse those damned lights. We can work with the night vision goggles in complete safety."

He threw all of the circuit breakers except those marked *main floor outlets*. When he did so, all of the lights went out. Within ten minutes he began cutting up the fountain. While he was doing that, Ray started taking down the paintings and carrying them out to the boat.

✳ Monday, September 3, 2012, 2:00 am ✳

It took Al more than two hours to cut up the fountain. Several of the larger pieces were too heavy for even Ray to carry so they had to be cut in two.

Ray could tell their boat was now sitting much lower in the water. "That stuff must weigh close to a ton. I hope we can still run the boat up the creek."

"That's why I got such a big boat, you idiot. I figured all of that out a long time ago. The boat could probably carry twice as much weight. Shut up with the damned worries and make sure we didn't leave anything. Did you pick up the extension cord?"

"It's in the back of the boat."

"Hold down the fort for a few minutes. I've gotta go take a dump before we leave."

Ray waited on one of several benches in the yard near the pier. After a few minutes he jumped up and ran to the broken doorway. Al was walking across the main room toward the door.

"A boat with a bright light is comin' toward the dock," he shouted, his voice shrill and excited. "It'll be here in a minute or two. What can we do?"

"Quick, into the boat house. They won't find us."

"They will see our boat with all the stuff."

"Shut up, Ray. Let me think."

"Damn, Al, look out the window, they're coming right to this pier."

"Ray, will you shut the fuck up. I want to try to hear what they're saying."

"They're pulling the boat into the lift. They must be staying in the house. A bunch of them are in the boat, men and women. I can hear 'em talkin'. What are we gonna do?"

"We're gonna stay right here till they go into the house. As soon as they leave the dock, we climb in our boat and high tail it up the lake. We'll be long gone before they are back down to the dock."

"I doubt that Al. From what I hear them saying, two of them, a girl and a guy, are staying with the boat while the rest are heading for the house. As soon as they find the busted door, they'll realize what's going on. We've gotta do something, now."

"If they see us, they'll be able to identify us. We'll take them out. What can we hit 'em with? Not a damn thing in here I can find."

"I don't need nothin' but my fists. I'll take the guy. You think you can handle the girl?"

"Don't be such a smart ass. Here's what we'll do. Let's walk out casual like. Act like we're lost or searching for someone. Better yet, we tell them our motor quit and we tied up at their pier until we could get help. That'll work. You move close to the guy while I get close to the gal. When we are close enough, I'll holler, NOW. We jump 'em. Make sure they are both out before we stop hittin' 'em."

They walked casually out on the pier. "Can you folks help us, or tell us where we might find some help?" Al asked. "Our motor conked out so we paddled in to your pier and tied up. We were going to head up to the road when you pulled in."

Before either of them could answer, Al shouted, "NOW."

By the time they stopped, Charlotte and Warren were beaten senseless and laying in the bottom of the boat.

"Ray, the keys are in the boat. Unhook those two ropes on the prow and we can take the boat out in the lake and dump them."

"We gonna drown 'em?"

"They both saw our faces. We can't let them go or they'll be able to identify us."

"What about the rest of 'em? By now they're in the house and sure as hell they saw the broken door and know something's goin' on."

"Let me think. . . . I told you not to, but did you bring your Glock?"

"Of course."

"I hope it's not in the truck."

"My Glock's wrapped in gun cloth in the bottom of my tool box in the boat."

"Good, go grab it, quickly."

A few minutes later Ray returned with his gun. "It's loaded, but the chamber's empty. I wouldn't want to accidently shoot myself in the leg."

"Give me the gun while you take them out and dump 'em. Did you bring your knife?"

"Of course. Why?"

"Just to make sure, slit their throats before they go in the drink. We don't want any live witnesses . . . and come back here as quick as you can. I'll try to do something about the rest of them."

Ray backed the boat out, turned and headed around Silver Point at full speed.

"Damned idiot," Al said out loud. "I sure hope no DNR officers heard him. All we need is for Ray to be stopped for speeding at night. . . . Idiot."

TWELVE

A s they approached the house, Walter noticed the broken door. "Oh shit. Someone broke in while we were away. That must be their boat tied up to the pier. That means they're still here. We'd best be careful," Walter reacted quickly. "Hurry to separate and spread out. If they're in the house that will make it more difficult for them than if we're together in one place. One of you call the police or sheriff on your cell phone. I'll go up the back stairs and turn the lights back on. As soon as the lights are on, head for the back door. We can hop in the cars and escape."

Blaze did not like that idea one bit. "What about Warren and Charlotte? They're down at the dock. We can't just leave them."

They heard the motor of the power boat accelerating away from the pier.

"I sure hope that was Warren and Charlotte getting away," Walter said.

Samantha knew immediately what to do. "Follow me, quickly, and boys, one of you please stay near the bottom of the stairs. Grab Walter as soon as he comes back and follow us upstairs. I found a perfect place to hide at the end of the hall to the bedrooms. The place will also take us out of the house. We should be able to rescue Warren and Charlotte as well."

Blaze dug in her purse and grabbed her cell phone. "Damn, no signal. We must be out of range down behind this hill. I'll try to find a regular phone in the master bedroom."

✳   ✳   ✳

At first the boys stayed together at the bottom of the stairs. After a few minutes, Fred started toward the side door. "We should duck out the side door. We could climb up the hill and be gone."

67

"I'm stayin' right here. Those gooks could be hangin' right outside the door. They sure as hell aren't in the house."

As Walter returned down the stairs, he turned on every light switch he could find. This lit the main room with it's two story ceiling as bright as daylight. Walter saw the empty walls. "So those crooks stole all those paintings that were hanging on the walls."

Fred hollered, "Quick Walter, up the stairs to the bedrooms. Samantha says she has a perfect hiding place."

As they started up the stairs, Fred hesitated, then started for the side door. Before he had taken two steps he changed his mind quickly, reversed course, and headed up the stairs behind the others.

Outside, Al watched Fred through the window, raised the Glock and then lowered it. *Those fools are trapped*, he thought. *No way can they come down except by those stairs and I've got that covered. No point in going after them till Ray is back.*

He went inside and sat down on the couch to wait for Ray to return, the Glock in his lap.

✳ Labor Day, September 3, 2012, 3:40 am ✳

Blaze entered the master bedroom on the second floor while the rest of them went up to the third floor. She turned on the lights to search for the phone. No phone was in sight.

Damn. She said to herself as she looked around. *A phone must be here somewhere, but where?*

After ten minutes of fruitless searching she thought, *the headboard of the bed. The phone must be somewhere in the headboard.* Frantically she opened every door she could find in the headboard—no phone. *It has to be here somewhere*, she thought.

As she stood at the end of the headboard, she checked behind the bed for a phone line. "Damn! No phone line means no phone. I can't believe a fancy place like this has no telephone," she said our loud. "I had better join the others upstairs."

As Blaze left the bedroom and headed upstairs, she peeked around the doorway and glanced down into the main room. She saw Al sitting on the couch, the Glock in his lap. He did not catch sight of her as she scampered up the stairs and ran down the hall to find the others. They were nowhere to be seen

When she reached the top of the stairs, Samantha ran down the hall to the maid's closet, opened the door, and turned on the light. "Hurry. In here."

"What the hell," Brandy cried out. "This is a damned closet. We'd be trapped."

"No—check this out," Samantha said as she walked to the back corner, pressed the wall and the door opened. "This stairway goes all the way down to the boathouse, a secret passage. We can all climb the stairway, turn off the light in the closet, shut the door, and they'll never find us. If we can stay quiet."

"We'll wait for Blaze," Brandy said.

"Where the hell is she?"

"She's trying to phone the police from the master bedroom. Cell phones don't work down behind this hill. No signal."

"You wait for her. Try to hurry her up. We don't want those thieves to find out where we are."

"Leave the secret door open. I'll close it as soon as Blaze returns."

Brandy waited an agonizing ten minutes before Blaze ran up the stairs. "I saw one of them sitting in the main room with a big gun in his lap. I hope Sam wasn't kidding when she said she had a good hiding place.".

"She wasn't. Hurry, you'll see."

Brandy turned off the overhead light. In the light from the stairwell she moved several buckets and a broom into the path they used to go to the corner door. "That should make our secret place a little less obvious. Once we pull the door shut behind us and douse the light they couldn't find or even suspect a door here."

"That's really slick. I wonder why they put in the stairway and hid the entrance."

"We'll ask Jake, if he's ever around."

Walter called softly from the bottom of the stairway, "Leave the light on so you can see. I found another switch down here."

When they were all together at the bottom of the stairway, Walter turned off the light and asked, "Blaze, did you call the police?"

"No. Apparently they put no hard wired phone in this place. I didn't find one in the master bedroom. No phone line anywhere. I searched all over the room. Damned cell phones are useless too. They don't work anywhere in the house."

Sam said, "I think they might work up on top of the hill, where the cars are parked."

"Hell, If we could go up to the road we could jump in the cars and go away," Fred said with a sneer.

"The kid's right except what about Warren and Charlotte?" Blaze commented. "We aren't sure they got away in the power boat. Hopefully they're somewhere safe in the boat on the lake."

"The rest of you might not be keen on gettin' away from here, but Randy and I are. I say those who want to should go out the door, climb the hill and get the hell away from here. That's a lot better than stayin' here hopin' those crooks don't find us."

Sam's voice came out of the inky blackness. "Why don't we let them go. That would mean two less to worry about. Now, everyone, please be quiet. I'm going to open the door and check outside. If no one is outside, the boys can head away from the house, climb the hill, and be gone. Anyway, I want to check on Warren and Charlotte—find out where they are."

"I don't think that's a good idea, Sam. Supposing they catch the boys and you. They'll tell them where we're hiding," Walter cautioned.

"I went out this door before. Outside is like a short tunnel through thick shrubbery. They wouldn't see me in broad daylight. The boys can head off to the right and find their way up the hill, even in the dark."

"Them leaving gives us another problem. A serious one you never even considered."

"What's that, Walter," Brandy asked.

"Suppose they go up the hill, and some of the crooks are waiting and catch them. How long would it take a few crooks with guns to convince these boys to reveal our secret hiding place—where we are? We have no idea how many of them are here, or where they are for that matter, other than the one guy with a gun in the main room. Be honest with me, boys. Wouldn't you tell them about our hiding place if faced with torture and death?"

The boys remained silent.

"I think that provides the answer. We stay together and in hiding," Walter was quite definite.

"I still think I should sneak outside to check on Warren and Charlotte," Sam pleaded.

"Okay," Walter said. "But please be careful. Stay in the dark as much as possible."

Sam crept outside to the boathouse. "The big boat's gone. Hopefully Warren and Charlotte left in the boat," She whispered. Then she had an idea. "I'm going to untie their boat and push it away from the pier. They won't be able to escape when the police come."

"**If** the police come you mean—**if**," Blaze corrected. "That's chancey, Sam."

"The only light is from the house. I don't think any one would see me."

Walter moved toward the doorway as Sam opened it. "I'll go with you. Two can work quicker than one."

When they reached the pier, they untied both ends of the big outboard, walked to the end of the pier and gave the heavy boat a healthy shove out into the lake. They hurried back into the stairway.

The light breeze from the northwest caught and moved the big outboard slowly but steadily up the lake to the southeast. A third quarter moon was rising above the eastern horizon.

When they returned to the group, Fred announced, "Randy and I are going out and up the hill. We can get away."

"It's pitch black outside," Blaze said. "You won't be able to see a thing."

"I think we'll be OK. Come on Randy. Let's go. The moon's coming up and will give us some light"

The two disappeared into the darkness before any one could try to stop them.

"I hope they don't run into any of those robbers," Walter said quietly. "What should we do now?" The sound of the rapidly approaching power boat drove them back quickly into the stairwell.

Sam stayed by the partially open door. "Let's find out who's in the boat before we do anything."

✳ Labor Day, September 3, 2012, 4:10 am ✳

The two boys struggled up the hill and out onto the road where a streetlight broke the night. Fred immediately ran for the other side of the house and started down the hill.

"Where in hell are you going?" Randy shouted.

"To get the stuff I stashed in the shed, stupid. It'll bring us a bundle of cash."

"Yeah, and maybe we'll be killed by one of those robbers."

"Damned chicken. Come on. Give me a hand."

Ten minutes later they struggled up the hill. Both were carrying as much as they could hold and still climb up the hill.

"Now, lets go to our car and drive home," Fred announced proudly. "You see, no problems. This weekend has turned out to be a winner for us in more ways than one."

"It's a mile or more on pavement in near complete darkness to our car in the parking lot. Lugging all this stuff in the bargain will be tough. It's heavy."

"Let's find someplace to stash our loot and come back with the car."

"And just where could we find such a place, Fred."

"Let's keep our eyes open as we walk. We would only need the place for a few minutes. If your little car is too small, you could borrow your mom's SUV and we could use that. She won't be workin' tomorrow. It's Labor Day."

"Why are we always borrowing **my** mom's car? You don't offer to ask your mom even once in awhile. That's not fair, Fred."

"Shit man, you know my mom goes berserk about her precious car. She told me if I wanted to drive I should buy my own car. I can after we sell this stuff."

About ten minutes later, "Look, Randy, over by the tree. Isn't that an old culvert pipe?" They could barely make it out by the light of the moon. "That would be a perfect place to hide this stuff. We can come back for as soon as we can latch on to a big enough car. Let's hide our stuff inside."

Fred took off across a yard with Randy soon following. They stacked their loot inside the piece of culvert and pulled up a small, woody bush to hide the opening.

"What will we do with this stuff? How can we turn it into cash?" Randy asked as they walked back to the road.

"We've got plenty of time. We can figure out a way."

✳   ✳   ✳

Ray took the boat down in front of the dance hall where the lights from the parking lot enabled him to see what he was doing in the boat.

Ray addressed the unconscious Warren. "Mister, those must be $500 boots you're wearing, and they are about my size. Since you won't be needing them anymore, I'll remove them. They'll look sharp on my feet."

He hoisted the now barefoot Warren over the side and held him by the chin. One swift stroke of his switchblade and blood spurted against the boat. Ray washed the blood spatter off as Warren's body sank out of sight.

"Now, little lady, you're gonna give me a bit of pleasure before I dump you," He said out loud as he stripped Charlotte's dress from her.

When he was finished, he hoisted her over the side and grabbed her by the chin to finish her off. As he started to position his knife to slit her throat, she suddenly twisted her head out of his grasp. His knife caught her chin as he tried to drive it into her ear when she twisted away from him. As he slashed with his knife, it flew out of his hand and slipped over her skull.

"Damn. My good knife. . . . No matter, little lady," he said as she quickly sank from view in the dark water. "You'll soon drown."

He fired up the boat and headed back around Silver Point toward the blue light marking his destination. The third quarter moon was bright in the eastern sky as he eased the boat into the lift. He noticed their boat was gone from where they tied it up when he left.

"That son of a bitch headed out with our loot and left me. I'll kill the bastard"

Hearing the power boat return, Al got up and went outside. "Hell, you took long enough."

Ray was confused. "Our boat's gone."

Al stared in disbelief at the empty spot by the pier. "It probably came loose."

"Not by a long shot. I tied the boat up good with triple clove hitches, front and back. Somebody had to untie it. I don't like that one tiny bit."

"I didn't hear the motor. I would hear the motor for sure if someone ran the starter. I think we'd better go in, find the rest of those people and take care of business."

The last thing Charlotte remembered was repeated crushing blows to her head, face and body, and of grasping a piece of paper from the deck of the boat. Then came the peace of unconsciousness. She awoke to the horror of realizing she was being raped. When she started to scream, she stopped and forced her self to remain limp and silent. She did not want any more of those savage blows. She was barely aware of what was happening. She was in a fog of semiconsciousness and in lots of pain. She was gripping the paper she picked up so hard her nails were cutting into her palm. The sudden shock of cold water covering her body brought her to full consciousness. Her head was being held just above the water. She twisted quickly out of the hand that held her. Immediately she felt a severe pain from her chin to the top of her head. Still, she did not move but let her body sink below the water. A strong swimmer, she immediately began swimming under the surface away from the boat.

When she heard the motor start, accelerate, and move away, she surfaced and paused to catch her breath. She recognized the lights of the Tippy parking lot and started swimming toward them. With each stroke of her arms the pain racking her head struck stronger. The cool water of late summer was chilling and numbing her. If only she could reach the shore.

Finally, the feel of gravel beneath her knees and hands buoyed her spirits. She had made the water's edge. She lay half in the water for a moment, then crawled on her hands and knees as far as she could go. She heard voices, children's voices, then silence. She was terribly confused and having difficulty making sense of what was happening.

"Walter," she cried out, "Walter," and passed out.

She vaguely sensed someone covering her convulsively shivering body and trying to comfort her. Strong, gentle hands lifted her onto a warm soft bed. She heard several soft voices, then she drifted off slowly and peacefully into a deep sleep.

They all heard the exchange between Al and Ray after Ray pulled the power boat into the lift. They had no idea what had happened to Warren and Charlotte but the fact they were no where to be seen and they were missing when the power boat returned, had a fairly obvious and ominous meaning

"As soon as they go inside to *take care of business* as they announced, let's hop in the power boat and go away from here," Walter suggested.

"Someone had better run out and check for the keys before we all expose ourselves. I'll bet they took them," Blaze said. "I suppose I volunteered."

A quick trip to the boat and back and she announced, "No keys. They took them, so back to the drawing board"

"Who has the keys to our BMW? I don't," Walter said.

"I do," Blaze answered. "Unfortunately they are in my purse and my purse is in our bedroom. If our friends find them, goodbye BMW."

"Not so," Walter corrected. "Don't you remember our little security lock on the ignition. The key will only provide entry into the car by using the buttons. Once the key is inserted in the ignition, a security code must be entered in the key pad to start the car. Blaze, you remember the code. You drove here."

"All I meant was we would not be able to use the BMW to leave. So the BMW is not in danger, but we four are. What do we do now?"

"We'd better find some way to use a cell phone," Walter said

"Or go away from here," Brandy said. "Light is starting to show in the east and we'll be able to find our way shortly. I say we head south away from the house and find some neighbors who can call the police or sheriff."

"What about my brother and Charlotte?"

Worry furrowed Blaze's face. "When the power boat came back with only one crook, I had a real bad feeling about the two of them. The last we saw of them, they were in that boat, waiting for the lights to come on. We haven't seen them since."

THIRTEEN

Al did not like the situation. "Okay, Ray. Chamber a bullet in your Glock and let's go hunting, one room at a time. Stay by the door so none of them come down past us. While you're watching the hall, I'll check the room and closet so we don't miss any of them."

"It'll be a turkey shoot."

"And Ray, head shots if possible, less of a mess that way. Lets start at the second level."

By the time they had searched every room frustration was setting in. "Where in hell are they, Ray? I saw them come up here. They must be here somewhere. Those plans showed those front stairs to be the only access to the third floor."

Al checked out the maid's closet. "No place to hide in here. Damn."

"I passed a spiral staircase at the other end of this hall? Could be they climbed those to escape."

"Damn, I bet you're right."

They ran to the staircase, climbed up and were stopped by the door with a locked deadbolt.

"Damn it, Ray. I bet they took these stairs to the roof and locked the door behind them. Shoot the lock open."

Five shots were needed to free the deadbolt and open the door. They rushed out onto a widow's walk with a railing. All around were steep roofs. No one was in sight.

Al scratched his head in disbelief. "This is impossible. They couldn't just vanish into thin air."

Ray turned around and headed for the staircase. "Let's leave here and fast. None of the rest of them got a good look at us so they probably couldn't identify us. Besides it'll soon be getting light. We'd better take the power boat and find our outboard. It will be floating somewhere down wind."

"I don't think that's a good idea. I hate leaving loose ends. Why don't you take the power boat and find our outboard. Tow the damned thing back here. When you are back, cover the boat with the cover so's nobody can see our loot and tie it up to the pier. While you're gone, I'm gonna sit on this place. No way could those people escape without our seeing them so they must still be inside and up those stairs. I'll wait right here till you are back. Then we'll go huntin' again only this time we'll find them."

Al sat down at the lawn table and faced the house, the Glock on the table in front of him.

Ray took the powerboat and headed east. He was soon searching fruitlessly for the boat by the light of the waning moon.

Half an hour later, Ray saw the light of the moon glistening and reflecting off of the outboard's windshield. He had found the fishing boat in close to shore. *I'm in luck,* he thought. *No one around.*

He finally reached the outboard. It took him nearly twenty minutes to tie the boat on to the rear of the power boat and start a slow trip back. The big outboard swished back and forth wallowing in the wake with the heavy load. By five o'clock the outboard was covered and retied to the pier.

✳ Labor Day, September 3, 2012, 6:20 am ✳

Deputy Paul Noonan was headed west on Armstrong road after completing a call in North Webster. He slowed as he passed the boat ramp on Armstrong Road. He made a mental note of a truck and boat trailer parked in the lot when he drove by earlier. Obviously the rig stayed parked all night, a most unusual situation. Not technically against the law as the time limit, clearly worded on the sign, is 24 hours. He made a U turn and headed back to the ramp parking lot to check it out. He checked out the truck plate first and found the owner was Ace Truck Rental of Indianapolis.

Checking he found no problems with the registration. The trailer license was also registered to Ace Truck Rental, and everything about the trailer was in order as well.

When he got back into his car, a call came in for him to go to KCH. "EMS brought in an injured girl with no ID. She may be the one you were searching for earlier."

"Would you ask Eric to contact Jerome Wells. If he can't come to the hospital, tell me and I'll pick him up. Otherwise, I'll be at the emergency room in about twelve minutes." He spun his car around and sped west toward KCH.

FOURTEEN

The sound of five shots rang through the house. "I hope that wasn't them finding the boys," Blaze said. "How about we go outside and away from here."

They all went to the bottom of the hidden stairs and waited. Walter decided to open the door and peeked out. After a few minutes of silence he heard Al and Ray rushing out of the house.

"Somebody's coming out of the house. Don't make a sound."

After a few minutes they heard the unmistakable sound of the powerboat starting up, backing out of the lift, and taking off fast. Walter cracked open the door. By the light of the moon he saw the boat with one man flying east at high speed. "Only one of them is in the boat so the other one is still here and he's the one with the gun. Oh oh, he's sitting down at the table right outside this entrance. When the sun get's bright enough he's bound to notice this doorway. I think we had better go upstairs and try to go out the back door."

Blaze led the group up the stairway and into the hallway. They carefully closed and latched the door behind them. Keeping in a tight group, they sneaked down the main staircase until they could see the front yard. Al was sitting facing the house and staring directly up toward the staircase.

"No way can we go to the back stairs without him seeing us," Walter said quietly. "I don't think those glass windows would keep bullets from hitting us if we tried."

Sam said, "How about this? He's sitting right near the doorway to those secret stairs. I'll go into the maid's closet and toss a bucket down the stairs. He's sure to hear the terrible racket and go to the door to investigate. As soon as he's out of sight we can all run down to the second floor and up the back stairs and out."

"Before you do that, let me grab our purses from our rooms," Blaze asked. "He can't see us in this hallway so I can pick up all of our purses including Charlotte's. Then we'll have the keys to both cars."

"I'll go too," Brandy said. "That way it will go twice as fast. The rest of you holler if he moves. When we are back, Sam, you can do your distraction and we'll all escape. What do you say?"

Walter was dubious. "Are you sure we can all run down and up those steps before he comes back?"

Sam said, "We can try. Go ahead girls, grab those purses. I'll keep an eye on him while you go."

It only took them a few minutes to pick up the purses and return. Blaze dangled the keys to the BMW triumphantly as she positioned herself to watch.

"I hope you are aware of what you're doing, Sam. Be careful," Walter cautioned.

"Don't worry, I will. He's bound to be curious, and if he goes inside the entranceway, we will be able to scoot out the back door. Someone tell the rest when he's out of sight."

Blaze said, "I'll tell everyone exactly what he's doing. Surely he won't see me peeking carefully around this corner. He didn't before, even when he seemed to be looking straight at me."

Sam ran down the hall and entered the closet. The metal bucket bouncing down the long flight of stairs made a lot of noise. Before it stopped at the bottom, Sam was back with the group waiting for the signal to run.

"That sure startled him," Blaze reported. "He jumped up, grabbed his gun and pointed it in the direction of the stairway. So far he hasn't moved from the spot. . . . He's staring intently in that direction. Oops, now he's looking back up this way. . . . I think he's trying to decide what to do. He took a slow step toward the stairway. Go on dummy. . . . He took a long look up the lake. It's still quite dark. We should wait until it is brighter out. . . . No . . . go now. He's gone inside. Go! Go!"

They all rushed down one flight of stairs, ran across the second floor hall and up the back stairs to the door. Walter stopped to set the alarm. Seeing Al's control box he grabbed it and ripped the connections off. He armed the alarm before leaving through the door which he deliberately left open. All four made the stairs without a shot being fired.

Blaze went out onto the road and checked her cell phone. *Two bars*, she said to herself. *Thank God.*

Right then the alarm, went off and was definitely not silent.

She dialed 911.

"Emergency operator. Your name and location please."

"My name is Blaze Phillips. I am a guest in a home on Lake Tippecanoe about a quarter mile east of the Tippy dance hall. Two men robbed the house. One of them just left in a powerboat going east on the lake. The other is in the front yard holding a gun, a big gun."

"What is the number of the house?"

"Walter, what's the house number?"

"Wait, the number is right here in my pocket. . . . 2965 Forest Glen."

"2965 Forest Glen."

"Thank you. Officers will be sent to investigate as soon as we can assign them to this call. From our map, I assume the road you are on is the one starting in the dance hall parking lot."

"Yes, that's the one. It only took us a few minutes to drive to the house from the parking lot."

"Our closest vehicle is about twenty minutes away. I'm sorry, but that's the best we can do."

"Right now we're Okay, I think we'll climb in our car and leave and go as far as the parking lot at the dance hall. In case the one with the gun decides to come up here."

"Can you stay close by and keep your phone connected until our officers arrive?"

"I certainly will. We'll stay nearby. I don't want to stay too close."

"How many are in your group?"

"Four, one guy and three gals. Two others of our group disappeared and we are afraid something bad happened to them. They are gone." She didn't include the two young boys thinking they were best left out of the situation and were already gone.

"Just don't disconnect the phone."

"I'll certainly try not to. We plan on staying within sight of the place until the officers arrive."

Walter joined Blaze and opened the door of the BMW. "Get in. Did you call the police?"

"I called 911. The operator said a car would be here in about twenty minutes. I told her about our missing friends."

Walter began to worry about all the stuff in their portable bar and the video cameras. He ran back into the house and collected the little TV cameras and put them into the portable bar. He closed the bar and rolled it out into the hall.

"Blaze! Brandy! Come down here and give me a hand, will you?"

As they came haltingly down the stairs, Blaze called out, "Walter, is it safe? What do you need?"

"Yes, they left in their boat right after the alarm went off. I better hide the bar in the trunk of my car before the cops are here."

Blaze ran down the stairs. "I forgot all about that stuff. I'm glad you remembered. Come on, Brandy. We need your help."

The bar was safely stowed in the trunk of the BMW long before the police arrived.

✳ Labor Day, September 3, 2012, 7:45 am ✳

Sargent Chase Johnson and Deputy Danny Sheridan of the sheriff's department introduced themselves, identified all four of the remaining group, and asked what had happened. Walter led them into the house and pointed out the empty walls where the paintings hanging earlier are now missing.

"Look at the front door. That's how they got in," As he pointed out the damaged door, Walter scanned the barren patio in the daylight. "My God, that beautiful fountain is gone. Only the pipe sticking up where the fountain stood yesterday is left. Jake told me about that fountain, pure silver. He bought it in Greece twenty years ago. Paid over half a million bucks for the damned thing. How in hell did they get away with that? I bet it weighs nearly a ton."

Sargent Johnson stepped through the door onto the patio. "My guess is the fountain was the main thing they wanted to steal. They obviously planned the entire thing around that fountain. The paintings and other similar items were probably taken because it was easy once they took down the fountain."

Deputy Sullivan kneeled down to examine the ground near where the fountain had been. "The ground is covered with these fine grindings. I'll bet they're silver. They probably cut the thing up somehow and carted one piece off at a time. They put the pieces in the outboard you described. You said they had a big boat, an outboard, right?"

"Yes, It was a big boat for an outboard, and heavy too," Walter explained. We know it was heavy because we untied it and pulled it out to the end of the pier and sent it out into the lake."

"You did that while they were in the house?"

Walter explained. "We wanted to keep them from getting away until you got here. Then our cell phones wouldn't work and we couldn't call in."

"You say one of them had a gun?"

"A big black one," Blaze added.

"So we can now add armed robbery to the charges. Danny, get on the horn and call for another car. I think we're going to need more of the troops."

FIFTEEN

Suddenly the scream of the burglar alarm rent the air. At the sound, Al sprinted out to the boat. "Take the damned cover off. We've gotta hurry out of here."

"What set off the alarm? I thought you disabled it?"

"It was only turned off. Someone turned it back on. Don't worry about taking the cover completely off. Just open it enough so we can climb in and operate the boat. We've gotta escape—fast."

It took the boat with the heavy load a long time to get up on a plane, but when it did they flew. Al pointed the prow directly at the opening to Grassy Creek two miles away. Though the sun was still below the horizon, the daylight was quite bright when they flew through the mouth of Grassy Creek and up the first straight stretch. Negotiating all the crooks and turns as the waterway narrowed required slowing down. Al kept the boat going fast enough to stay on a plane until a sharp left put a stop to that. As soon as the boat dropped off planing, the motor began churning up mud and chunks of big roots. Al used the automatic tilt to angle the motor and bring the prop away from the bottom before any damage was done. This made the unwieldy boat even more difficult to control.

Ray was visibly disturbed. "Damn, we're going slow. At this rate we will take forever to reach the ramp."

"We're going as fast as we can with the motor tilted up like this. I don't think we have another choice. Ah, there's the culvert up ahead. We are almost to the ramp."

"The water in the culvert is shallow. Do you think we'll get through?"

"According to the boat specs, yes, but we may need to do so without the motor."

"How?"

"I put a heavy rope in the box of the truck. When we reach the culvert, jump out, run across the road and grab the rope. Go up on the road and drop one end into the stream. The current will carry the end down to the boat where I can grab it. I'll tie it on and you can go back around to the ramp and pull the boat through from the bank opposite. I'll hold onto the inside of the culvert to keep the boat steady."

"I hope this works."

After I tied my end to the boat, Ray tied the rope around a tree by the water's edge and planned to use a sideways force on the taut rope to pull the boat. Everything went as planned until Ray tried to pull the boat through the culvert. Al hadn't planned on the strong current flowing through the culvert. When Ray could make no headway against the current, Al decided to help by starting the motor. As soon as he released his hold on the culvert to start the motor, the boat lurched to the right and was turned out sideways into the flowing stream. It tipped precariously and almost went over. Fortunately, the motor started immediately and powered the boat out of the culvert into the still water of the little bay in front of the ramp.

"That was close," Ray shouted. Should I pull the boat up on the ramp now?"

Al sighed with relief, shut off the motor and tilted it up for the trailer. "Pull up beside the ramp so I can step out . . . unless you want to back the trailer into the water?"

"I'll leave that up to you, old buddy, seein' as how I've never backed up a boat trailer."

Working as quickly as they could, they cranked the heavy boat onto the trailer, drew the cover tight and checked everything. One walk around and they pulled out onto Armstrong Road headed east.

Ray turned to Al from the passenger seat. "Murphy's law."

"What? Oh, Yeah. Well, we're not out of the woods yet, not by a long shot. Pull the police scanner out of the glove box and turn it on every once in a while. Try to find any police activity on the radio. Leave it on only as long as we need to. The guy I bought it from says it probably has a GPS so we should use it sparingly. If we leave it on too long they might be able to track us. Oh, and should we be stopped for any reason, stuff the scanner back in the glove box. Scanners like this are strictly illegal for civilians to own."

As they turned south on SR 13 Ray asked. "Do you think they made us?"

"Nah! The truck and trailer are both clean and it was too dark for anyone to read the numbers on the boat. I'll drive carefully at the speed limit and try not to break any traffic laws. We don't want to be stopped by any cops."

"What about the truck and trailer? Couldn't they trace them back to you?"

Al laughed. "Planning, old buddy, planning. I rented the truck using one of those license/credit card combos I bought from one of my suppliers. My photo is on the license, and the card was never used. When we return the truck and trailer, we pay in cash so the credit card doesn't show up, and we're home free. Nothing can tie us to either one in the unlikely event that someone checks. Like I said earlier, I've been planning this for a long time. I even opened a checking account under the name on this license in case we need to pay for something costing more than our pocket cash. We don't want to ever charge anything using that credit card or those records will cross us up."

"We left quite a few loose ends back at the house."

"Nothing that leads to us, nothing. We made sure of that. The only real witnesses are at the bottom of the lake. They won't even show up for a while. You did take care of that, didn't you?"

"Yeah, for sure. Only, I lost my knife when I did the girl. Dropped out of my hand."

"Well, don't worry. No one will find it in that deep water."

"That was my favorite knife. My name is on it."

"What?"

"Well, only my first name. I had "Ray" engraved on the little silver inlay on the handle."

"It's a good thing Ray is a common name. Even in the extremely unlikely event someone found it, they would have a hard time tracing the knife to you, and even harder to tie it to those two slit throats."

"Oh my God, Al. A cop car is coming up behind us fast, with flashers on. What will we do?"

"Not much we can do. We sure as hell can't out run him in this rig. I'll pull over and stop—act like nothin's wrong. Let me do the talkin'.'"

As they rolled to a stop, the police car roared by and kept going.

Al was shaking as he gripped the wheel with whitened hands."Damn! that sure scared the shit out of me."

"Me two. I thought we was goners. I don't think I ever saw a more beautiful sight than those flashing light disappearing in the distance. We're lucky neither of us had a heart attack."

Al pulled slowly back into the roadway. "I'm gonna take things easy till my heart calms down. I don't scare easy, but that sure scared the crap outta me."

They continued talking about the incident for some time as they drove south toward Wabash.

When they reached the intersection of SR115, Al turned right and headed for US 24. "I'm changing our route home, Ray, I had a thought."

"I thought you had this all planned out. Why change?"

"By now, the police will know what we stole and be searchin' for it. They are also sure to realize we took it away in a boat, a big outboard. Soon they will be stopping outfits like ours and searching them. I think we should take all the stuff out of the boat as soon as possible."

"How in hell can we do that? I thought the plan was to transfer everything into the storage building at the back of your lot."

"That's more than eighty miles away. We'd probably be Okay, but I don't want to take a chance. One of those rental storage places on US 24 near Peru, is a few miles down the road. If we rent one of those spaces, we can store everything until we figure out what to do."

"Isn't that a bit far for us to go for our stuff?"

"Sure, but parking things will make them hard to tie to us. This place is only two hours away from Indy. When the pressure is off we can take the silver and convert it into bars so we can sell them. We may need to leave those paintings in storage for several years. That will be like money in the bank as long as we aren't in a rush."

"I don't like the stuff being so far from home."

"Well, we can always move them to Indy after things cool down, when and if we decide to."

"I'll feel a lot better when we've converted the silver to cash and those paintings are stored closer to home."

"So will I, but we must be realistic. A lot of risk sits in the trailer and we will risk a lot less if we drop everything off about ten miles down the road. It's off to the left at the next traffic light."

Fifteen minutes later they pulled into the storage place. They took two hours to arrange for one of the storage units and unload their loot. They stacked all of the paintings in the back of the unit. All but two pieces of silver were piled in front of the paintings and covered with a small tarp. The two pieces of the silver fountain were stashed behind the driver's seat. Al used the phony license for an ID and paid using the checking account he had under that name.

As they headed south on US 31 Ray grinned and patted Al on the back. "I gotta hand it to you, Al, having that license and check in a fictitious name was a stroke of genius."

"It's not a fictitious name. George Mann is a real person. That original license was stolen, no, actually borrowed, copied, and returned, without Mann ever knowing. Everything is as clean as a whistle no matter who checks."

"What's the point?"

"Fake names and fictitious licenses are red flags to police. Real ones are not. As long as they are not used directly, no one knows. I can pay for anything using that checkbook and as long as the check clears, no red flags go up. Now that all that stuff is no longer in our boat, we are home free should the cops stop us for any reason."

"What about those two pieces of silver behind the seat?"

"I need them in Indy. I plan on turnin' them into cash as soon as I can. I need to recover the money I spent on the things we needed for this job, and especially the cost of the rental space I didn't anticipate. I doubt they would find where we stuck them even if we are stopped and searched anyway."

"I sure hope you're right."

SIXTEEN
✳ Labor Day, September 3, 2012, 6:50 am ✳

Jerome had just gotten to sleep when his mother awakened him. "A man on the phone wants to talk to you. He says it's extremely urgent. Here, take it."

At those words, he was wide awake. "Thanks mom. . . . Hello?"

"Jerome, this is deputy Blanding. Deputy Paul Noonan asked me to call you. We need you to come down to KCH as soon as you can. Your missing girlfriend might be here."

"At KCH? Is she hurt? What happened?" he asked while struggling into his clothes.

"I can't discuss her over the phone. Please come as soon as you can. When you are here your questions will be answered. If you can't get here. Deputy Noonan will come and pick you up."

"No need. I can drive."

"He'll meet you at the emergency room entrance."

"OK. Bye."

His mother asked, "What's wrong? Who's hurt?"

"A friend, Mom. No time to talk," he said as he finished pulling on pants, shirt, and shoes and rushed out to his car.

He broke most speed limits driving and worrying about how badly Susan was hurt.

Deputy Noonan was waiting as he rushed in. "Follow me this way, please, and be quiet. I want you to look at someone and tell me if she's your girlfriend."

Jerome was ushered into a room with a bed with a woman attached to tubes and all kinds of monitoring devices. A nurse directed him. "Take a good look until you're sure. Don't touch anything and leave quietly."

"That's not Susan," he told deputy Noonan.

"You're absolutely sure? Her face is badly bruised and swollen."

Jerome was a bit relieved. "Absolutely. That woman is a brunette. Susan's hair is ash blonde. She also is taller than Susan."

"I hope your Susan turns up soon, and in much better health than our Jane Doe here. She's in terribly bad shape, beaten up unmercifully. They don't give her much chance of surviving."

"That's terrible. She must be about Susan's age."

"They guess late teens. Thanks for coming down. Sorry to drag you out so soon after you got home, but we must do these things. You understand."

"Sure. Can I go now?"

"Of course. I hope your Susan turns up in good health. Someone will call you if we find her."

"Thanks."

Jerome headed for home and bed once more, thinking, *thank goodness Susan's not that poor girl.*

✳ Labor Day, September 3, 10:00 am ✳

Skip slid into the water off the back of his dive boat. He held a 300 foot long white rope with markers of colored tape every five feet. The end was anchored by a stake driven deep into the beach in the middle of the path the young woman made when she crawled out. He descended slowly, paying out the rope as he moved down the sloping bottom. He swam as straight as he could away from the shore. By the time he passed the 200 foot marker on the rope, the bottom had flattened out. A lot of junk was strewn on the bottom, mostly cans and bottles covered with silt settled out of the water. His work cut out for him, Skip began searching in a pattern crossing the rope as soon as he reached the end of his search pattern. He was careful to stay high enough above the bottom so he did not kick up any silt.

By the time Skip surfaced for another air tank, he had photographed and picked up several items. The next time he surfaced he had photographed and picked up eleven items which he carefully placed on a white towel on the beach. None of them had any silt on them and had probably dropped to the bottom no more than a week earlier. Anything with even the slightest amount of silt was ignored.

Skip was explaining where each item was found to Captain Yoder. "The most significant items I found are this switchblade knife and the dress," he said, holding the knife in a small towel so as not to disturb any possible fingerprints. "The fact that it is open is significant. Also, I found it more than 320 feet from the shoreline. The dress was about fifty feet from the knife. Both were obviously recently deposited."

"I'll wager that's the knife used to cut the young woman," Captain Yoder said. "The one who wielded it probably dropped it when he botched the job of cutting her throat. I bet it slipped out of his hand when he botched the murder. Perhaps our lab can lift a print or two. The dress was certainly the girl's. I didn't find anything else but beer cans and bottles. What's that pile of paper?"

"The piece of paper is a napkin. I don't think we can open it up without destroying the entire piece."

"They can do that in the lab. It is printed inside. I'd like to be able to read the printing and find out where it is from."

"Should we widen the search range? that would require hours of searching and I don't think you'd find much more. Captain Yoder, because of its shape, I bet the knife sank almost straight down and clearly marks where she was attacked."

Ragan grinned at Skip. "Probably, but more important, it probably belongs to Jane Doe's attacker. I hope it will help us find and convict him."

"If you don't need me any more I'd like to go back to Chapman."

"Thanks, Skip. You can go find the lost motor now."

SEVENTEEN

The morning of Tuesday after Labor Day, a fisherman, Gary Cross, hauled in a grisly catch near the Sand Bar in front of Patona Bay Marina. Sherif's deputy, Danny Sullivan happened to be in Paton's, about to remove the patrol boat from the lake when a breathless boater rushed in and pointed to the place where the body was.

"A fisherman found a dead man." he shouted when he saw Deputy Sullivan. "Caught him on his fishing line."

Danny quickly started the outboard on the small patrol craft and headed out for the sand bar. He pulled up beside the fisherman's boat less than three minutes after hearing the boater's shouts. The fisherman was clinging to the man's shirt not knowing what to do. He was visibly shaken. In spite of being distressed, he helped Danny pull the body into the patrol boat. The fisherman's casting plug was still hooked in the man's shirt.

He immediately radioed his findings to the sheriff's department. "No need to send an ambulance, the Coroner's hearse will do. He's clearly been dead for some time. His throat's been slit. He's in the boat. I will be in Paton's waiting for the body to be picked up . . . no, he doesn't seem to be carrying any identification. His pockets are all empty and he's wearing no jewelry. His face shows he was beaten before his throat was cut. I'd guess him to be about thirty. Also, he's wearing an expensive shirt. I recognize it as one of those fancy, expensive brands. . . . I 'm not sure about the trousers, but they don't look cheap either. No shoes or socks.

Quite a crowd of onlookers had collected in the little park next to the channel into the marina by the time the coroner's hearse arrived. Soon sheriff's investigators Lully and Carson were at the park as well. They rushed over when the call from deputy Sullivan came in. They wondered if there might be some connection with the young woman they found on Monday. The four officials took fifteen minutes to transfer the body from the boat into the hearse. Folks in the crowd were rubber necking, trying to catch a glimpse of the gruesome sight. As soon as the hearse was closed, the crowd dispersed. Some gathered into small groups discussing the event. This was an unusual and exciting thing for this small resort community—grist for the usual rumor mills. They would all be listening with rapt attention to the next local news on radio and watching TV news from nearby Fort Wayne and South Bend.

✳   ✳   ✳

The people who made the original call had identified the girl barely clinging to life in KCH. They also reported a man of their group was unaccounted for. His description fit the man's body they found. The girl first, and now a real and obvious murder awakened hundreds if not thousands of rumors among the local residents. This would likely expand quickly into the surrounding counties and eventually into the national news.

✳ Wednesday, September 5, 2012, 10:50 am ✳

Ragan arrived at the coroner's office around 10:50 am. Coroner Wilson Morgan had only glanced at and photographed the man's body fished out of Lake Tippecanoe.

"I though you'd be showing up," Wilson said as Ragan walked in.

"You only started, but what did you find so far?"

"One male, healthy other than a bashed in face and slit throat. I'd say 30 to 35. Soft manicured hands and expensive clothes are signs of the idle rich. His pockets were cleaned out and he is wearing no shoes or socks. The last part's weird. I don't need an autopsy to determine the cause of death. The deep slit of his throat emptied his body of blood. He was dead long before he had a chance to drown."

"When do you think your final report will be ready?"

"Before noon tomorrow. Probably about this time. I will provide more details, but I doubt I will make any different conclusions from what I said."

"Put his belongings in an evidence bag. We could be lucky and the lab will find something we can use."

"Do you want to wait? I can pack them up for you in fifteen minutes?"

"No, I've got to work on the puzzle pieces with a few of KC's finest. Someone from the lab will pick them up," With that, Ragan turned and left.

✳ Wednesday, September 5, 2012, 1:00 pm ✳

Captain Yoder and several officers met at the sheriff's office to put together everything they could about the seemingly connected crimes and people involved. Captain Yoder addressed the group which included, Eric Blanding, Gordon Genoa, Paul Noonan, and their lab specialist, Emil Han.

"We've put up on boards what information we recorded about our suspects and the evidence we collected. I want each of you to read through what we displayed and offer any additional information or corrections. I'll tell you verbally the known facts. Our perps are two men in their late thirties or early forties most likely living in Indianapolis. From the name on the knife Skip found in the lake we are fairly certain one of them is named Ray. The victims who were in the house gave us a good description of both men.

"Thanks to the curiosity of Deputy Paul Noonan, we have a lead on where they rented the truck, boat and trailer. Paul made note of an unusual truck and trailer parked overnight at the boat ramp on Armstrong Road and recorded their license numbers. The rental company in Indianapolis was not a completely dead end. The name on the license and credit card they used to secure the rental was a stolen identity. No red flags went up since they paid for the rental with cash, only using the credit card as security. The card was not processed. Emil is checking for any other records of the credit card or license being used as identity followed by payment in cash. The rental agent said he could identify the man who rented the outfit. That will be useful if we ever find him.

"The stolen paintings and fountain must be in storage somewhere between North Manchester and Indianapolis, probably in one of those storage complexes or even in a barn or garage. At this time we haven't a clue. Hopefully some record will turn up from our check on that credit card.

"A state police officer from North Manchester noted passing a heavily loaded boat and trailer going south on SR 13 when he was on an urgent call early the morning of Labor Day. He noted the trailer was riding low and the tires appeared to be overloaded, but couldn't make out the license number or take time to check it out because of the urgency of the call he was on. The description he gave fit with the truck and trailer Paul saw at the boat ramp on Armstrong Road. How important investigating anything out of the ordinary can be.

"The people who were in the big lake house were quite helpful if a bit strange. The twin brother of the murdered man identified his body and the young lady at KCH. All he knew was her name, she was from Goshen, and lived with her brother. We did not find the brother yet. Incidently, doctors at KCH say she took a good turn and will probably win her battle to live."

With this, a cheer went up from the officers followed by a mumble of exchanges of expressions of gratitude. Captain Yoder resumed.

"It's nice to learn you are all so concerned about the young lady. What's really amazing is she has not aborted. KCH doctors say the fetus is healthy, active, and about three months along. They expressed amazement. The doctors are having her transferred by helicopter to the trauma unit of the IU Medical Center in Indy where they are better prepared to handle severe trauma cases. The DNA we assume to be from her rapist will help us guarantee he will be found, convicted, and punished.

"The other occupants of the house are a rather strange assortment. The Germain girl is a Warsaw resident who lives with her parents. She was an honors student at the high school. She graduated in June and is enrolled at IU for the fall term. She identified two young men from Huntington who were in the house overnight. These two already earned a significant record of petty crimes and other mischief. For this reason, we will question them extensively to determine if they had any part in the crimes committed. Considering them as innocent bystanders would be a stupid mistake. Believe me, we will find they are involved if only as opportunists. I'll bet dollars to doughnuts. Gordy, will you arrange to pick up those two no later than tomorrow morning and bring them here for questioning? The two other young women are sisters, long-time Ft.Wayne residents, and friends of the twin brothers."

Several low whistles, chuckles, and comments came from the officers who had met these two.

"I'm inclined to agree with those expressions," Ragan said with a broad smile. "Those two are a bit should I say unusual? For your information, one of them happens to be a rather highly regarded psychologist for the state and is working on her doctorate. That surprised me.

"Paul, several cottages are across Grassy Creek from the boat ramp. I'd like you to check with the people in those cottages. Find out if anyone noticed any activity with that truck and trailer.

"These two perps are a pair of nasties. They think they are clever but already made a number of stupid mistakes. We sent their descriptions and the name, Ray, to the Indy police and asked for the names of any local bad guys that fit their descriptions. We should hear from them soon and add that information to our suspects list. Hopefully they will provide several names. Let's catch these bastards by the book so they don't get off on some technicality. Now let's go to work. Let's all meet back here tomorrow morning at eight.

Gordy, try to bring one of those two juvenile delinquents in here by then, earlier if possible. The one named Fred is the leader of the duo and should be questioned first. Bring him in early to question if you can. Call me if you run into a problem. We should receive some info on the perps from the Indy police before then."

EIGHTEEN

R andy and Fred were together for the first time since they stashed their loot in the old culvert. They were in the kitchen of Fred's house. Randy opened the refrigerator.

"Mind if I drink a beer?"

"Be sure you take the can out of the six pak. The ones loose on the shelf are my mom's and she counts 'em. I snuck the six pak in for us and all six had better be gone by the time my mom is home or I'll catch hell."

"When will she be home?"

"Not till real late, two, or three in the morning."

"You sure?"

"Yeah, I can tell by the way she got fixed up and what she told me. She has a new boy friend. She may not be home till late morning. She told me to stay at home and not go out. She only tells me that when she's gonna be late."

"Okay so what are we going to do? Why'd you call me over tonight? Did you find a way to sell any of the stuff?

"No, but I am getting a bit nervous about our loot since the guy was murdered. The cops will eventually find out we were in the house and question us. I want us to be prepared."

"What can we tell them, Fred, nothing. So what's the problem?"

"First thing they will check are our juvenile records and that ain't so great. I guarantee you they will bring us in for questioning."

"So what? We've been through that crap before including those good cop, bad cop acts."

"What should we tell them? We went to a party in a private home? That's nothing."

"Well, for one thing, we're both juveniles and those babes could be in a lot of trouble for having sex with us and for giving us liquor and drugs."

"Come on, Randy, we can lie about that. We don't need to tell them anything, just that we were having a dance party. That's all, a dance party after the Tippy dance hall closed."

"I don't think they would ever buy that story."

"As long as we stick to our stories and don't say anything about what we were doin' they can't touch us. Just stick to our story no matter what. We've been through brow beating before. We understand how that goes, what to say and what not to say."

"I'm not so sure, with one twin being murdered and all. They're bound to press us hard."

"I've been thinking about this for two days and came up with a great idea. Let's throw them a fish, a red herring."

"A what? That makes no sense. A fish?"

"Not a real fish, that's only a saying. We feed them some of the stuff we took, say we're really sorry, act remorseful and stare down at the floor when we talk to them."

"We're gonna admit we stole the stuff?"

"No, not in those terms and not right off the bat. That would be a give away. We hold out for a long time and act real sorry before finally admitting we took those silver platters."

"What about the rest of the stuff, the little painting, the clock, and the chess set? That's a lot of stuff. We could be faced with grand larceny. That would take us out of juvenile protection."

"We don't give up any of the real good stuff, just a few pieces of sterling. We keep the three things you mentioned plus the sword. I've been checking on ebay for the value of those things and they're worth a whole lot more than those sterling platters and serving dishes. I couldn't find out anything about the small painting, but I bet that little painting's the most valuable of all our loot."

"So how do we do this and where can we stash the valuable ones?"

"I think the culvert is by far the best place for us to keep the good stuff. Nobody, and I mean nobody would ever find our stuff there as long as we stay away."

"I don't know, leaving those things for a few days was Okay, no rain. What if we get rain or a storm? The water could damage things and make our stuff worthless."

"We will take care of that tonight. I picked up a box of huge zip lock bags, bags big enough for everything but the sword. I took a couple of contractor bags from our garage. After we put everything that will fit onto double zip lock bags, we put everything including the sword into one of those contractor bags and seal it up with packaging tape. We put this bag inside the other one and do the same sealing job. Remember how the culvert is broken with one part almost like a shelf against the inside? We can stick the bag on the broken piece and slide it back against the outside. It will stay up off the ground that way and will even be harder to find if someone did happen to look inside. Perfect!"

"What about those sterling platters? Where will we hide those? We sure can't leave them in the culvert."

"There's an old sump in our garage covered with a wooden piece made out of two by sixes. When it's in place with dirt from the floor covering it, no one would know. The hole has plenty of room for those platters and the sump's dry."

"Sounds like you worked things out."

"Pretty much, but we must do everything tonight."

"Why so?"

Fred took a single key from his pocket and held it up. "I managed to take my mom's car keys long enough to make a duplicate."

"What good will that do ya? Your mom took her car."

"Wrong old man. Her new boy friend picked her up in his car. Hers is in the garage. Ta da!"

"Can we get all that done before she is back?"

"Piece of cake old buddy. Piece of cake. Now, let's move. It's almost dark out."

"How we gonna do that in the dark?"

"First we go grab all the stuff and bring it here where we can wrap it all up in the light where we can see. When the package is wrapped snug and tight, we take it back and place it in the culvert like I said. Enough light from the one street light shines in so we can finish the job. We can take a small flashlight to use inside the culvert, but only for a few seconds. We don't want anyone to catch us poking around the culvert. Let's go."

They took half an hour to go to the street near the culvert.

"Why are you parking way back here? We're two blocks from the culvert."

"Dumb ass! You want everyone to see us getting out of my mom's car and traipsing over to the culvert? This way we can stay low along the hedge and fence till we are near the culvert. We check to make sure on one is around and make a quick run to the culvert. Plenty of brush grows around the culvert to hide us while we pick the stuff up. We will need to make three more trips back and forth the same way. We'll make sure no one is out and around. If we see someone, drop down low and freeze until they are gone. Piece of cake."

"I hope you're right."

"Okay dummy. Let's go."

NINETEEN

* Thursday, September 6, 2012, 6:00 am *

Gordy stopped at Fred's house and had to bang on the door a number of times to wake Mrs. Fuzario. She was furious when Gordy said he had to take Fred down to the station.

She screamed, "Fred, get your butt dressed and down here, now! The police are here to take you in for questioning. What the hell did you do now?"

No answer.

"I'll go for him. This may take a while."

"If you need my help, yell for me. The threat of handcuffs usually does the trick."

She goes upstairs, into his bedroom and shakes him. "Fred. Wake up. A cop is downstairs who wants to take you down to the station. If you don't come right now he'll handcuff you and take you in as you are. What did you do this time?"

"Aw, Mom."

"Up with you damn it. Get up right now. I don't want all the neighbors to see my son handcuffed and hauled off to jail. Hurry up now. I'm going down to talk to the policeman, try to stall him. Dress and come downstairs immediately or else I'll light into you. Now move."

"OK! OK! I'm gettin' up. I'll be right down."

She went back down stairs and told Officer Genoa, "He was sound asleep. He'll be down as soon as he washes and is dressed. It should only be a few minutes."

Realizing her appearance after being awakened at such an early hour and that officer Genoa was a good looking man about her age, Mae Fuzario excused herself and went to fix her hair and put on makeup. A different Mae pranced back out in a much better looking robe, make up on, and hair now in place.

"I'm sorry, officer, I'm not hospitable. Can I fix you a cup of coffee?"

"No thank you ma'am. I'm in a bit of a rush. I'd like your son to be at the station as soon as possible."

"What's this all about? Why do you want my son?"

"Routine questioning, ma'am. He may have information that would help us in a murder case we are investigating."

"What murder case, and how is he involved?"

"I can't discuss details of an ongoing investigation, ma'am, but I can say your son is not a suspect."

"Thank God, but why question him?"

"As I said, ma'am, he's not a suspect. That's all I can say. You understand."

"Not really, but I guess I'll accept your words. I wonder what's taking that boy so long?" She yells up stairs, "Fred, come down here this minute or you're going to be in real trouble."

From upstairs Fred answers slowly and sleepily, "I'm coming. I'm coming, as soon as I put my shoes on."

"I'm sorry, officer . . . I didn't even ask, what's your name, please."

"Deputy Sheriff Genoa, ma'am, Gordon Genoa."

"Nice to meet you officer Genoa. I'm Mae, Mae Fuzario. But you probably knew that, didn't you?"

"No ma'am, only that this is where Fred Fuzario lives."

Fred stumbled sleepily down the last few steps, tucking his shirt into his pants. "I'm ready."

"I'll probably bring him back in a few hours," Gordy said as they headed out the door.

"Good bye officer Genoa," Mae said musically as Gordy put Fred in the car.

✳ Thursday, September 6, 2012, 7:00 am ✳

Gordy faced Fred across the desk in the interrogation room. They were both seated.

"All right young man, tell me everything you can remember about that night in the big house on Tippy, everything that happened after you left Pie Eyed Petey's."

Fred gave his version of what happened along the lines of what he and Randy had discussed.

Gordy let him complete his story, then asked, "So you are quite sure Warren Simmons and Charlotte Woods left with the bigger of the two perpetrators in the power boat and were not in the boat when it came back about half an hour later. Is that right?"

"I didn't see them leave, but they were both in the boat when I last saw them and they were not when it returned about half an hour later. I never saw either of them again. How long is this going to take? Today is a school day and I'm supposed to be in class by 9:00."

"Do you need anything from home?"

"No. Everything I need will be in my locker at school."

Gordy continued questioning Fred up until a few minutes before the scheduled meeting with Ragan. He learned no other useful information so he had one of the other deputies drive Fred to his school.

✳ Thursday, September 6, 2012, 8:00 am ✳

Everyone except Gordy was in the room when Ragan walked in right before eight.

"I added a few more facts to the board. The kid, Fred Fuzario, is quite certain Warren Simmons and Charlotte Woods left with the larger of the two perpetrators in the power boat and were not in the boat when he returned about half an hour later.

"The Indianapolis police gave us names of several criminals who fit the descriptions we sent them. The only pair known to work together before are Al Jonas and Ray Walters. My guess is they are the perps. We already requested a warrant for their arrest. If neither will voluntarily provide us with a DNA sample, we can still use the fingerprints on Ray's knife to nail the bastard. That and Fred's testimony will bring us an indictment.

"We got a hit on a search for credit card activity on the stolen ID. They used it to rent a storage room at a complex near Peru. As soon as we can get a warrant to open and search the unit we'll send Eric down to Peru with a truck to check and bring back whatever we find in the locker."

"Paul checked with all of the people from the houses in view of the boat ramp. No one will admit to seeing the big outboard or trailer on or near the ramp, or anything unusual happening there, a dead end.

"I want you each to do your job by the book, no shortcuts. We don't want some hot-shot criminal lawyer getting these crooks off on a technicality. I'm sure we all want them to spend the rest of their lives behind bars with no chance for parole. Do you understand?"

After several quiet yeses, Ragan shouted, "Do you understand?"

There was a responding shout, "YES!" from everyone.

"That's more like KC deputy sheriffs," Ragan said, smiling. "If anyone has a question, ask now. . . . No? . . . Okay, let's do this as quickly and efficiently as possible with no screw ups."

TWENTY

In Indianapolis, Al returned the rented truck, boat and trailer to the rental place and paid cash. He did not realize the holding transaction is recorded at the credit card company even though he paid cash and didn't use the card for payment.

✳ Thursday, September 6, 2012, 8:30 am ✳

Two days after returning the rented boat, trailer and truck, Al stopped to talk to his friend at the foundry hoping to pick up a bundle of cash. As he walked in, his friend, Luthor, motioned him to go to the office. By the time he walked into the office, Luthor was sitting at his desk, a scowl on his face.

"I thought you were bringing me some silver scrap. Those two pieces you left are pot metal, worthless pot metal."

"I don't understand. Are you sure?"

Luthor grabbed one of the pieces. "Absolutely! Here, watch this," he said as he placed one of the pieces on his anvil and hit it with a hammer, shattering the part.

"One blow with my hammer and the piece shattered. Silver would not shatter. The metal can only be cheap die cast metal, almost worthless as scrap. Those two pieces are worth two bucks max as scrap. Who told you it was silver?"

"A guy I'll never trust again for sure," Al said with growing anger.

"My guess is whoever you got those pieces from either thought they were silver, or flat out stiffed you. I hope they didn't cost you much."

Al stormed out of the foundry shouting his anger. "That son of s bitch. I'll kill the bastard. Wait till I catch hold of him. He'll be sorry he cheated Al Jonas."

As soon as he got back to his trailer he dug up the emergency number the owner of the house had given him and called.

"Hello."

"Jake? This is Al Jonas and I am pissed. You lied to me you bastard. I did my job and now my money is gone."

"Hold on Al. Don't you remember what I told you, the specific instructions I gave you when we set this up?"

"Yeah. Something about calling you before I did anything with the loot. So what? So I found out your fountain was junk and not silver. I end up with useless metal and you get all that insurance money. You told me the job would be worth a hundred grand or more."

"I did and I did not lie. Just cool down and listen. I assume you kept the fountain."

"Yeah, for what it's worth."

"Well, there is a sack with a number of bars of .999 silver in the base of the fountain. You should realize $50,000 minimum from those bars. They are clean, fully legal, and untraceable. How about the painting above the mantle and the two miniatures, the small paintings in the book case?"

"Yeah, we got the big painting from over the mantle, but there was only one miniature. So what?"

"That painting from above the mantle is worth more than a hundred grand. Of course, it won't bring that much since it is shown in my insurance photos and is one of those listed as stolen. Still, it should net you 50 Gs or even more depending on how long you can hold it and who you find to sell it for you. I can help there. You certainly shouldn't try to sell it for at least a couple of years."

"A couple of years? Damn, I don't want to wait that long. It will be necessary to store it carefully somewhere."

"I told you that when we were going through what was worth selling. Did you say you only found one of those miniatures? There were two, a matched set. They should be worth $60,000 each and should bring that or more in any auction. They are fully legal and not reported as stolen."

"We only found one of them. Are you sure you kept two in the cabinet?"

"Absolutely. You missed one of them."

"I checked. There was only one in the cabinet. Your guests probably stole the other one. Speaking of those guests, You told me no one would be there."

"Those people were supposed to be there the previous week end. I told them not to use the house Labor day weekend, but they did anyway. Sorry."

"Not as sorry as they ended up being."

"Yeah, so I learned."

"Any suggestions of how I can track down the other painting?"

"Not really. I should add the miniature to the list of things stolen. Problem is that would cut in half the value of the remaining one."

"Let me try to learn what happened to the painting. I remember a few things that might help me find it."

"Okay. Try to find out what happened to it. You wouldn't be so upset if you had followed my instructions. Do you feel better about the job now?"

"I'll feel a lot better when that stuff is turned into cash and know for sure how much we netted for the job. Incidently, how much did the insurance pay you?"

"They won't tell me for six months or more. Why did you ask?"

"Curiosity. I was wondering how you made out."

"If I were you, I'd be trying to find out what happened to the other miniature. It should be worth fifty to sixty thou, especially with the other one."

"Your friends probably stole the damned painting."

"Not a chance."

"Are you sure? Quite a few more people were in the house besides your two friends. One of them probably took it."

"You should check out who those others are and find out what you can."

"You don't know?"

"Of course not. I'd tell you if I did. I'll try to find out about those other people and let you know. I planned my part in this carefully because I didn't want any problems and already things are screwed up big time for both of us."

"That's for sure. Damn. I hate to go back, but we may need to. Wait until I tell Ray. He ain't gonna be happy about this."

✳ 9:30 am ✳

Ray slammed his fist down on Al's kitchen table with a bang, bouncing Al's beer to the floor. "Damn it Al, I can't wait for my money. Now we must go clear back to Peru for the silver."

"Calm down, Ray. Look at the mess you made. I'll need to use the mop. Damn you made a mess. Why'd you hit the table so hard?"

"I'm sorry Al, but after all the fucking around we are still out of money. I'm pissed."

"Okay, we can go tomorrow and pick up the silver. I'll rent another small truck and we can bring those two paintings down here so we won't need to go back again. We can leave the rest there and forget about them."

"What about the other small painting? I can't believe it's worth so much. Now we must go back and try and run it down. I don't like that one bit, not one damned bit."

"We should go to the lake first and find the miniature. We can stop in Peru on our way back and pick up the rest of the stuff."

"Where will we stay?"

"In a little motel in North Webster. We stay there, pay cash and leave no trail."

"More of our money down the drain. I'm getting so I don't like this deal, not one damned bit."

"Come on, Ray. We will still net between 200 and 250 Gs when we finish."

"Only if we can find the other painting."

"Leave that to me. I am sure I can find it."

"Oh? How? How will Mr. genius find the painting when we don't have the slightest idea who has the damned thing?"

"The police reports of the incident. They'll be in the local paper and should list the names of everyone who was involved. We can figure out who has it by process of elimination."

"Yeah. How are we going to find a nine day old paper?"

"The library."

"The library keeps copies of old papers?"

"If not actual copies, they store microfilm or digitized copies we can view."

"Well, you know a lot more about police reports than I do. Once we figure out who has the painting, how do we get hold of it?"

"First off, we can try to buy it."

"Why buy it? Whoever has it stole it. We can just take it."

"Offering to buy it could bring whoever has it out in the open. When we meet to buy it, we take it. Since the damned thing is already stolen, they can't go to the police. We'll rip them off."

"I don't know. More people involved. We might be found out."

"Whatever happens, let me do the talking."

"Any choice for me? No! If we get into any real trouble, I'll be the one to bail us out with my fists, knife, or Glock."

"Don't do anything hasty. I'll tell you if any muscle is needed."

"Yeah! In the end I always do the dirty work."

They pick up a rented truck and head north.

TWENTY-ONE

The first place they stopped when they got to Warsaw was the library. It didn't take Al long to locate the paper and find the police report.

"Damn! Damn!. Damn!" Al uttered when he read the report. "It says right here they don't reveal the names of juveniles. Obviously some kids were involved and probably took our painting. I remember seeing two boys. There could be others."

Ray cursed. "I knew it. One more of your Goddamn plans shot to hell. Now what do we do? How in hell are we gonna find out who those kids are? You're guessing they took that painting. It could be somewhere else with some other thief."

"Wait a minute. I got a real good look at one of those kids. The article did say they were from Huntington. The Huntington library will keep a copy of the school yearbook. We'll head there right now. Let's go."

"Another wild goose chase, damn you."

"Shit, Ray, you give up too easy. The library will be open till late so let's go. It's less than an hour away. I'm sure the kid's picture will be in the yearbook. I won't forget that face. He stared right my way and at me."

"If he sees you he might recognize you."

"Not a chance. I saw him, but he didn't see me since I was outside in the dark."

✳ 3:30 pm ✳

As they walked up the steps to the Huntington library, Ray was still unhappy. "You'll take forever to go through all those faces in the yearbook What will we do if you can't find him?"

"Oh, for Christ's sake, Ray, save your bitchin' till we've gone through the book. If I don't find him, then we will deal with a problem."

It took Al fifteen minutes to locate the latest yearbook and go to a table. Another half hour and Al points and says, "That's him for sure. Fred Fuzario. I was sure I'd remember his face."

"Okay, smart guy, what do we do now?" Ray said with a sneer.

"We look Fuzario up in the phone directory. How many Fuzarios can live in this hick town. We call and talk to him after we find him."

"What good will that do?"

"Ray, why don't you just listen. Quit complaining till something real comes up to complain about. Now I'll use the library phone directory and find a number and an address."

Thirty minutes later they were out in the truck parked a few houses away from the address of the only Fuzario in the phone book. Al punched the number into his cell phone. No answer and he didn't leave a message. About half an hour later, Fred walked down the street. Al recognized him.

"That's him, the Fuzario kid. He's the one we want."

Al waited for him to enter the house and placed the call.

"Hello."

"Is this the Fuzario residence?"

"Yes, what do you want?"

"I'm calling for a Fred Fuzario."

"I'm Fred. Who are you?"

"I'm Eldon Gordon of American United Insurance. We insured the residence that was recently broken into on Lake Tippecanoe. One of our informants told us you were in the residence when it was robbed and might hold something we are trying to recover."

"What are you talking about. Who told you that?"

"Fred, we are only interested in recovering the property of our insured. We will pay a substantial reward for its return, no questions asked. We were told you probably took the painting. If you can help us recover the miniature, there's a thousand dollars for you. Your name will never be mentioned."

"Really? How can I be sure? I don't know you from Adam."

"I hold a thousand in cash in my hands. We can meet you somewhere private. Is the painting with you?"

"Naw, it's near Leesburg, hidden away."

"Near Leesburg you say? We are going to pick up several other large paintings while on this trip. We brought a truck to hold those other paintings if we find them. Do you have any idea where we might find those large paintings taken from the house?"

"Naw, I haven't a clue. All I have is one small painting of a scene with lots of people in a garden. We hid the picture outside of Leesburg, north of Warsaw."

"How can we get it? We could pick you up and take you to it?"

"I'd gotta be paid first."

"Tell you what, I'll give you half when you are in the truck and the other half when the painting is in our hands. That should assure you."

"That sounds fair. You do pay in cash, don't you?"

"I'll give you five $100 bills as soon as we are together, and five more when you deliver the painting."

"Deal. When will you pick me up?"

"Walk outside and you'll find a dark blue Ford van a couple of doors down from your house. Come over to the van and talk to us."

After he ends the call Al turns to Ray, "Climb in the back and keep your damned mouth shut. I don't want this kid to be suspicious. You understand?"

"Not really, but I'll do what you want. Do I have a choice?"

"Ignore anything I say or do, and don't say a damned word."

Fred comes to the truck, and Al opens the front door for him. As soon as he is in and sits, Al peels off five $100 bills and hands them to Fred.

"Here's the first payment, just like I promised. Now, where do we go?"

"Drive to Warsaw and head north out of town on 15. I'll show you where to stop."

The man in the back is another one like you. He's hoping to receive a big reward for recovering some large paintings for us."

Ray rolled his eyes.

TWENTY-TWO

Al turned the radio on and found some country music. They listened as they drove. No one spoke a word until they were several miles north out of Warsaw on 15.

Fred explained. "The little town ahead is Leesburg. Turn right opposite the Marathon gas station, go through town and turn right after crossing the railroad tracks."

"Where do we go next?"

"The Tippy dance hall is a few miles up Armstrong Road. We go through the little town of Oswego and turn left at the road with the brick gateway."

It took about ten minutes to reach and turn at the gateway.

"Now turn right at the first road and stop when I tell you."

After traveling about a mile down the road, Fred pointed and said, "Stop right where the shoulder is wide."

Al pulled onto the shoulder and parked. "Okay, what now?"

"Wait here and I'll go get the painting."

"Don't try to run off with my $500 or you'll be sorry. I should send Ray here with you."

"I'm not stupid. I want the other 500 bucks. I also don't want to show anybody our secret hiding place. Understand?"

"Yeah, I understand, but if you are not on your way back in no more than fifteen minutes we're coming after you. Remember, we saw where you live."

"Mister, I may be a kid, but I learned long ago what not to do and I want no trouble. Give me twenty minutes. I may take that long to get the painting. I'll be coming out from behind the bunch of bushes right there," he said, pointing.

＊ 5:20 pm ＊

In less than fifteen minutes Fred came running from behind the bushes.

"Ray, you see? In a few minutes we'll own the second painting. I told you it would work. All your frettin' was for nothin'."

"I'll agree when the money is in our hands, and not before. Okay, genius, what do we do now?"

"We drive to the park on Center Lake, take the kid out behind the building on the shore and dump his body in the lake. Simple. He's almost here so don't say a thing except follow my lead."

Fred walked up to the truck and opened the door. "Here's the painting. How about the rest of the money?"

Al said, "Step in and I'll give you the money and take you home."

As soon as Fred sat down, Al peeled five more $100 bills and gave them to him. Fred pocketed the money with a smile.

"While you were getting the painting, Ray's contact called so we are going to stop at the park on Center Lake to meet him. We shouldn't be long. Afterwards we'll take you home."

No one said a word while they drove to the park and parked in front of the pavilion about twenty minutes later.

As he and Ray got out of the truck, Al said, "Fred, would you come with us? The guy we are meeting is extremely skittish. Your presence will ease his mind. If you walk with us I'll give you another hundred bucks."

"Sure, might as well," Fred said as he stepped out of the car. "I could use another hundred."

As soon as they were behind the building Ray hit him with a sap from behind. Fred dropped like a stone. As Ray dropped down to finish the job a siren sounded and flashing police lights came on from the west entrance to the park.

"Run for the truck!" Al shouted.

They sprinted for the truck, jumped in and drove out the entrance with tires screeching onto State Road 15 and headed north.

＊ 5:45 pm ＊

Sherrif's Deputy, Eric Blanding left the sheriff's office after a meeting and was on his way to Milford. As he entered the Center Lake Park, three men walked around the pavilion toward the lake. He saw one of the men hit another with a sap and jump on him as he fell. He hit the siren and lights and accelerated toward the pavilion. In the time Eric took to cover the distance, two of them ran to a blue van, jumped in, and raced out of the park heading north on 15. He drove directly over the grass to where the third man was lying on the ground, got out and found him bleeding from the head wound, unconscious, but alive. He immediately contacted his dispatcher.

"I found an injured, unconscious young man on the ground on the lake side of the Center Lake Pavilion. Send an EMS here as soon as possible. I'll stay with him until they arrive. The two who attacked him are headed north on 15 in a dark blue Ford van, license number letters KJB. I could not catch the numbers. Any officer on 15 should be able to intercept them unless they turn off."

Dispatcher Lois Noonan confirmed the information and immediately put out the necessary calls. Within minutes she received a confirmation from an ambulance on the US 30 bypass a few minutes away from the injured man.

Lois notified Eric. "Eric, an EMS is on the way and will be at the pavilion in about seven minutes. What's the condition of your injured man?"

"My guess is he has a fractured skull. With EMS so close I'll wait for them to treat him. He is unconscious, but breathing regularly. He's just a kid, Lois. I'd say about sixteen or seventeen."

✳ 5:55 pm ✳

Ragan Yoder was sitting down for dinner with friends at Stacy's on State Road 15 in Leesburg when the call came in.

"Excuse me boys, I may be gone for awhile," he tells them as he stood up. "Perps coming our way on 15," he called out as he ran out into the parking lot.

Before he could even reach his truck a blue van barreled by and through town at a high rate of speed. By the time he was in his truck and on the road, he was about a mile behind them. He flipped on his flashing lights and accelerated after them as fast as he could. His greatly modified little truck was soon gaining on them. He was close enough to see them turn west on W 900 N, but not close enough to read their license.

✳ 5:56 pm ✳

Seeing distant flashing red and blue lights in his mirror, Al said, "We picked up a cop in the little town we just blasted through."

"I told you we should slow down going through those small towns."

"Don't worry, those little hick town cops don't drive cars that can catch this big V8."

"Yeah, but their radios can."

"I'll take a left at the next county road. These back country roads wander all over the place. We can lose them easy."

Al braked hard and barely made the corner west onto W 900 N. They went airborne over the rise above a culvert a short distance after turning.

"Damn it Al, if you wreck this baby we're done for."

"Agh, that wasn't even close. We'll make a right at the second paved road."

"Why not the first?"

"They'll probably assume we turned on the first road. We turn west again on the next road and they'll be off our tail. There's one road, now check for the next one."

"There's one coming up. Wait, it's a service road to a group of buildings."

"Can't take a chance. We need a through road."

"Another intersection with houses on both sides is just ahead, right where those two houses are."

"Yeah, hang on."

Al cut the corner, drove partly through the yard of one house and blew through a wire fence around a garden. He straightened out and accelerated north on county road N 425 W, straight as an arrow. About a mile down the road he once more saw flashing lights in his mirror. He held the big V8 wide open. In spite of this he could tell the lights were gaining on them.

"Find me a road left and quick."

"I can't find a road that doesn't exist, damn. Wait, one is coming up. Damn, it's a dirt road."

"No good. We need a paved one."

"Up ahead is a farm with a house and several white buildings on the left, and another house on the right. That must be a road."

Before they reached the road Al saw the intersection was a T. Beyond was no road, just a field.

"Hang on, Ray!"

Al stood on the brakes and steered into the yard on the right. Pumping the brakes, he turned left onto W 1050 N. The truck got partially sideways as it drifted through the intersection. The rear wheels slid off the pavement as Al turned the wheels to the right to try to stay on the roadway. They slid sideways along the shoulder for about fifty feet at which point the rear tires caught on the pavement where a driveway entered the road. The truck shot forward across the road and onto the driveway of Marci Yoder's house. Parked in the driveway was her ex husband's eight wheeled dump truck filled with sand. Their truck struck the left rear of the dump truck at about fifty miles per hour. The bed of the dump truck sheared off the top of the truck from where the windshield met the body back to the rear of the doors. The dump truck barely moved.

✳ 6:10 pm ✳

A minute later, Ragan drove around the corner and pulled his S10 up next to the wreck. He got out, examined the truck and the occupants. He immediately contacted Lois, the dispatcher.

"I'm at the corner of county road N 425 W and W 1050 N where a single vehicle accident with two fatalities occurred no more than five minutes ago. You can cancel the APB on the blue truck from the reported attack at the Center Lake pavilion. You don't need to send an EMS. Enough blood is pouring out of the wreckage to assure the occupants are beyond help even if we could get them out. Someone with the capability of cutting two bodies out of a Ford truck crunched down to about half of normal size would be appropriate. Removing enough crushed metal to extract the bodies will take quite a long time, so the Coroner need not be in a rush."

Lois replied, "Ragan, you don't seem too concerned. A sheriff's deputy will be with you soon, probably my hubby. He's the closest one. I'll also start the ball rolling on all the paperwork. You must know something about the fatalities I don't."

"I do. The license number of the truck indicates it is one rented by Al Jonas in Indy using a stolen identity. He and Ray Walters almost certainly committed one murder on Tippy recently and probably more during a criminal career going back many years. I find it hard to feel any regrets about their deaths. Actually, I'm rather pleased. Indiana will save zillions of dollars convicting and incarcerating them. The taxpayers should be delighted."

"Oh, those two. I understand what you mean. I'll notify the coroner and send a wrecker with the needed equipment. You said the corner of county road N 425 W and W 1050 N, right."

"Right! I'll stay here till everything is wrapped up."

"Paul should be with you shortly to help. Out."

TWENTY-THREE

By the time Ragan finished his call, a small crowd of people had gathered. Six were from passing cars that stopped and several were from houses on the corner. The crowd stayed back from the truck and its growing pool of blood. An attractive lady about forty was the first to rush to the truck. She turned to Ragan.

"From the flashing lights I assume you are an officer of the law. I'm a trauma nurse at Goshen Hospital. From the amount of blood, I doubt anything could be done for the occupants, even if we could get to them. I'm sure removing them will take too much time and be extremely difficult. Besides, they are obviously quite dead."

"I'm Ragan Yoder, a homicide detective working with the sheriff's department. I fully concur with your assessment of the occupants. I notified the sheriff's department, and they are sending a deputy. What's your name, ma'am?"

"I'm sorry. I'm Marci Yoder and I live in this house. The accident is on our property and the dump truck belongs to my ex husband."

"Well, Marci, would you help me string some yellow guard tape around the accident to keep people back?"

"Gladly. Tell me what to do."

Ragan retrieved a roll of yellow police line tape, a small sledge hammer, and a number of wooden stakes from the back of his pickup.

"I'll drive these stakes. If you will unroll the tape, I'll fasten it to the stakes to cordon off the area around the truck."

They took about twenty minutes to ring the two trucks with tape twenty-five feet away from the trucks. By the time they were finished about forty rubberneckers were milling about. Marci was upset when several people walked carelessly through her flower garden. Deputy Noonan arrived about this time and helped them expand the taped-off section to include the house, the flower garden, and most of her yard.

✳ 7:15 pm ✳

A wrecker vehicle with cutting torches arrived about the same time as the coroner. They needed nearly an hour to figure out and accomplish the best way to separate the two trucks and extract the bodies. While this was going on, Marci invited Ragan to come into her house for coffee while he waited. They sat down at her kitchen table across from each other.

"I gather from your conversation with the deputy you are involved in an unusual relationship with local law enforcement. I was also wondering, why would a homicide detective be chasing criminals in his own private vehicle?"

Ragan grinned. "You are quite perceptive. Here's the short version. I grew up on Lake Tippecanoe before moving to Chicago and becoming a homicide detective. That took more years than I care to think about. When I retired a few years ago, I came back and bought a house on Willow Bend about a mile from the country club. My wife died about five years before I retired. Since she had been my Chicago anchor, I decided to move back to the place I had loved while growing up. I was fifty-five when I retired."

"That's interesting, but it doesn't answer my question. How come you are here in your own vehicle, chasing crooks? It does not make sense."

"Here's the rest of the short version. The son of one of my closest friends is a member of the KC Sheriff's department. Soon after I moved into my house on Tippy we were talking about a difficult murder case he was working on, and I offered some suggestions. He invited me to help on the case. One thing lead to another and before long I found myself officially sworn in as an honorary captain in the sheriff's department. I worked numerous homicide cases for both the police and sheriff's department after the first one. It's been rewarding, and I loved every minute. End of story."

"That's quite unusual. You use your own car, the little Chevy S10? Isn't your truck unsuitable for a sheriff's vehicle?"

Ragan laughed and proceeded to explain how his docile little S10 had been converted into a fire-breathing, 150 mile per hour dragon.

"The locals provided me with the hidden light bar, It's the only thing they had to pay for. Strange enough, today was the first time I ever used those lights."

"How about you? How did you end up as a nurse in Goshen?"

While waiting for the coroner they talked, sharing many life stories. During this time, which stretched into an hour, Ragan began having warm, fuzzy feelings about this attractive woman. He definitely wanted to see her again. This was something quite new to him. He had not been interested in any woman since his wife died. He had no idea what to do or say. Then Wilson, the coroner, called for him, shattering his thoughts.

"Excuse me, Marci, duty calls."

"Come back in when you can. I want to ask you another question. Just knock on the door."

"Okay, I will," he said as he walked out to talk to Wilson.

"We're all done here," Wilson said. "The bodies are in my vehicle and the wrecker loaded the remains of the truck and is ready to haul it wherever you want. I'm good to go. Oh, here's a small painting we found in the truck. It was wrapped up in a towel and looks to be undamaged."

"Thanks, Wilson. I'll tell him to take the truck to the impound lot in Warsaw. That painting may be important evidence so thanks for recovering it. Where's Noonan? Do you know?"

"He lit out on another emergency call about fifteen minutes ago. Told me to tell you he was through with the accident report and to call for him if you need him."

Ragan said good bye to Wilson, told the wrecker what to do with the wreckage, and headed back to Marci's door. A knock brought an immediate response.

"Come in, Ragan, I'm fixing dinner, would you care to join me? I'd like you to if you could."

"I'd love to. You gave me an invitation I will not turn down. Besides, this event cancelled my dinner at a restaurant and I would love a home cooked meal. I'm starving. Oh, and take a look at this small painting. Tell me what you think."

"I'm no expert on art, but that's a real painting and I think quite old. It could be valuable."

"Thanks, you confirmed my non expert opinion."

They talked about the painting while Marci finished dinner preparations and the two sat down to eat.

✳ 11:45 pm ✳

It was nearly midnight when Ragan stood at her door saying good night. Marci finally said, "I certainly enjoyed talking with you. I can't believe we talked away the entire evening. Now I'll be quite forward and say I'd like to do it again, and soon."

Ragan was afraid to say what was on his mind. "I too would like to do it again. How about Saturday? Nurses are sometimes on strange schedules, but does that fit?"

"Saturday is fine. Be here at about six, OK?"

"Perfect. Do you prefer anywhere special to eat, or should I pick the place?"

"Actually, I'd rather fix dinner for you right here. Is that okay with you."

"You'll be two up on me. Okay only if you promise I can return the favor, twice."

Marci laughed. "It's a deal. Now, one more forward thing I want to ask if you don't mind. Would you give me a hug before leaving? I would like a hug from you."

"What a pleasant surprise. I'd love to. I haven't hugged a woman in nearly ten years."

They held each other gently, leaned their heads back, and gazed into each other's eyes for a long moment. Their lips suddenly sought each other.

It was past one when Ragan finally walked to his truck and left. He was flying ten feet off the ground all the way home. All thoughts of police work were gone from his mind.

TWENTY-FOUR

Ragan awoke a bit later than usual, last evening's unusual experience filled his mind. He was experiencing feelings he had not had in years.

I'd better begin thinking about the case, he thought. *I need to examine the stuff Eric brought back from the locker.*

He gulped down a bowl of cereal and fruit and headed for the sheriff's department. Eric was already back from Peru and had the doors of the van open. Nothing had been removed as yet.

"That's quite a haul," Eric said. "It's hard to believe they moved all that in a boat and up Grassy Creek. I counted twenty-four paintings, all but a few are big and one is small. In front of the paintings is a pile of metal pieces of the fountain. It took us more than three hours to pack the stuff in the truck. We had to be especially careful with those paintings. We packed the metal at the front and used mover's blankets between each painting. I understand they are quite valuable."

"Did you find a secure place to store them?"

"Pete suggested we use an empty holding cell. They will be locked safely away. He went next door to borrow a wheeled cart to move them. . . . Ah, here he comes now."

"I would like to photograph, number, and catalog each piece as they are taken out of the van. I will photograph both sides of each painting."

Eric and Pete uncovered and held each painting so Ragan could photograph each side.

Half way through photographing the paintings, Ragan said, "Wait a minute. One painting back is different from the others, much older. All of the rest of the them are different with much newer backing. You can tell even the edges are quite new. I wonder why this one is so old, and all the others are so new?"

"Perhaps the other paintings were refurbished, had new backs put on," Eric said, looking at both groups of paintings. "All the rest are exactly the same. All except this one."

Ragan was puzzled. "We will ask the painting appraiser. One is being sent down next week from Chicago to examine the paintings. He may know. After we move all of the paintings to the holding cell, I want to take a close look at the pieces of the fountain."

✳ 9:30 am ✳

When all of the paintings were photographed, cataloged, and stored, they started moving the pieces of the fountain onto the cart. The last piece to be removed was the base.

"Damn, this piece is heavy," Eric said as he struggled to put the awkward piece of metal on the cart.

When he and Pete finally accomplished their task, the piece fell over and a canvas bag fell out of the opening. Pete picked up the bag.

"This is what made that piece so heavy. I wonder what makes that bag weighs so much?" he said as he set the bag on the ground.

Ragan proceeded to open the bag and remove several metal bars marked, .999 Ag.

"That's strange," he said. "I wonder why those silver bars were in the fountain? It makes no sense."

"Eric said, "I wonder why the metal of the fountain is so different from those silver bars. The bars are much lighter in color."

Pete replied, "Maybe it's because the fountain is a silver alloy, like sterling. Pure silver is much too soft to make anything useful. That's why all silver pieces are made with 92% silver alloyed with copper or other metals. Still, it should not appear as dark as the metal in the fountain. I'll take a closer look."

"How do you know so much about silver?" Eric asked.

"My father worked silver and made jewelry in Mexico. He taught me all about it. Incidentally, I examined one piece closely. I'm quite sure that fountain is not silver or even an alloy of silver. I never saw anything silver that was so dark. The surface is silver. I'll give you that, but the entire fountain is probably plated. The inside is definitely another metal, probably something cheap."

Ragan said, "Someone at Dalton Foundry can help. Their lab could tell us what the fountain is made of. Let's give them a call. I'll take some close ups of each piece, and the bars as soon as I can. We'll stick the metal in the cell with the paintings and lock the door. Everything is supposed to be worth scads of money so we don't want anything to disappear. I bet we uncovered evidence of another crime, a huge fraud of millions of dollars."

"How so?" Eric asked.

"I'd like to wait until the insurance people report their findings before saying anything. My guess is with their report we will be able to present more than enough evidence to go to a grand jury. I don't want to jeopardize that."

Ragan called Dalton and sent Eric to the lab with a small piece of the fountain. They said they would call with the results of their analysis by afternoon today. Next he called the insurance company and brought them up to date on the recent developments. They were most appreciative and said they were immediately sending an investigator from Ft. Wayne. The painting expert would be in Warsaw on Monday. As soon as Eric returned, they all headed out for lunch.

✷ 12:30 pm ✷

They returned from lunch and found the insurance investigator waiting.

"I'm Captain Ragan and this is Deputy Eric Blanding, and Pete Ramirez of the sheriff's office staff. And you are?"

"Andy Mulholland of Acme Insurance Investigators. We do investigations for several insurance companies."

They all shook hands. Ragan guided them back to the holding cell where the paintings and fountain parts were stored. After they entered the cell, Ragan picked up a piece of the fountain.

"Andy, Pete here says this metal is not silver and he is something of an expert on silver. We sent a sample over to the lab at Dalton Foundries for chemical tests. They promised the results would be in our hands this afternoon."

Pete said, "You can tell how different the inside is from the outside. The fountain was silver plated so a thin layer of silver covered the entire outside."

Andy said. "If true that means the insured, or someone, replaced the original silver fountain which we insured for $1.5 million with a nearly worthless copy. That's big time fraud or theft and we will prosecute. We certainly won't be paying off on that claim. What about the paintings? The list with photos of those reported stolen shows twenty-five paintings."

Ragan said, "Including the one in my truck, we count twenty-five, so they are all here. An expert on paintings is coming here Monday to examine them. Until he gets here, they will remain locked in this cell."

"Let me check those paintings. I'm no expert, but I can tell what copies should look like."

After checking over several of the paintings with new paper on the frames and comparing them with the one old appearing one, Andy announced, "I'm quite sure all those with new backings are copies and not originals, but since I'm no expert, I'll wait and not make a report. A remote possibility is all of those could be originals and were restored with new paper added to the backs of the frames. I've never looked at a restored painting so my opinion doesn't carry much weight. Monday we should find out for sure."

Eric said, "For my money, all of those paintings except the old looking one and the two miniatures are fakes. I'll bet money I'm right."

Andy said, "I'm inclined to agree with you. I'll wait for a copy of the chemical analysis of the fountain metal before going back. That will be essential. Once the company has the report we will proceed to sue for restitution and punitive damages. Law enforcement and the local district attorney will be the ones to file criminal charges."

✳ 2:30 pm ✳

Someone from the Dalton lab called and reported the metal was spin cast die cast metal, pot metal is the common term. "It has little or no salvage value," they reported.

"Well, that confirms what we already knew, but the written report will be admissible in court," Ragan said.

"I would appreciate you sending me a copy of the written report," Andy said.

"Consider it done," Pete said.

Andy said, "Nothing to hold me here so I'm off for home. Thanks for everything. When exactly will the art expert be here? I'd like to be present when to hear what he has to say. I'd also like a copy of what ever reports he makes."

"He's scheduled to be here Monday morning about eleven. We asked him to call when he was leaving so we could predict when he would arrive," Eric said. "Our experience with those kind of experts is they often miss appointments so I'll call you after he calls and says he is on his way. Even then we can't be sure. Artists can be quite casual and forgetful about meetings and appointments."

"I hear what you say and thanks for telling me. I'll probably talk to you again on Monday, or in court if I don't see you Monday. Bye for now."

Ragan turned to the other two. "We've done about as much with the paintings as we could until the art expert is here, and also with the fake silver fountain. We collected enough evidence on Jake Ramsey to obtain a warrant for his arrest. I'd like to bring him here for questioning . Pete, will you start the process going?"

"Right away. Unfortunately with all the publicity this has been getting I would be surprised if he didn't already fly the coop and leave the country. He's surely hidden most if not all of his assets somewhere out of the country a long time ago. This didn't happen recently. He's been involved in the process for years."

Ragan cursed. "That bastard was the cause of this entire crime spree that already cost three lives and us a lot of grief. Ask Eric to put a trace on his credit cards. We might find out where he went. I'm going to KCH to check on the kid with the fractured skull. I wonder if any one told him what happened to the two who bashed him? I'll talk to you both on Monday."

Ragan drove to KCH and asked about the young man from his nurse.

The nurse said, "He has a bad skull fracture and was in surgery for more than two hours. His surgeon says he is lucky to be alive, but he came through well and should recover fully. He will not be able to talk to anyone until tomorrow afternoon however."

"Wow, it was that bad? If Eric hadn't chanced to catch those two bums in the act, he would certainly be dead. It's good to rescue a live attack victim for a change. Call and tell me when he will be conscious and able to talk. I'll call tomorrow afternoon if I don't hear from you."

"One more thing. We found ten one hundred dollar bills wadded up in his pocket. What's a kid doing with so much cash?"

Ragan smiled. "I think I know. What did you do with the money?"

"It's with all of his belongings in a locker. Because he had so much cash, we cataloged everything and locked it all in one of our lockers. It's quite secure."

"Keep it locked up. Don't let anyone even look at any of his things until you clear it with me or the Sheriff, OK?"

"Don't worry. It's locked away safely and here's the key," she said, dangling a key on a small chain.

"Good! Just don't let anyone talk you into giving them the key without approval from me or the Sheriff."

"You can be sure of that," she said.

"Now I'd better be going," Ragan said as he headed for the door.

✳ 5:15 pm ✳

As soon as he got home, Ragan grabbed a beer, hit his couch, and turned on the TV. The tense day after a short night took its toll. He fell asleep long before the six o'clock news started. His phone woke him at nine o'clock. It was Marci.

"Hi Ragan," greeted him when he answered. "Can we delay our dinner date tomorrow an hour to seven? The hospital asked me to work till six. That's two hours later than my work day usually ends."

"No problem. Is one hour enough? I could come at eight if it would help."

"No, one hour is plenty. If history repeats itself I'll probably only work until quarter after five, five thirty at the latest. Besides, if I'm still fixing dinner when you arrive, I'll put you to work."

"Fair enough. I'm anticipating another fine evening with you. I wasn't prepared for last evening, but I am now."

"I hope that wasn't a negative."

"To the extreme contrary. It was a huge positive. Our dinner was a most pleasant evening I will never forget."

"I feel the same way. I'm looking forward to tomorrow evening, no preconceptions."

They talked for almost an hour before saying good bye. He poured out most of a bottle of warm, flat beer and went to bed. He lay thinking about Marci and reliving the evening. It was delicious, remembering. *Ragan, you old goat. I believe you're falling in love. It's been a long time since you had any of those feelings. I hope she doesn't break your heart. Somehow, I don't think she will.*

TWENTY-FIVE

Ragan headed out with his fly rod and bass flies. Eight days went past since he last wet a fly. Daylight was beginning to show in the east when he rowed out in front of his house toward one of his favorite spots for bass in the early morning. His hot spot was a bit to the north of his pier and about a hundred yards from shore.

The second time his fly hit the water it disappeared in a swirl. He was soon battling a fair sized bass. *Come on, baby, you'd make a luscious pair of filets for Marci to fix for dinner,* he thought as he played the bass trying to keep him out of the weeds toward shore. In about ten minutes a two pound bass was netted and placed on his stringer.

Now I wonder if your brother or sister is out and about, he thought as he sent the fly on its way to the same spot knowing bass often move in schools. After several dozen fruitless casts he moved the fly a good sixty feet to the south. *That's probably where your buddies went,* he said to the one on the stringer.

About fifteen minutes later another swirl, a sharp lift to the fly rod, another ten minute battle and a twin of the first bass was added to the stinger. *okay guys, I'll leave you alone. I've plenty of food for the next few days. Probably be back later in the week,* Ragan thought as he returned the boat to the pier.

By seven he had cleaned and fileted the two bass and placed them in his fridge wrapped in wax paper. He called Marci.

"Hello, Marci."

"Ragan, this is a pleasant surprise. What's up?"

"I caught and fileted two beautiful bass. I'll bring them with me tonight. You can cook them for our dinner or freeze them for another meal. Your choice."

"Wonderful, I love fresh fish. I can easily shift gears and fix them for our dinner. Fish are so easy and quick to fix. Thank you. Till about seven. No, on second thought, make it six-thirty with the fish. You are so thoughtful."

"Six-thirty it is."

Ragan sat down in his favorite chair, stared out at the lake and started doing some serious thinking about Marci and what happened at her house. *How could I develop such strong feelings in just a few hours?* He thought about his late wife, Rita, and suddenly missed her a lot. He recalled clearly how they had met at eighteen and how he decided within a few hours he was going to marry her. Of course, it took him nearly three years to propose. He hadn't thought that about Marci, but he was definitely enthralled. She is the first woman he kissed since Rita died. Something was definitely cooking and Marci seemed to be in the same state. He needed someone to talk to before things became complicated.

Doc Miller! I'll call Doc and ask if he will talk to me. He knows more about me than anyone, he thought. He picked up the phone and called.

Doris, Doc's daughter answered. "Hello?"

"Hi Doris. This is Ragan. Is Doc around?"

"Ragan, it's good to hear from you. Dad's out in back. I can call him for you. Is this a police matter?"

Ragan laughed. "No, Doris, a personal matter, and not a medical one either. I need some advice and Doc's about the only one around I can ask and can trust completely."

"That sounds serious."

"No. Not really . . . well . . . yes, it certainly could be. Would you ask him to call me when he can."

"No, hang on. He's just puttering around out back. I'll get him right now."

In about five minutes Doc Miller's gravely voice came on. "Ragan you old rascal, what's this personal problem Doris said you wanted to talk to me about?"

"Doc, I'd like to sit down with you and talk about it in person. It's not medical, but I'd truly like your opinion. Could you join me for lunch, today?"

"Certainly. Why don't you come here for lunch? How about twelve thirty? Doris and I usually eat about then. We can sit out on the porch before and after lunch where it's quite private. Better yet, why don't you come over now if you can. We can chat till lunch is ready."

"Thanks, Doc. I'll be at your house in about twenty minutes."

Ragan walked up the familiar steps to Doc's house in Milford which had also been his office until he retired. Almost the same time as Doc's wife died, Doris's husband was killed in an accident at work. A year later she moved in with her dad to help care for him. She lived with him ever since. Doris greeted him at the door and gave him a hug.

"Come in, Ragan. You're looking fit. It's good to see you."

"Good to be see you too. How long since your party? A couple of years? that's the last time I was here."

"That was in August so it has been more than two years. Doc's waiting out on the porch. Can I bring you something to drink? Iced tea or lemonade?"

"Lemonade sounds pretty good in this heat."

"Go on out. You know the way. I'll bring your lemonade."

Ragan walked where he had walked many times since he was a boy and out onto the porch. He sat down next to Doc.

Doc got right to the point. "Okay, young man, what's this big problem you need help with?"

"You don't beat around the bush, do you? I should remember after all those years. Well, I met a lovely woman and now I'm involved. It happened so suddenly I'm at a total loss as to what to do. I really need help."

"I provide one standard bit of advice which applies to anyone in that situation. Follow your heart, but CYA. Recognize plenty of predatory women are out prowling so don't do anything stupid. Who is this femme fatale? Is she local? I might know her if she is."

"She lives out west of here on 1050N. Her name is Marci Yoder."

"I can't believe this. Ragan, Marci is my niece, my brother Andrew's daughter. She's a wonderful lady, one of the Miller family. How did you meet her?"

Ragan explained his car chase and the end in Marci's yard. "First she invited me in for coffee while I was waiting for the wrecker and coroner to finish. We talked for a long time. She asked me to knock on her door when they were finished and I did. One thing led to another and she asked me to stay for dinner. A few hours of conversation and she said she would like to do dinner with me again. We made a date. I finally left after one in the morning. I was flying ten feet off the ground and she seemed to be in the same intoxicated condition. I'm going back to her house for dinner tonight. I wonder if I'm prepared for this. I do feel wonderful. I've not had any kind of a relationship with a woman since Rita died. My mind is a complete blank. I can't think of anything or come up with any idea what to do, especially since things happened so fast. That's why I wanted to talk with you."

"It's amazing, you hooking up with Marci. You are definitely one lucky man. Half the eligible males in the area are after her since the divorce. She has shown no interest in any of them. She must see something in you she likes and respects. I'll be damned. You and Marci. Ragan, I delivered you as a baby and learned almost everything about you ever since. I think you and Marci would be a good match up. Go for it.

"Fortunately her ex, Alan, is a decent man, a poor intellectual match for her but a nice person. They had a friendly divorce five years ago and are still on a friendly basis. He'll cause you no problems. Did she tell you about their two children?"

"Yes, she spoke about her son, an engineer in Chicago with a terrific job. She seemed quite proud of him. She mentioned a daughter at IU but didn't say much about her."

"Well, her daughter, Iris, is a genuine pain in the ass. I don't understand how two children of the same parents could be so different. Iris is drop-dead gorgeous and uses it to get what she wants. She's been like that since she was a little girl. She's also extremely bright. In her, that's a bad combination. She wants to move to Hollywood and become a movie or TV star. Her major at IU is drama and she's good. She hardly speaks to any of the family any more. Treats both of her parents like dirt. Only calls them when she needs money. I personally hope she goes to Hollywood and becomes a success. Her moving should keep her away from all of us. It's a terrible thing to say, but true. Last year Marci gave up trying to bring her into the family fold. I think she has been much happier since."

"Wow, I'll not ask about Iris. What's her son's name? She told me, but I forgot."

"Bruce, Alan Bruce Yoder. He uses his middle name to save being confused with his father. He's on excellent terms with both parents. He and Iris do not speak."

"That's sad, like a lost member of a family. How old are the two of them? Iris must be about twenty."

"Right on the money. Bruce will be thirty-one his next birthday."

"How's that possible? I took Marci to be about forty."

"She's a real fooler. Everyone thinks she is much younger than she is. She'll be fifty-three her next birthday."

"Wow, I feel much better about our age difference. Five years sounds a lot better than eighteen."

Doris stuck her head out the door and said, "Lunch is ready. Come and get it."

As soon as we sat down, Doc said to Doris, "You'll never guess who Ragan here has fallen for, and who has probably fallen for him."

Doris turned to Ragan. "Doc's an old blabbermouth. Are you sure you want him to tell me?"

Ragan laughed. "I'm sure lots of people will find out eventually, so why not? You're family anyway."

Doc grinned. "Doris, she's someone you know well, in fact, someone in the family. Guess."

"I'm not good at guessing."

"We were talking to her yesterday, after the terrible accident in her yard."

"My God, Marci . . . Marci for God's sake. You are a lucky man, Ragan. She's a gem. We are close. More like sisters than cousins."

"I would appreciated your not telling her I talked to you until after tonight. We've only had a single impromptu date. Tonight will be our first real date."

"Don't worry, we won't," Doc said. "I sure wouldn't want to jinx things for two of our favorite people."

Doris sported a sneaky grin. "You don't mind if I ask her what happened after the accident, do you? We only spoke briefly right after it happened and I did tell her I wanted to hear all the details. She usually calls me during her lunch break about ten minutes from now. You'll still be here."

"Who am I to stop family conversations. Don't tell her I told you about us. Let me tell her first."

"Don't you worry. Can I ask what are your plans? I'm sorry, I'm being quite nosy, but Marci. I can't get over it. We're in touch daily."

"Our only plans are for dinner tonight at her house, and my saying she would be two ahead of me and she must accept two of my future invitations."

"And did she agree?"

"Yes."

"Delicious! I can't wait to hear her side of this story. It's so wonderfully romantic. Two of our favorite people who didn't even know each other yesterday morning are now romantically connected. It's wonderful, a storybook happening."

Doc frowned at his daughter. "Don't go off the deep end, Doris. It's far too early. Let's wait for whatever happens."

"Don't worry. I can be inquisitive about yesterday and the accident. That's normal. I just want to hear what she says completely on her own."

The phone rang. Doris picked it up.

"Hello," Doris vigorously shook her head up and down.

"Oh, hi Marci. I thought it might be you . . . You did? . . . Tell me about it . . . *long pause* . . . a retired detective from Chicago . . . *another pause* . . . you actually invited a complete stranger into your house for dinner? That was either brave or foolish . . . he was a complete gentleman," Doris repeated, grinning at Ragan.

"You what? You invited him back for another dinner, tonight? . . you can't be serious. He's bringing some fresh fish he caught this morning . . . You'll give me a full report tomorrow . . . Of course I won't tell anyone . . . *another long pause* . . . what?"

Doris put her hand over the mouthpiece and said to Ragan, "You didn't tell us she kissed you goodnight."

Ragan got up and excused himself saying, "I don't think I should be listening to this conversation when she doesn't know I'm here. I'll be out on the porch."

Doc followed him out. "I'm sorry about that, but I don't think any harm was done. I'll see to it she never tells Marci you were here when she called. Those two are so close, almost like twins since they were tiny."

"I don't care if she learns I was here. I would like to be the one who picks the time and place to tell her about it. This relationship has quickly become precious to me and I don't want to do anything to mess it up. Right here and now I decided to ask your niece to marry me, some time in the future, of course. That is now my number one goal. There is no turning back."

"I couldn't be happier for both of you. I'm sure Doris feels the same way. We'll sit on the sidelines and cheer you on."

"And thanks, Doc. You and Doris solved my problem for me far better than I expected. I'm now on the right track and know it. Now I'd better go home and prepare for a special dinner with a special lady. Tell Doris thanks and good bye. Sometime soon the four of us will get together."

"Right on, Ragan, right on."

TWENTY-SIX

After dressing for the occasion, Ragan searched through his wines and selected a light German Liebfraumilch-Spätlese to compliment the fish. He took the filets out of the fridge and carefully packed them in a small cooler with ice. Knowing he would take 15 minutes to goto her house, Ragan left at exactly six-fifteen and drove into her driveway at six-thirty sharp. He walked onto the porch and knocked on her door. . . no answer.

He only waited a couple of minutes when a bright red Mustang convertible turned in the driveway. Marci hopped out quickly and ran to the porch, still in her nurse's uniform.

"I'm so sorry, Ragan. I was late getting away,"she said as she hurriedly unlocked and opened the door and ushered him inside. "I wanted to be all ready for you, but they kept me nearly an hour more than usual. I'm frazzled."

"Relax, we're in no hurry now. Take your time and do what you need to do. First of all, I would like a hug and kiss."

"I'm all sweaty and smelly from work. I need a shower and to change. Are you sure you want to be close to me?"

"I don't care. You are beautiful to me, and I need a hug."

After a hug and warm kiss, Ragan held her while he said, "Now, go do what you want to, and take all the time you need. We are in no rush. I'll put the fish and the wine in your fridge and sit here and read the paper till you are ready."

"Thanks. You are such a gentleman. I am impressed. I shouldn't be long."

"Like I said, relax and take your time. The entire evening is ours to do with as we choose."

About twenty minutes later, a scrubbed, quaffed, and sweet smelling lady in a slinky green dress pranced into the room. She was tastefully and minimally made up.

"Wow, what a transformation. You are beautiful."

"And you are quite the handsome gentleman. I too am impressed. Now I feel much more kissable. Come here."

It was several minutes later when Marci finally turned and headed for the kitchen. Ragan noticed the dining room table was all set with flowers and a pair of candlesticks.

"You were busy," he said, indicating the table. "It's lovely. Can I be of any help?"

"I set the table this morning before I left, just in case. Good thing I did. Now it's my turn to ask you to sit and relax. Everything is under control. Should I need any help, I'll ask."

"That does not surprise me," I said as I sat and picked up the paper. "One glance around your house and I can tell you are neat and efficient. It's lovely."

Marci called from the kitchen, "How do you like your fish, broiled or fried?"

"Your choice. Either is okay with me."

"Broiled is my choice. I'm making some dill sauce for the fish. Is that okay with you?"

Ragan got up and walked to the kitchen arch. "Perfect. Your kitchen layout is quite efficient and such beautiful wood cabinets too. Are they new?"

"Actually, they are almost twenty years old. Real wood cabinets stay like new with reasonable care."

"I bet I can tell you where they came from."

"Oh, how can you?"

"My new kitchen cabinets are similar to yours, They are hickory about the same color and with the same hinges. The door designs are a bit different. Yoder Kitchens made them and installed them soon after I bought the place. Sean Yoder is a distant cousin. Of course scads of Yoders live hereabouts as you know."

"It's a small world. Sean designed my kitchen. You say yours are also hickory? I like hickory a lot. We used hickory in all the cabinets in the house when we redid everything nearly twenty years ago. Did you know a lot of hickory is sold as pecan? The two are related. Sean told me and even the experts can't always tell which is which."

"I knew I liked your taste. Your home is an attractive place, livable I call it, livable and comfortable."

"Yes, I love this place. Sadly, I am going to move in about ten months. I hate having to move and try to find another place I like."

"Why?"

"It's part of our divorce settlement. I was given full use of the house until our daughter graduates from college even though our farm remained titled to my ex, Alan. She graduates in June and I must move out by July 31."

"That's a shame."

"It was my choice. We had another farm about five miles south of here which is now in my name. It's about twice the size of this one and has a lovely woods with a small stream. It has no house so I will need to build one. We had a friendly and fair settlement. Alan's a decent guy, but our lives began diverging not long after Iris was born. Our divorce was a mutual one, no rancor, quite unusual. We are still friends."

"You were fortunate. About ten years ago my sis had a nasty divorce. It divided her kids. I doubt they will ever be on family friendly terms again."

"Yes, I think that's more the rule than ours. Alan keeps his trucks and equipment here in the big white building. He came over to check his truck yesterday. Told me it was driveable. The left rear outside wheel and tail light were damaged, but nothing else. The Ford van was sure a mess."

"Everyone did receive one blessing. Two nasty career criminals died and the state saved bundles of money on trials and incarceration to boot."

"I agree. Now, dinner is ready. Grab those two serving dishes and put them on the table. I'll get the rest."

"You bet."

"Sit on the end. I'll sit on the side. Lots of my family live around here so I kept the big dining room table for family gatherings. Otherwise we'd eat in the kitchen like we did Thursday. I decided to eat here for this special occasion. Please open the wine. I'll bet it's terrific."

I poured two glasses. "I will make a special toast. To the start of something truly beautiful. May this be long lasting."

"Wonderful toast. I couldn't agree more."

✳   ✳   ✳

"The meal was wonderful. The fish, asparagus, corn-on-the-cob, and salad were perfect. You are an accomplished cook."

"I enjoyed everything as well. Fresh bass is one of my favorites. The wine was great. I love German white wines. All of the vegetables came from my garden I'm proud to say. I must tell you that you are the first man I invited to dinner for years, except for family of course."

"That makes us about even. You are the first lady I had dinner with since Rita died."

"Tell me about her, if your comfortable doing so."

"I'm quite comfortable talking about Rita, thank you. She was quite special. We were highschool sweethearts at Warsaw High. She grew up on a farm south of town. We married right after I graduated from the Chicago Police Academy. Her family was upset at first when I took her away from

Warsaw, but soon got over it. Her mother especially warned her I had a dangerous job in a dangerous city. She was all for our marriage, just warned Rita what she could be in for."

They continued talking while clearing the table, then moved to the living room couch.

"I can understand her mother's concerns. What about children?"

"No sadly. Rita would have been a wonderful mom, but she was unable to conceive. She went to a number of doctors but to no avail. With eight siblings, she had lots of nieces and nephews, but of course they were not the same."

"I assume she worked. What did she do?"

"She majored in business at IU and ended up as a CPA. She worked for the same large accounting firm till she got sick. She had moved up to a vice presidency before she died."

"She sounds like a sharp lady."

"That she was, bright, kind and caring too."

"You must miss her much."

"Sometimes terribly. I think about all the good times we had and much of the pain goes away."

"What did she die of."

"Complications from the flu. She developed pneumonia and didn't make it. She was far too young. Hers was one of the saddest funerals I ever attended. She was from a huge, close family who were all at the funeral. Buckets of tears flowed, a lot of them mine. I never cried so much for so long in my entire life."

"You are a caring, compassionate man. I saw that in you soon after we met. That's why I . . . I am so attracted to you. I might as well say so right now, I'm falling for you, Ragan. I haven't felt anything like this for many years, maybe never."

"Marci, I'm in the same condition. These kinds of feelings were absent from my life for so long I almost forgot how good they are and how scary, not because of the feelings, but mostly because of how strong those feelings are and how quickly they came on."

"I feel exactly the same. I'm terrified, but wouldn't consider changing anything for the world."

Ragan decided this was the time to tell her about Doc. "I must make a confession."

"Oh?"

"My growing concern about how to handle this prompted me to contact an old friend and advisor, the doctor who brought me into the world. I talked to him and told him about my concerns. Guess who my doc is?"

"Not a single clue."

"Doc Miller, your uncle."

"Oh my God. What did he say?"

"That I was a lucky man and he would be cheering us on. His daughter, Doris, said the same."

Marci raised her hand to her mouth. "You were listening when I called, weren't you? I thought something was unusual about how Doris was talking. That scalawag. Wait till I get my hands on her. So you heard all of her side of our conversation?"

"No. I walked out of the room about midway, as soon as I realized I shouldn't be listening. I'm sorry, but I did hear quite a bit. Are you angry with me?"

"Not one bit. You didn't deliberately eavesdrop, but Doris, I'll speak a few words with her."

"Don't be too hard on her. She had wonderful things to say about you. She obviously cares a lot for you."

"We've been like close sisters since we were babies. I'm not really angry. We'll laugh about it, but I will give her a hard time," she said with a laugh. "That's an amazing coincidence, you going to my uncle to ask for advice. I'll bet our paths crossed before. I worked for my uncle for several years, right after I finished nurses training between 1981 and 1983."

"I was in Chicago then. I don't think I ever saw you or I would remember. Yours is not a face a man would forget."

"That's a nice thing to say, thank you. Incidentally, neither Doris nor Doc are gossips so all of this will stay in the family. We will certainly raise some eyebrows in the family. Several of my cousins tried to fix me up with dates. I never took them up on their offers, so they gave up trying long ago."

"Why so?"

"I got so sick of Alan's buddies pestering me for dates I got in the habit of refusing all offers of any kind. I got so I ignored or reacted negatively to all passes or male contacts of any kind from anyone. I was happy with my life the way it was. I didn't want a man to mess me up. I guess I was afraid of a replay of my years with Alan."

"Why me? What was so different?"

"I can tell you exactly why. First of all, I invited you into my house for coffee, remember?"

"Yes, pleasantly, and after a nasty experience."

"My invitation for you to say for dinner was one of those spur-of-the-moment decisions, a necessary one. I simply pegged you as a real gentleman and wanted to learn more about you. The more we talked, the more I liked what was happening. When I began having those telltale warm feelings I let them happen for some reason. I surprised myself by being so forward with you. When we were holding each other as we said goodbye, I had to kiss you. That surprised me even more and was the first time in my life I ever did such a thing. After you left I wondered if I gave you the wrong idea. Did I?"

"I never even considered anything negative. I was pleasantly surprised. Right away I knew you were a special lady. Frankly, I was hooked, caught in the tender trap as the song writers say."

"We both seem to be in the same trap."

"One more confession."

"Oh?"

"I told Doc and Doris, and I quote my words, 'I decided to ask your niece to marry me, some time in the future.' Ask them if you doubt my words."

"Ragan, it's much too soon for such a question."

"For actually asking you are right. To make the decision to do so in the future? That's who I am. Perhaps I shouldn't have told you, but since I told Doris and Doc, I wanted to be the one who did tell you."

"We'll find out if and when the time comes, won't we.

"Yes, but I would not say if, only when. It's the second time in my life I've known."

"I can't think of a thing to say."

"You don't need to say a thing, but I would like a kiss."

This was followed with hours of new lovers sharing, planning, and growing in their love. After two in the morning Ragan finally arrived home and went to bed. All he could think about was Marci coming to spend Sunday with him at the lake. He wondered what he should do to ready the place. An hour later he finally went to sleep, the only thing stopping him from thinking about their future plans.

TWENTY-SEVEN

Ragan could hardly believe he had slept so late. He jumped out of bed and dressed quickly so he could get everything done before Marci arrived at eleven. Fortunately he kept a rather neat house, and since he was gone most of the time, cleaning and vacuuming did not take long. The weather was warm and sunny so they planned to spend most of the day out of doors. They would not eat on the patio because of the many flies. He packed a soft sided cooler with sandwich makings and another hard sided one with beer, pop, and iced tea. They would take the coolers with them on the deck boat when they went cruising on the lake.

When this was done, he cleaned and checked the sailboat to make sure everything was ready in case they had some wind. He took the cover off the deck boat and vacuumed the carpet. The boat was a twenty-five year old Viking he rescued and refurbished soon after he moved in. Next he mowed the lawn and pulled a few dandelions.

At ten thirty he made a quick tour of the property and picked up a few errant pieces of plastic and paper before heading in to shower and dress. He had just pulled on his shorts when Marci pulled in and parked behind the house. He stepped out to greet her.

"You had no trouble finding the place."

"Of course not and good morning, I've been to the Tippy Country Club numerous times so I knew exactly where your house was. This is a delightful place with a huge yard, and you're right on the lake."

"Lets go around front so you can enjoy the view for a while."

"Let me grab my case and take it inside on the way. Here's a little something for our meal. Why don't you put it in the kitchen while I stow my things. And where should I put my case?"

"Right here in the first bedroom," he said as they walked in. He pointed to the left.

"This is a beautiful place. I love the view through those picture windows. Look at all the boating activity. Today is Sunday of course, and a warm sunny one.

"It could be the last warm summer weekend so everyone's come out to enjoy it. It's possible we won't experience another one like this till next June, but you understand that, don't you, living in the same area."

"What's first on the agenda?"

"Why don't we dress for a day on the water and take a cruise on the deck boat. I can put up the canopy if it's too sunny. You are tan so you are used to being out in the sun."

"Yeah, I enjoy the sun. I brought my bathing suit and a coverup. Will that do?"

"Should be fine. We can take the two coolers along and eat lunch on the water. I'll meet you in the kitchen when you're ready to go."

Several minutes later they cast off and backed away from the pier.

"I'll point out things as we cruise by. First we'll pass Kalorama Park. It's one of the oldest sections of cottages on the lake. Many were built in the 90's when the country club was developed. You seem quite at home on the water."

"My brother, Terry, owns a place on Dewart Lake north of Tippy. I spent a lot of time for years, swimming, boating and water skiing. I love being on the water. Strange enough, this is the first time I've been on Tippy. Seen the lake many times from the Country Club dining room, but being on the water here is a first for me and I am enjoying the ride."

"Now's a good time for a cruise. It's not terribly busy. By two o'clock a lot more boats and PWCs will be on the water. Everywhere will be busy. We'll go for a sail if the wind is up.

"Sounds exciting. That's one thing on the water I have never done—been on a sailboat. I am excited about sailing with you."

We cruised slowly all around the shoreline and reached the far eastern end of the lake before one. I headed the boat up Grassy Creek.

"This is one of my favorite places to go. We'll discover lots of critters, turtles, frogs, fish, birds, especially red wings, even a beaver or muskrat. I always think it's like a primeval place, especially with no signs of civilization visible at all."

"I know exactly what you mean. It's so quiet and peaceful."

"Up ahead after the next few curves in the creek is a little beach, a sandbar in a farmers field actually. We'll pull the boat up on the sand and eat our lunch."

Ragan cut the motor as they slid up on the shore. The quiet was overpowering after the noisy watercraft on the lake. He got out and tied the boat to a small tree on the bank. Marci began making sandwiches while Ragan opened the drink cooler.

"I'm having a beer. What would you like? We have several flavors of soda, iced tea, and bottled water."

"Beer please. I'm not much of a drinker, but nothing satisfies thirst on a hot day like beer."

"Coming up."

As they sat for lunch, Marci removed her cover up. She was wearing a stunning, light green, one-piece bathing suit. Ragan carefully took her all in from head to toe.

"You certainly are a lovely, youthful woman, athletic even. Do you work out?"

Marci smiled. "Thanks for the compliment. I try to stay fit and trim. When I first entered nursing I realized how many nurses got heavy, even obese, so I vowed never to let myself go. I was careful about my diet, exercised regularly several ways, walked, ran, biked, and sometimes worked out in the exercise room at the hospital. It paid off in good health as well. I'm proud to say I weigh now almost exactly what I did when I graduated from high school. I inherited good genes which certainly does help. Most of my family are fit and trim as well."

"It shows. You are one of the loveliest ladies I know. You are better looking every time I see you. When I first saw you I guessed your age at about forty. You sure fooled me."

"My goodness, Ragan, compliments can turn a girl's head. You seem to be in quite good shape yourself, no paunch at all. Few men your age are in that kind of shape, many men much younger even."

"The Chicago police had an excellent weight control program which was suggested, but not mandatory. I adhered religiously and even continued after retiring. I'm also careful what I eat—try to maintain a healthy diet."

"My mother always told me to find a man who takes good care of himself, and he will take good care of you. I think she was quite correct, except for narcissists of course."

"I'll bet it's just as true if you reverse the sexes."

While they sat relaxing and having lunch, several boats passed by and waved. They both smiled and waved back.

Marci made an observation. "Folks on the water are so friendly, helpful too, especially if anyone gets in trouble on the water. Actually, I think that's normal human behavior, behavior we sometimes forget about in other places and circumstances."

"Like in big cities?"

Marci thought for a moment. "Probably, but I've spent little time in big cities so I really don't know. Could be because of the different circumstances. People behave differently in a crowd than they do in small groups or alone."

"Being a cop in Chicago for so many years, I saw all kinds, some good, some bad, and some really evil. Of course, because of our job, we dealt with the worst, rarely the best people. Speaking of evil people, I want to show you where those two who died in the truck put in and removed their boat with the stolen goods. The ramp is a short distance upstream from here and as far as we can go in my deck boat. The creek is dammed with a concrete spillway. Next to the dam is a boat lock that cannot accommodate a boat as big as this one. I've used the lock many times in smaller boats."

Ragan pushed off and headed the boat upstream. They soon came to a culvert under a county road.

"What do we do now?" Marci asked. "That's too small for us to go through isn't it?"

"No, the deck boat barely fits. We must guide the railings through carefully, but this time of year we can go through. In spring and early summer, the water in the creek is so much higher the boat can't go through."

Ragan guided the boat slowly and carefully through, using his hands against the metal of the culvert. The side railings only missed the metal culvert by a few inches and bumped the metal several times. Once through, they were in a small lagoon with a concrete boat ramp among a grove of trees to the left. Several tiny cottages were close together on the right side of the lagoon. Beyond the lagoon, water spilled over the dam. The lock at the left end of the dam was about seven feet wide by twenty-five feet long. The lock had a steel apparatus to raise and lower the gates for a lift of about two feet. The entire apparatus was painted bright yellow.

"That ramp is where those crooks launched and retrieved their boat. I'll bet they had a hassle taking the boat with so much weight up the creek and under the culvert. It's a wonder they even made it."

Ragan took the boat over by the dam and explained how the lock worked. As he did, a boat came downstream and went through the lock so Marci was able to see the process in action. They followed the boat downstream through the culvert and all the way back to Tippy. They finished cruising back along the north shore to Ragan's and tied up to his pier, went inside for a potty stop, and ended up sitting in the living room.

TWENTY-EIGHT

After relaxing for about half an hour Ragan asked. "Are you up for a sail? A fairly good wind is blowing so we should enjoy a nice ride."

"Absolutely, but you must show me the ropes. I've never been on a sailboat."

"I'm sure you're agile enough. My Hobie 16 is a catamaran. We sit on a canvas trampoline, not down in a hull. You won't want the coverup and we'll be wearing life jackets. They are required by law, a fortunate rule. It's a big fine if they catch you without an adequate number of approved life jackets easily accessible. They are right on the porch. Let's go."

They donned the jackets and walked out to the pier where the Hobie was pulled up onto a rack made of two inch galvanized pipe. Ragan showed her around the craft, pointing out its features and gadgets. He showed her where she would sit and what to do when they *came about*. The sheltered part of the lake where they were was quiet so he raised and set the sails while the Hobie was still on the rack. He unhooked and launched the boat into the shallow water. He helped Marci aboard, walked the Hobie out to deeper water, and gave a big shove as he jumped on board. In the light air near shore they moved slowly at first. An unusual east wind was blowing so he set the sail to starboard and sailed downwind toward Silver Point.

"We'll sail with this setting almost to the far end of the lake and tack back. This is called a port reach because the wind is coming from the port or left side, even to the stern. The boom and both sails are on the starboard side."

"Port is left, starboard is right. Stern is rear. I'm learning. . . . We seem to be going faster and faster."

"As we move out into the middle of the lake the wind is stronger so we do go faster. You'll notice I am pulling in or tightening both the jib - the

154

front sail - and the main sail. That's because we are moving at an angle to the wind direction and not moving directly down wind. As we move faster, the angle of the wind to the sails changes and I must tighten them to put the most power into the sails while holding on any heading."

"I think I understand, a little anyway. This is fun. I like sailing, especially the silence, no motor sound. What happens when you run out of lake? Surely you can't sail against the wind?"

Ragan laughed. "You're clueless about sailing, aren't you?"

"I told you I have never been on a sailboat. Of course I am clueless."

"When we go as far downwind as we can go, we simply sail upwind."

"How is that possible?"

"I'll show you. First, I'll begin tightening both sails as I ease the rudder over. See, we are turning to port. As I continue turning I pull both sails as tight as I can. See those little orange ribbons on the sail?"

"Yes."

"They are called tell tales. When they are streaming straight back like they are now, the wind is moving smoothly over the sail and we are getting the most power out of the wind. Now look what happens when I turn a bit more into the wind. Keep your eye on the tell tales."

"They are beginning to flutter, to move around erratically."

"When the tell tales flutter, the sail is luffing or losing power. Now, watch when I turn downwind or fall off as sailors say."

"They are straight again. No, wait, now they flutter a bit every once in a while. Why is that?"

"We are sailing as close into the wind as possible. That's called being close-hauled. For most sailboats, sailing right at this point is the fastest way to sail upwind. We are now close-hauled and are sailing upwind. You said "impossible." So show me what direction the wind is coming from."

"How can I tell? I think from that way," she says pointing forward and to port.

"Very good. You are close to correct. The tell tales attached to the wire stays holding the mast indicate wind direction relative to the boat, not true wind direction. That's the direction we use to set the sails. Now we are sailing upwind?"

"Amazing. How'd you learn all this, sailing I mean?"

"Mostly from friends in races and by observing and listening to other sailors. I also bought a book on sailing the Hobie. I learned lots about how to trim the sails for racing from my Hobie book. See how fast we are going? We're gaining on the motorboat in front of us and it's not going slow."

"My gosh, Ragan, this is exciting. I never dreamed a sailboat could go so fast. I am impressed."

The rest of the sail they tacked back and forth southeast from the Country Club to near Ragan's. They turned on their last starboard tack and headed across the lake toward Ragan's place. They had just come about when a large power boat moving slowly and making a huge wake cut across their prow a bit too close for comfort.

"Hang on," Ragan shouted.

The first wave raised the Hobie's bows high in the air. It came down the other side and dug deeply into the next wave, the trampoline actually going completely under water. Marci was washed off the boat as the wave surged over the trampoline. With a sickening crash a fast moving PWC with two teens aboard struck the back of the Hobie right where Ragan was clinging to everything he could to stay with the boat. The teens were jumping the waves behind the power boat and never saw the Hobie.

Marci bobbed to the surface between two demolished boats. The Hobie was hanging almost upside down supported only by the intact port hull. Nothing else of the catamaran was visible on the surface. The PWC was also upside down, its prow smashed in, but raised above the water so it stayed afloat. One of the teens, a boy, was clinging to the hull of the Hobie, dazed and barely conscious. Ragan and the other teen were nowhere to be seen. Several boats rushed to the scene to help.

Marci screamed. "Ragan, Ragan, my God, where are you?"

An accomplished swimmer and scuba diver, Marci slipped out of her life jacket and dove below the surface. She found Ragan almost immediately. He was pinned to the submerged hull, held down firmly by a thin shard of broken fiberglass driven through his upper arm. She saw lots of blood in the water coming in spurts from Ragan's arm. With the extreme strength often shown in such instances, she broke the fiberglass shard off of the hull with her hands, unwound the main sheet from his arm, swam up to the surface, and took him to the nearest boat.

"Hold his head above water and give me something I can use as a tourniquet and hurry please. A belt or thick rope will do. I also need a stick or large screwdriver to tighten the tourniquet. I'm a trauma nurse and he has a severed artery. If I don't stop the bleeding he will bleed to death quite soon so hurry. Do not try to pull him out of the water until the bleeding stops."

Someone handed her a thick rope and a square stick.

While Marci wrapped the rope around Ragan's upper arm, she yelled. "Someone use your cell phone. Call the Sheriff. We need help."

Marci tightened the rope until the blood stopped spurting. Finally able to relax a bit, she thanked those in the boats helping, The welcome sound of a siren announced the sheriff's patrol boat was coming. The officer was Gordy Genoa who had lake patrol duty. He had seen the collection of boats and knew something was amiss. The boats parted to let him through and he was soon next to the boat with the people holding Ragan above the surface.

"Oh, God no, Ragan," he said as soon as he saw.

Marci said, "Deputy, he has a severed artery in his upper arm and possibly other injuries. I stopped the bleeding with an improvised tourniquet, but he must go to a hospital as soon as possible."

"Who are you, ma'am?"

"I'm Marci Yoder, a trauma nurse at Goshen Hospital. This man is Ragan Yoder who lives right across the lake. Can you pull him into your boat and take him to an EMS as soon as possible. And be careful with that piece of fiberglass. He will probably require extensive surgery. Also, an injured boy is clinging to that hull. He needs help as well."

One of the men in a nearby boat called out, "The boy is in our boat. He seems dazed, but unhurt. He says his brother was with him."

Seeing Ragan being carefully lifted into the patrol boat. Marci was torn, but turned, took several deep breaths, and dove beneath the surface once more. After several dives she followed some bubbles and dove deeper. She grabbed the hand she saw and swam for the surface. She thought she might not make it, but finally burst through the surface and pulled the boy to the nearest boat as she gasped for air. One look at the boy's face and she began to cry. His skull was crushed and he was quite dead. A man in a nearby boat took the body.

A man in a fast speedboat asked, "Lady, do you want to go with the man in the sheriff's boat? I can take you there in a hurry."

"Yes, please. That would be wonderful."

He pulled her in quickly and headed for Paton's at high speed. He knew exactly where the patrol boat was going. They pulled in to Paton's just as the patrol boat was tying up.

"How did you know?" Marci asked when the boat slowed so he could hear.

The man smiled. "I saw you together on the sailboat as you came about before the accident. I take my hat off to you. You are one brave and resourceful lady. I was close enough to follow your dives and rescues. You are amazing. What's your name, ma'am?"

"Marci, Marci Yoder. Who are you."

"I'm a neighbor of Ragan's, live two doors south of him. Tell him Tim Long wishes him well. I'll tell him what an amazing lady you are as soon as I see him. You were unbelievable."

As they pulled up to the dock Marci said, "Thank you so much for being so thoughtful. Ragan may not be out of the woods yet. That's going to be big time surgery to remove the piece of fiberglass and he could be suffering other injuries."

"Somehow I think he will be Okay. Go! Take good care of him."

"I will, Tim, I will. And thanks again."

She ran over to the patrol boat and asked, "How close is the EMS and where from?"

Gordy was quite official. "Ma'am, I don't know who you are, but everything is under control. He is on monitors and his blood pressure and other vitals are holding steady. The EMS is coming from Milford and should be here in no more than fifteen minutes, ten more likely. I'm a life long friend of this man and will make sure he receives the best of care."

"I'm Marci Yoder, the head trauma nurse at Goshen Hospital. I was on the sailboat with Ragan when he was injured. Not only were we sailing, but Ragan told me yesterday that he was going to marry me. Is your question answered now?"

"Yes, ma'am, definitely. We are both on the same side."

"I would like to call Goshen Hospital and set up their trauma section, arrange for the surgeons and other personnel and prepare everything for him. KCH is closer and I understand the rules, but I also know that with my help he can be examined and in surgery far quicker than if he goes to KCH."

"We must follow the rules, and KCH is closer. Can't you do the same thing with KCH? Prepare them the same sway?"

"Absolutely not. I maintain no standing at KCH and none of their trauma doctors or nurses would have any idea who I am or what I can do. To them I would be just another civilian. All of the EMS people in Milford know me. I can even do some of the necessary prep in the Ambulance on the way. Ask them when they are here."

"Wait a minute. I know who you are. You're the one who dove down and pulled Ragan up. You even applied his tourniquet. How in the devil did you get here so soon? Last I remember you were diving after that other kid."

Marci told Gordy about Tim and his fast run to Paton's with her.

"Okay, Marci. I'll set things up from this end. You can even use my radio to talk to Goshen Hospital if it will help."

"Yes, let me use your radio right now, please."

After a few minutes on the radio, she turned to Gordy. "It's all set up. I'll give them the rest of what they will need from the ambulance."

"Can I ask you, did Ragan really say he was going to ask you to marry him?"

"On my honor, but please don't tell anyone . . . except Ragan of course."

"Don't worry, I won't. I wonder about one thing."

"Oh, what's that?"

"How'd you ever get so close to Ragan. I would bet a mint he would never even consider marriage."

"I'm sure you heard about the death of those two criminals in an accident on Thursday. The accident happened in my yard. I met Ragan in my yard because of the accident. We had coffee in my kitchen, and later, two dinners in my dining room. That did it. Boom."

Lady, you are amazing. Adding what you told me to what you did today is unbelievable. Oh, I'm sure it happened, just like you said, but still unbelievable. Please notify me when you decide to go public, will you?"

Marci laughed. "You bet."

The EMS arrived. Ragan was carefully loaded and Marci jumped in before it sped away. The head trauma nurse arriving in an ambulance clothed in a bathing suit created quite a stir at the hospital. She quickly changed into a surgical gown and faded in among others.

The surgery took more than four hours as they carefully removed the shattered fiberglass and tied the artery back together. Ragan had been lucky. Other than the damaged arm, three broken ribs, a badly bruised hip, and a mild concussion, he had no other injuries. At nine-thirty they wheeled him into the recovery room. Doc, Doris, Gordy, Eric and several others from the sheriff's office were waiting in the room. Doris had gone to Marci's and picked up clothing and toiletries for her.

Close to eleven Gordy, Doc, Doris and Marci were the only ones still in the room. Gordy stopped and spoke to Marci as he walked out. "I don't quite know what to say except thank you and bless you for all you did today. I'm glad you ignored my misguided official efforts. You're one fantastic human being. If you ever find anything I can do for you, consider it done." He leaned close and whispered in her ear, "My lips are sealed, until you make things public."

After the others left, Marci said, "Why don't you two go home? it's late and I'm going to stay here with him. The staff here is taking good care of him and all we can do is wait anyway."

"Are you sure you're all right?" Doris said. "I could stay here and keep you company."

"I'll be fine. The chair lays back and I'll most likely be asleep most of the time. Go!"

"If you're sure."

"I'm sure."

"Doc and I will go pick up your car in the morning. We have Ragan's address. Where are the keys?"

"Oh my gosh. I never thought about my things till now. They're in my purse sitting on the dining room table at Ragan's. We only took our bathing suits and life jackets with us when we left on the sailboat. I'll bet Ragan's things are right where we left them as well. The house is wide open."

"Should we go now?"

"I'm sure they'll be all right for tonight. Get a good night's sleep and go in the morning. The lights are all off."

After they left, Marci lay back in the chair and promptly went to sleep. She awoke each time anyone came in to check on the patient and went back to sleep immediately after they left. Every time Ragan moved or made a sound, she was instantly awake, then fell back asleep when she knew he was okay.

TWENTY-NINE

Doc and Doris arrived at Ragan's, found the door was locked, and read this note they found: *I locked up and the keys are at my house two doors south, Tim.*

They walked to Tim's and knocked on the door. A pleasant elderly lady answered.

"Yes?"

"We saw the note on Ragan's door. We came to retrieve some things from the house and to pick up Marci's car."

"Oh yes, Tim said someone would probably be coming for things. I'm Tim's mother. He's at work. Come in, please. How is Ragan doing? Such a good man."

Doris answered, "He came through surgery well. This morning Marci told us they expect a complete recovery. He will need time of course, several months."

"Such a terrible accident, Ragan being hurt so bad and that young boy killed. What a pity. Those little water bugs go so fast. Most of them are kids and they go way too fast. I know, I see them all the time. I wonder why there aren't more serious accidents."

"Yes, they are dangerous, and we all understand about kids. They can be wild."

"And the young woman, the one who dove down and saved Ragan, Tim raved on about how brave and clever she was. What was her name?"

"Marci, Marci Yoder," Doc said. "She's my niece. I'm Doc Miller from Milford, and this is my daughter, Doris."

Mrs. Long introduced herself. She was sweet, but quite a talker. Half an hour later they manage to pick up the keys and return to the house. Doris packed Marci's case while Doc picked up all the things on the table including Ragan's and put them in a plastic bag. Noticing the coolers on the porch they examined them and emptied the one with the drinks.

Doris opened the refrigerator. "There are only a few perishables in here. Let's put them in the cooler and take them. They'll be green science projects by the time Ragan is back here."

They took a walk through the house to find out if anything else needed their attention. Finding all in good order they headed out for the hospital.

✳ 10:20 am ✳

They arrived and found Ragan awake but befuddled. Marci was waiting for her car so she could go home.

"How's the patient doing?" Doc asked.

"He's groggy but awake off and on. He'd be in a lot of pain if not sedated. The trauma to his arm was severe. Doc thinks he will regain full use, but a lot of painful therapy will be needed. They spent time with surgical binocular microscopes finding all the bits of fiberglass and picking them out of his arm. The surgery took so long for that reason."

Doris explained, "Here's your purse and some things of Ragan's we found on the table too. We emptied his fridge and put all of the perishables in his cooler which is now in the trunk of your car. A thoughtful neighbor, Tim, had closed up and locked the house. He left a note on the door so we went to his house and retrieved the key."

"Oh, yes, Tim. He's the one who ran me down to the sheriff's boat and Ragan right after the accident. He's a thoughtful gentleman who saw the accident and came to help."

Ragan was awake and trying to sit up.

"Who's there?" was his groggy question.

Marci was instantly at his bed. "It's me, Marci. Don't try to sit, Ragan, lie still."

"Where am I?"

"In Goshen Hospital. You were in an accident and seriously hurt. You've had surgery and will recover fully, but now you must rest and not move."

Ragan spoke slowly and groggily, "The last I remember was seeing you washed off the Hobie by that damned power boat. Are you all right?"

"Yes, Ragan, I'm fine. I only got wet, but you were hit by one of those PWCs going extremely fast."

"I can hardly feel anything. Why am I so numb?"

"Your left arm had major surgery to remove a lot of broken fiberglass. Your entire arm will be numb from anesthetic for some time so you will not experience much pain. You also broke several ribs and sustained a seriously bruised hip. Relax and try to sleep as much as you can. Doris, will you go tell the floor nurse he's awake and trying to move."

"Sure, right away."

She returned shortly, following Sarah, his assigned nurse. At about six feet, Sarah was a tall woman. She checked his monitors and went to his side.

"Okay, Mr. Yoder, you are awake. Here are some important instructions for you. Do you hear me?"

A groggy yes came from the bed.

"First and most important, I don't want you to move at all until I say you can. Is that clear? . . . You can answer me you know."

Another mumbled yes.

"Louder young man. I need to hear if you are still alive," she said in an authoritarian voice."

A much stronger yes was the result.

"That's better. I wonder how you rate a head nurse as your private nurse and companion, but I can handle it. That's never happened before in this hospital as far as I know. If you need anything, anything at all, press the orange button, Okay?"

"Okay."

Sarah turned to Marci who was one of her good friends, "Why don't you go home? I'll make sure he's well cared for. So will everyone else here. Where'd he come from anyway? I never knew you to have a boy friend—thought you didn't even date. That's the word around here."

Marci laughed. "It's a short but complicated story. I will say this, he is a special man in my life. I'll tell you all about him some time when we can talk. Now's not the time."

"Okay, I get the message. I'll wait. Just don't forget. Now go on home before I throw you out."

Marci kissed Ragan goodbye and walked out with Doc and Doris.

As they walked to their cars, Doris asked, "Isn't nurse, Sarah, a bit rough, even crude with her patient?"

Marci smiled. "That's her way with patients like Ragan. Her male patients love the way she treats them. She uses a whole different manner with women. In fact, she varies her attitude and treats each patient individually, not all the same, male, female or children. Some of her patients, the ones who need it, receive treatment tailored for them. She always seems to choose the best treatment and makes few mistakes. She's also a good friend."

As they stood by Marci's car Doris said, "Your overnight case is in the trunk. I picked up everything of yours I found and put them in your case, even your coverup from the living room."

"Thanks for getting my car and stuff and for everything else. I'll talk to you later, bye."

"You're certainly welcome. Take care."

THIRTY

Pete and Eric were sitting in the sheriff's office, anticipating a call from the Chicago art expert who was already an hour late with his promised call. They were talking about Ragan and his accident.

"I am so sorry I was away and wasn't able to visit Ragan," Pete said. "I only heard about his accident this morning during our seven o'clock briefing. Gordy told us about his part and about Ragan's lady. He couldn't stop talking about her. She sounds like some sort of superwoman according to Gordy, real good looking too. I didn't think Ragan had a girl friend. No one in the department seemed to know either. Gordy even said he only learned about her after the accident and he is so tight with Ragan. Makes you wonder."

"You probably didn't know, Gordy's dad and Ragan played on the same Warsaw High School basketball team that went to the state finals. They were best friends and stayed friends through the years. I never saw a grown man cry like Ragan did at his funeral."

"How long ago was that? I didn't realize Gordy lost his dad."

"It was several years before you joined the department. He was killed when some drunk ran the downtown red light and hit into the driver's door of his cruiser. The slob wasn't even hurt, but Greg Genoa died instantly."

"What will happen to Ragan's case now that he's in the hospital?"

"First of all, with no disrespect, the case is not Ragan's, it's our case, the department's. He's working on it, like we all are, more or less. He was the acting point man on this one so Sheriff Rabb will appoint another one of us to take the point, probably Gordy or Chase Johnson. We'll wait and see."

"Yeah, I guess so. But isn't it a new case now, a case of fraud? The other was a murder case and it's all over."

"A lot of the same players and evidence will be involved, so logically the same officers will stay assigned."

Ellen announced, "Your art expert is on the phone. Will one of you talk to him?"

Eric picked up the phone. "Deputy Eric Blanding . . . Half an hour? . . . I thought you were going to call when you were leaving . . . Our people will need some time to get here. . . right! . . . bye . . . Ellen?"

"Yes."

"Call the insurance guy, Andy, and tell him the art expert will be here in a half hour. He just called."

Turning to Pete, "Maybe you should get a hold of Gordy. He's somewhere in the building. He'll want to speak with the art expert. Damn, I wish he had called like he promised."

"Okay."

✳ 9:30 am ✳

Pete found Gordy in the sheriff's office and told him about the art expert.

Gordy stepped to the door. "I'll be a while longer with Sheriff Raab. We're discussing who is going to do what now that Ragan's unavailable. Go back to the main office and meet with the expert. Don't wait for me. After he examines the paintings, don't let him leave till I talk to him."

"Okay, Gordy."

By the time Pete returned to the main office, Dr. Wiesse arrived. He wasted no time and began examining the paintings as soon as Eric showed him where they were. After going through the entire stack of paintings he walked back to Eric.

"I can say right off, all but the one painting you had set aside are copies, no originals. They are excellent copies worth maybe two hundred each. The one original would sell at auction somewhere between a hundred and a hundred and fifty thousand, possibly more."

"You're sure?" Eric asked.

"Absolutely! Whoever made them had the originals to copy. He even tried to imitate the brush strokes. One quick examination and I saw no cracks in the paint. Old paintings always show tiny cracks in the paint. On originals the paint is always cracked unless they are quite recent. All of these are supposed to be more than a hundred years old and I found no cracks at all, none, even with my magnifying glass. They cannot be originals."

"You will, of course, provide us with a written copy of your findings, signed and witnessed," Eric said.

"Absolutely. If a secretary is available I can dictate my report and she can type it. I will sign and you can sign as witness. That should serve you in court. I've done this numerous times before and am familiar with the format to use."

Eric said, "Ellen Cross, our indispensable office manager, can handle the typing for you."

He escorted Dr. Wiesse to Ellen's desk and asked her for three copies.

"Come back to the main office when the copies are ready and we'll get them signed and witnessed. I also must ask you to stay here until the insurance investigator from Fort Wayne is here in about half an hour. He has some questions for you and may want a copy of your report as well.

✳ 10.30 am ✳

Dr. Wiesse met with Andy, the insurance investigator, and gave him a copy of his report. Dr. Wiesse and Andy had their discussion about the paintings and left. They did not wait for Gordy."

✳ 11.00 am ✳

Pete and Eric waited until Gordy finally came into the main office.

"Okay, guys, listen up," Gordy called out. "Lots of things are progressing on this fraud case. Sargent Johnson and Emil are busy chasing information on Jake Ramsey including his bank records. He had about thirty thousand in two local accounts he cleaned out a week ago. The bank managers report he took cash in hundreds, packed the bills in an aluminum suitcase, and walked out with hardly a word. That was the day they fished the body out at Paton's. He's obviously been running ever since. No activity shows up on the records of any of his credit cards or cell phone since. He's hiding his tracks well. We're still digging."

Eric said, "He has obviously been planning this for a long time. He probably established another identity with credit cards, bank accounts, and a cell phone. It's anyone's guess what alias he established. Is there any procedure we can use to find aliases the person wants to hide?"

"Emil is searching everything he can find on Jake in any computer record. With good luck and determination we may be able to find his new identity. Once we learn that we should be able to find him."

The task would prove daunting. After three weeks and three days had passed with no results of any kind, their efforts were stalled completely.

THIRTY-ONE

Marci picked Ragan up at the hospital and took him to her house. His arm is healing well and he is about to start therapy. Ragan is showing signs of resenting his limitations and is thrilled to be out of the hospital.

"I'm well enough to go to my own house, Marci. I can take care of myself with one hand."

"Sure you can, but you are still a bit shaky on your feet because of your injured hip and one fall could mess up your arm. I will feel much better if I can keep my eyes on you most of the time until you show some improvement with therapy. You aced your evaluation session yesterday and tomorrow you start therapy. Let's see how you do for a week or so, then we might consider your moving back to your own house. Besides, I rather like having you around."

"I suppose you're right. I rather enjoy having you with me. I could get used to that."

"Don't get too used to it, big guy. I plan on sending you home as soon as I think you're ready. You heard what your doctor said."

"Yeah, three weeks or more. I'm afraid I might wear out my welcome."

"You'll wear your welcome out quickly if you don't behave yourself, and if you misbehave, I'll throw you out."

"You say the nicest and most encouraging things"

"Now I must return to the hospital for the rest of the day. I'll be home around six. Several dishes for lunch are in the fridge. I'm sure you can handle them with one hand. Please don't do too much. There are books to read, TV, and you can listen to my music system."

"Where's my cell phone? I couldn't use it in the hospital, but can now."

"Your iphone and charger are in the box of your stuff. It's not been charged so you'll need to charge it. I'll plug it in for you. Once charged, keep it in your pocket. That way you can call me if you need anything or get into difficulties. You're still weak so please don't over do."

"Okay, mother hen. Now, off to work with you. I'll be fine."

"Gimme a kiss and I'm outta here!"

"How romantic. See you at six."

"Just wait till you are all healed. I've missed those hugs and real kisses. We'll do lots of catching up. Bye!"

✻ 10.00 am ✻

As soon as his iphone was charged, Ragan called the sheriff's office. Ellen was delighted to hear his voice.

"How are you doing, Ragan, we've been getting all the reports of your progress, but it's good to actually talk to you."

"I'm doing quite well all things considered. I'm recovering at Marci's with her insistence. She wouldn't let me go to my house."

"Good for her. You listen to that lady. From what I hear you got yourself hooked up with quite a woman. You're a lucky man."

"I certainly am and thank the Lord. Now, I'd like to catch up with the Ramsey case. No one who came to visit me would talk about it. They kept saying wait till I'm well. What's going on?"

"Because they are without any leads on Ramsey—no answers. He vanished without a trace. They're stymied. Why don't you speak with Gary, he's one of the investigators assigned to the case and he's here."

"Yeah, let me talk to him."

In a few minutes Gary answered. "Yeah, Ragan, how are you doing?"

"Okay, I guess. Frustrated by not being able to do much. What's with the case anyway? Ellen tells me Ramsey disappeared without a trace."

Gary spent the next twenty minutes bringing Ragan up to date on where the case stood, definitely at a dead end. Every suggestion Ragan made was answered with, "We did that."

"I'm sorry, Ragan, that's everything. We are stumped. Every avenue we went down was a dead end, nothing."

"I hate hearing that and I really hate thinking that bastard got away with all that money without a trace."

"Yeah, me too. Andy, the insurance investigator said he scammed them out of several million, quite a haul."

"There must be some way to find him. He surely made a mistake or two. All we need to do is find them. I'll give that some thought. I surely can come up with something."

"You tell us if you do."

"Don't worry, I will. Bye for now."

✳ 11.45 am ✳

Ragan called back. "Ellen, is Gary still around?"

"Right at his desk. I'll call him for you."

"What's cooking, Ragan, a new idea?"

"Yes, Gary, a good one. Has anyone gone through his house thoroughly? I mean collected every personal item, every scrap of paper, all the stuff from any desk or writing area?"

"Only once checking for obvious clues. Ramsey cleaned out all those things when he left since we cataloged almost nothing but a desk pad, a few pens and pencils, some note pads and a few other items. That's all we found. It's all in a box in the evidence locker. Eric thinks he went through the house thoroughly sometime right after the robbery and gathered up all his personal belongings.."

"I'll bet he's right. Was a search for hidden papers done? I mean checking the bottoms of drawers or under cabinet tops for things hidden by being taped to those hidden surfaces?"

"I don't think our search was that thorough. You're talking a lot of work. Why would he hide things like that in his own house?"

"You'd be surprised what people hide and where. A detailed search will be a lot of work, but under the circumstances, the search should probably be done."

"I can authorize a search. In fact, I'll do the search myself and take Emil with me to help. He's good at that sort of thing."

"Tell me what you find if you find anything. I'd also like to go through the things in the evidence box if you can bring the box to me. I'm not home yet. I'm staying with a friend until my therapy is well underway. The house is at the southwest corner of county road N 425 W and W 1050 N ."

"I'll see what I can do. I have some time so I'll gather up Emil and head to the house. We'll check all the places you mentioned. I imagine we will need several hours. We'll try not to miss anything."

✳ 4.45 pm ✳

Gary shows up at Marci's door carrying a large corrugated box.

"Here's the evidence box. It's been inventoried, and I signed for it so don't lose anything."

"Great! Never lost a piece of evidence in thirty years so I think you're safe."

"Our search found one scrap of paper taped to the underside of a desk drawer. He tore the corner from some sort of travel brochure when he removed it. It's not much but does show a sailing vessel and the letters, b-b-e-a-n on the other side. That must refer to the Caribbean. Why would he hide a travel brochure?"

"Most likely because he didn't want anyone to find it. I'll bet that's where he's gone, somewhere in the Caribbean. Lots of islands all over, big and little. Some are independent nations and may not have extradition treaties with us. That's the best lead so far. Good work. Now, if I can only find something in this box."

"Not much in the box I'm afraid. We found one interesting book behind the cushions of a couch. It's especially interesting considering that scrap of the travel brochure. The title is *Islands of the Caribbean*. It's an old book though, around ten years old."

"That is interesting. I'll go through it carefully looking for any markings. Thanks, Gary, I'll give you a complete report on my findings as soon as I can."

"Unfortunately, we can provide no funds to send anyone to the Caribbean even if we knew where he was."

"No problem. My attorney says I should receive a sizeable settlement from the Insurance company that covered the PWC that hit me. I always wanted to cruise the Caribbean. This is my chance to do so, and I can pay for it myself. "

"Ragan, you are something else. You answer nearly everything."

"Just thinking ahead, Gary, thinking ahead."

"You be sure you are completely healed before heading for any Caribbean adventure."

"Don't worry, Marci will see to that. She's been riding herd on me since the accident."

"Good for her. I've not met your lady, but Gordy raves about her every time her name comes up. I'd like to meet her some day. I hear she is quite something."

"That she is. She certainly is. I'll bring her to one of the holiday gatherings the department holds."

"Great. Now I'd better head back. I'll write a report of our search and describe what we found. Put that scrap of paper in the evidence box with the other things. I'll come pick everything up when you've finished examining the contents."

"Safe travels."

THIRTY-TWO

Marci walked in the door and found Ragan sitting on the living room floor, items of evidence scattered all around him.

"What's all this and what are you doing?"

"This stuff, dear one, is everything personal found in Jake Ramsey's house when we searched. Gary brought it for me a couple of hours ago. He left almost nothing, and obviously cleaned out his things before he skipped. I'll put everything but these two note pads back in the box. I want to examine the pads closely to find and examine any impressions of writing that might be of use. I planned on having this all picked up by the time you got home, but you came early."

"I don't mind, but you shouldn't be down on the floor. How are you going to get up without using your left arm?"

"I can do it easily."

He grabbed the arm of a chair with his right hand and pulled himself up into it and stood.

"See? I'm not helpless. I can pull myself up from the floor."

Marci laughed. "I never ever thought of you as helpless. Well, right after the accident, but that was a rarity. Now, you can help me fix dinner. You'd better learn to earn your keep around here."

"Yes boss."

"And I would prefer you do not use that term for me. I am most definitely not your boss."

"Boy, that sure got a reaction. Should I call you master?"

She smiled. "Okay, so you're aching for a bruise."

"No, but I would like a hug and maybe a kiss."

"Okay. . . . Now let's fix dinner."

✳ 7.45 pm ✳

After the dishes were done, Ragan showed her what he was doing.

"What do you see on this pad?"

"Nothing, it's blank."

"Not completely. Look carefully at the surface when I hold the pad at this angle to the light."

"Still nothing, wait, I can see faint lines like writing. Oh, I understand. Whoever wrote on the earlier page pressed hard enough to make a slight impression on the sheet underneath. Unfortunately, it's too faint to read."

"Now I take this soft pencil and use the side of the lead to rub over those lines. Presto."

"I can make out some writing now. It's script and still hard to read. Looks to me like I-l-h-e-n-e-y. That makes no sense. Wait, add Mc and the letters become McIlheney, a name. The first name and Mc are completely illegible."

"Wait, isn't that a D or B, or an H, right where the first name would start?"

"That's a stretch, but could be. Now what?"

"Now, my dear, we have lots more to go on than we've had since we started looking for Ramsey, a name, possibly his alias. The scrap of a travel brochure for a cruise ship in the Caribbean and a book about islands in the Caribbean are certainly important. They give us a possible search area. I'll call Eric with this information. He'll ask Emil to search through travel bookings for passengers named McIlheney going anywhere in the Caribbean in the last month, especially on cruise ships. That old book on islands of the Caribbean had a single page corner that had once been folded over. On that page was an ad for a real estate company on Dominica."

"That's fascinating, coming to such conclusions from a few pieces of evidence. No wonder you enjoy police work."

"Not every part is enjoyable, but the rewards of solving a crime and putting the perps behind bars are beyond measure. Seeing two murderers get their just deserts has it's rewards. The happening in your yard makes up for the times I've experienced hardened criminals go scot free because of a minor technicality. Every officer of the law sees that happen once in a while, too often in my book. Because of sloppy police work those errors happen more than they should and could be prevented."

"Do I detect some rather strong feelings on the subject?"

"Definitely, but don't get me started. I'd like to concentrate on the good and positive. Hopefully these leads will take us somewhere and not be dead ends. Some time will be needed before we know. Now I'd better call Eric. He should still be working at the office today."

Eric was excited. "That's terrific work, Ragan. I hope it leads to our suspect. Even if we can't go after him we'll pin down his location and can track him and his money. He might even make the mistake of going somewhere we could nab him."

"Okay, tell me right away if Emil comes up with anything."

"I will, and Ragan, it's great for you to be back working with us. You've been missed."

"Thanks, Eric, it's good to be able to do anything. Being confined in that hospital room for so long was a real downer. I still can't use my left arm, but I begin therapy tomorrow so hopefully my arm will grow stronger quickly."

Therapy turned out to be slow and painful. Still, Ragan pushed himself. His therapist, Melody, told him he was one of her best patients and progressing rapidly.

＊ Monday, October 8, 2012, 10:15 am ＊

Eric called Ragan. "Another dead end. We could only find one passenger named McIlheney in all the bookings we checked, Beth McIlheney. She booked passage on a cruise ship called the Oosterdam at the last minute. We were even able to download a photo of her from the ship's photo gallery. She's in a bikini and I don't think Ramsey could possibly be like her."

"Did you check if she was traveling alone or with a companion?"

"Oops! No we didn't. Sorry. I'll start Emil on it right away."

"If she is traveling with a companion find his name and check for a photo. If it's Ramsey, he would not let them post a photo. They take ID photos of all passengers. Make a formal police request for a copy of her companion's ID photo. Also ask them to keep the request a confidential police matter. If it's Ramsey he will probably ask if any inquiries were made about him. Call me as soon as you learn anything. Oh and try to find out if they stayed on for the entire voyage or disembarked in one of the ports visited. Ask if any credit card or cell phone info on either of them is available. Use those words in your formal police request. If they can't provide us with the information as requested, ask them what hoops we need to jump through to obtain that info, be creative, and treat the entire request as a matter of urgency, but don't say what. If she has no traveling companion, let's still find all we can on her, just in case."

"Okay, Emil will add that to his search. This time we'll find all the peripheral information we can. Sorry I didn't do that in the first place."

"Don't be sorry. I had thirty years experience on the Chicago police to teach me. We had many more instances of this type of checking than the KC Sheriff's department ever will. I neglected to instruct you about what I needed and how to go about it, my error."

"We'll correct that omission immediately and I'll call right back as soon as I find anything. Now I better get busy."

"Go! Talk to you later, bye."

✳ 4:35 pm ✳

Ragan received a phone call from Emil.

"Ragan, this is Emil. Eric had to leave so I'm providing most of what you asked for. The lady is traveling with a male companion named, Jerome Rumsford. They boarded the Oosterdam in Port Everglades on Saturday, September eighth about three in the afternoon and disembarked in Barbados on Thursday the fourteenth. I searched for a departure from Barbados, but found none. I've been searching for merchant ships and small passenger vessels but so far no luck. Many do not list passenger names. I did find some valuable information. The Oosterdam would not provide ID photos or credit information as we requested. However, the headquarters of Holland America did wire the information directly to the KC Sheriff's department in response to our formal request. From the ID photographs they sent us, Jake Ramsey now sports a full beard and is using the name Jerome Rumsford. We've tagged him, Ragan. We don't know where he went, but we found one new name he is using and his different appearance."

"Hoop-la-dee and hallelujah! Great work, Emil. Now all we need to do is find him and figure out how to arrest him. That's not going to be easy.'

"We found even more good information. By researching credit card information on the two cards we learned about we found two more bank accounts. One is in Barbados, the First Citizens Bank, under the name Jerome Rumsford. That account had a current balance of around eighteen thousand. The other accounts were quite a surprise. Two are joint accounts in Banco do Brasil in Manaus way up the Amazon. The checking account has a balance of ten thousand, but the savings account has a balance of nearly half a million dollars. The other name on the accounts is Jerry Reese. We think Reese is another alias and are researching that name as well. So far no additional results."

"That's fantastic. Andy, the insurance guy will love the new information. He has more resources to locate bank accounts and investments than we do. I'm sure he will share any information he finds. My knowledge of how international banking works is zilch, other than being complicated. We'll rely on Andy or someone in his organization who has the necessary knowledge. Of course I care about the money, but mostly I'd like to get my hands on the bastard and put him away for a long time. My guess is Jake is headed for Manaus if he's not already there. Fortunately we do maintain a good extradition treaty with Brazil."

"After all the red tape of extradition is in order, someone still must find and arrest him before turning him over to American authorities. I'll bet that can be complicated. His having all that money to bribe officials is not going to make the job any easier."

"Andy may be able to help us. Will you or Ellen call and tell him what we've got on Jake and set up a meeting with me. An idea is running around in my head that might be the answer. Make sure Sheriff Rabb, Eric, Gordy, and Emil are notified of the meeting and asked to attend."

THIRTY-THREE

Ragan, Andy, Sheriff Rabb, Eric, Gordy and Emil sat around the table in the conference room in the sheriff's office. On the white board Emil had written an organized chart of all the names, aliases, locations, travels and associates known about Jake Ramsey. Also listed were credit cards, bank accounts and owned assets belonging to him.

Emil listed three houses he owned. The one on Tippy valued at three million was in his name and the two he found recently, one in Manaus valued at two and a half million, and a cottage on Dominica valued at three hundred thousand. The cottage on Dominica was found because of a book with the page marked. The two in Manaus and Dominica were titled under the name Jerry Reese. All three had mortgages close to 100% of their value. Also listed were three businesses: a hotel services company including a laundry, a small shipping company including five river freighters, and a quarter interest in a gold mining company. All of the businesses were in the name of Jerry Reese and headquartered in Manaus. The total value of his business assets were about two million. Their debt was not known as yet. Jake Ramsey built the house on Tippy. Jerry Reese had owned the house in Manaus for twelve years and the cottage on Dominica for seven. His total net worth is about five million less whatever debt he owes on the businesses.

Andy listed the total value of the items his company insured. That total was two and a half million dollars. They would deny payment of any amount since the stolen items were all recovered and most were found to be fakes. A lot of mumbled conversations were heard as the viewers commented to each other about the items on display.

Sheriff Rabb spoke, "I think it's quite clear Jake Ramsey spent a lot of time and effort removing his assets from the US and investing them in Brazil. He's obviously been doing this for years. His last known whereabouts was the ship terminal in Barbados on Saturday, September fifteen. From Barbados he probably went to either Manaus or Dominica. Unfortunately, we could find no departures of any kind from Barbados under any of his aliases or in his lady friend's name. No activity on any of his credit cards or bank accounts has shown up. He either has accounts we did not uncover or is paying cash. Twenty-five days passed since his last known whereabouts, and we can only guess as to where he is now. His cottage on Dominica is one possibility, but my bet is he's in Manaus using the name Jerry Reese, has connections in high places, and a fortress for a house to live in. He probably thinks he is quite safe where he is and he may be right."

Gordy asked, "What can we do from here? He's certainly outside of our jurisdiction."

Ragan said, "I had several experiences using extradition to try and get a criminal returned for prosecution. It's a long, drawn out affair requiring the cooperation and efforts of local police where the criminal can be apprehended. Once a warrant is issued, in this instance by the county, the sheriff's department must contact the extradition office of the U.S. State Department. They in turn contact their counterparts in Brazil, if he is in Manaus. The Brazilian government must approve the extradition and take the paperwork to the appropriate court in Brazil which issues a proper arrest warrant. Police in Brazil must find and arrest the suspect. Once Jake is arrested, the Brazilian court must approve the transfer to the U.S. This procedure will take a year or more if all of the necessary paperwork is approved and the arrest goes without incident. Unfortunately, Jake or Jerry as he is known in Brazil, has quite a bit of money at his disposal. He has had years to build up connections and friendships in Brazil, Bribery and payoffs are a way of life in the entire of the Americas south of the states. I'm betting Jake cultivated friendly relationships with some high officials in Manaus."

Gordy asked, "What can we do? that sounds like an impossible task. You seem to suggest he'll get away scot free."

Ragan grinned. "Two alternatives are all we can come up with. We can forget about Jake and let him get away with all he has done, or we can do a lot of paperwork and try to extradite him. That's about it."

Sheriff Rabb said, "The department doesn't possess the financial resources to spend on this case in preference to others. As much as I and every other officer of the law in the county would like to put him behind bars, many other criminals we can catch and prosecute are far more accessible. Let's be realistic and shelve this case until and unless he makes the mistake of coming back here, a remote possibility. I'll approve obtaining a warrant and filing the extradition papers with the State Department, but that's all for now. We will wait to find out if something happens. Who knows?"

Andy stood up. "I thought of an idea how we might be able to coax this clown back here all on his own. How much of the information about him has been released to the public, especially the news media?"

"The warrant for his arrest has been requested," Emil said. "That's all. The rest of the information on him stayed within the department. Except for the art expert from Chicago, Dr. Wiesse"

"Can we call Dr. Wiesse and make sure he doesn't tell anyone about those fakes?" Gordy asked.

Sheriff Rabb called out. "Ellen, will you call Dr. Wiesse as quickly as you can? it's important."

Ellen called back from her desk, "Right away, Sheriff."

The sheriff continued. "We may be lucky knowing he has flown the country. Andy, you said you had an idea because of the lack of publicity on him. What is it?"

"The robbery was in the papers and on the TV news with photos of the house and all. Lots of publicity centered around those two crooks and what happened to them. The local paper even did a piece about your lady friend, Ragan, and how she saved your life. The guy who wrote that piece would not divulge where he got all the information or the name of the mystery woman."

Ragan interrupted. "Thank God for that. Marci did not want any publicity and she got her wish. Go on Andy. Sorry I interrupted."

"Ragan, I'm glad you did. The bit about her, the accident and your injuries actually eclipsed the story about the robbers in the news. If we can keep any new information about the robbery out of the news, he could take the bait, which would help a lot. Here's my plan. I will institute a search for the beneficiary of the insurance policy on the house. We can make a big deal out of a wealthy guy whose house was robbed of paintings and a silver statue worth several million. I can say our company has a check for four million dollars waiting for him, but we can't find him. We can ask his friends and neighbors where he might be. That will be a huge human interest story for the media. If he bites and comes to collect the check, Bingo!"

"Andy, that's a clever idea. Now all we must do is figure out a way of using it."

Eric said, "Do you really think he'll fall for that? I'll bet he'll smell a rat and will not bite."

"Maybe so, but we should still try," Andy said. "It won't cost much and the media will eat it up as an interesting story."

Gordy asked, " What about the extradition? that might make the news. It's public record you know."

Ragan said, "We can request secrecy for both the warrants and the extradition paperwork. We do that by formally stating in the requests that any public knowledge of the proceedings would alert the subject. That won't guarantee confidentiality, but will prevent all but the most determined individuals from learning about them. We should at least try."

Sheriff Rabb said, "I'll ask Ellen to prepare the necessary requests. Then we'll tough it out. One way or another we'll do our best to catch that bum. First we must prevent Dr. Wiesse from talking about those paintings. Ellen's trying to contact him right now. Hope for good luck and that he hasn't said anything damaging."

It was noon when the meeting broke up right after Elen talked to Dr.Wiesse. Fortunately he had not told anyone and promised not to do so.

Sheriff Rabb said, "There is no point in our getting together until we get new information from the field."

They would not meet again for more than a month.

THIRTY-FOUR

Marci and Ragan finished cleaning up after dinner and went into the living room. Ragan plopped down in what had become his favorite chair. Marci walked in behind his chair, put her arms around him carefully.

"How's your arm doing?" she said giving a light squeeze.

"It doesn't hurt nearly as much as it did when I started therapy."

"Does it hurt if I sit in your lap like this?" she said as she came around the chair, sat carefully sideways on his lap, and snuggled up with her head on his shoulder.

"No, not a bit, and you could cause serous trouble doing what you're doing," he said as he put his arms around her.

"Oh, I certainly hope so," she said and stuck her tongue in his ear.

✳ 10:15 pm ✳

They were wrapped in each other's arms in her bed in the half awake, physically and emotionally drained state that follows serious love making. Finally some verbal communication broke through.

"Wow!" she said softly.

"Wow yourself."

"I don't quite know how to say it, but that was a long time coming."

"A confession."

"Yes?"

"After our sail I was hoping to entice you into my bedroom."

"While we were sailing I was thinking exactly the same thing."

"The damned accident messed things up."

"How does your arm feel?"

"Doesn't hurt a bit. You understand don't you, how those passion juices make all pain disappear."

"I'm a nurse, remember? We know about things like endorphins."

"Well, nurse, we must apply such often to alleviate my pain."

"You'll need to move in here permanently for that to happen."

"I thought you'd never ask."

"Thank God it's Friday. We can sleep in tomorrow."

"I like the way you think."

They would wake up several times during the night.

✳ Saturday, October 13, 2012, 11:30 am ✳

Ragan awoke to the pleasant sensation of a soft warm body entangled with his. He lay quietly, not wanting to move.

"Are you awake?" the warm body whispered in his ear.

"Just woke up. Didn't want to move."

"Eventually we are going to get up."

"Yes, I know. Mother nature is calling."

"Mother nature called us throughout the night."

"This is different."

"Yes, I know. You first."

"After we get our calls taken care of, would you join me in the shower? My shower stall is big enough for two."

"I'd be delighted."

Two soapy bodies rubbing against each other soon had all those hormones and passion juices flowing.

✳   ✳   ✳

"That was an amazing first," Marci said breathlessly, still clinging to her man.

"You've never made love in the shower?"

"Not before this."

"I can guarantee we'll repeat, lots of times."

"Oh, you say the nicest things."

"You, my dear, are one unbelievably sexy lady."

"Last night was amazing. I never thought I could feel so passionate. You may have created a monster."

"Nope. I didn't create it, I just woke it up. I tell you true, those feelings go both ways. You did the same to me. I'll never be the same again. Remember the toast I made the evening we had fish and German wine?"

"Do I ever."

"I'm betting it will be the story of our lives from now on."

"I never dreamed I could feel like this. We are something special, aren't we?"

"My sentiments exactly. Now we should rinse off, dry, and go down and fix breakfast."

"Spoilsport! . . . not really. I'm glad one of us is practical."

✳ 1:00 pm ✳

After everything but their coffee was cleared away, they sat at the table talking tenderly, the conversation of new lovers. Then Ragan turned serious.

"You know, Marci, I've been thinking a lot about us since the accident. I started while I was recovering in the hospital. You told me you had to leave this house in June. You could not possibly build a house on your farm in the time you before you must move. Why don't you move in with me? You could make a leisurely move since you are not under any immediate time deadline. Think about it."

"Some time before we met I started checking those manufactured housing units. I decided to buy and erect one on the farm. I even picked out the one I wanted. I would be on site watching over the building of my house without a deadline. Since you came into my life I quit thinking about the house until this minute. Off the top of my head it sounds like a good idea. Let's talk about it and what problems we can anticipate."

"Always the careful planner, aren't you?"

"You don't like that?"

"To the contrary, I like it a lot. You have around eight months before you must move. That's plenty of time. One of the first things we should talk about are any changes to my house you would like to make. I made a list of changes I'd like to make, a minor remodel like a new bathroom. The kitchen has already been completely remodeled as you know. I've been thinking long range of adding a second floor above the bedrooms. I even made some preliminary drawings."

"Why don't we go to your house right now so I can examine the place carefully and look at your plans. I'm beginning to be excited about all of this . . . putting our lives together in one place I mean. I need to do some work in the garden, but I can put my gardening off until tomorrow. It's not critical."

"Sounds like a plan. Let's."

"First I'm going to grab a few spare things to take to your house. I will only take a few minutes."

✳ 2:00 pm ✳

Ragan retrieved the plans he had been working on and spread them out on his desk.

"Here's the new staircase on this end of the living room. By placing the staircase here, I can expand the master bathroom and replace the tub with a large stall shower. We lose four feet from the end of the living room and the double-hung window next to this picture window. The staircase starts right here by the hall and makes a straight shot from the back door and up the stairs. "

"What did you plan for upstairs?"

"I haven't decided as yet. I thought about a large master bedroom with a big bathroom, or a combination office, craft, and workout room which would be the easiest since I wouldn't need a bathroom or lavatory."

Marci studied the plans for a few minutes and walked through the house inspecting everything.

"I wouldn't go to the bother of a second floor. Add another room and bathroom, in back of those two existing bedrooms. Your back yard has plenty of room for an addition. Is this the only copy?"

"No, I can print as many as I want from my PC."

"I'll show you what I mean by drawing on this plan. First we take the two bathrooms and the closets and make them into one master bathroom, a dressing room, and a walk in closet for the master bedroom. See, they would be something like this."

She sketched in the new layout and added the room in back.

"That leaves no access to a bathroom for those bedrooms."

"Here's how we take care of the bathroom."

She drew in a short hall, a bathroom in the new section with access from all four rooms via the hall.

"This way you would not lose all the square footage required for a staircase. You could do the bathrooms first and leave the door in place so everyone could access the one bathroom. After finishing the bathroom, make the addition to the rear of the house. You could do what you wanted with the resulting four rooms and all would be able to access the new full bath. Once you completed the rear addition, you could close the door, turn it into a closet, or leave it as an entrance to the master bath from the hall."

"You could be right. Expanding at ground level would probably cost a lot less than adding a second floor and I would gain a lot more useable space. Fortunately we have time to check out all the options. I'll call the contractor who did my kitchen. Jacob is my cousin. He will give me an idea about costs and some practical ideas we can consider. Thanks for the input. I keep finding out these neat things about you. I'm impressed."

"Those suggestions are good old Hoosier common sense. One more thing, if you do this before I move, you could stay at my house."

"You think of everything, don't you?"

"I try to be thorough and study the big picture. Growing up on a family farm teaches a person to be realistic."

"I was planning to move back here in a couple of weeks. With what happened the last few days, maybe I should put off moving until I've done the remodeling. I'll reconsider as will you. The first thing we should do is finalize the plans for remodeling. The sooner we finish them the sooner we can start. I drew another different plan for remodeling in here somewhere. . . . Oh, here it is."

"That's interesting, connecting the house with the garage, a completely different concept. I found a big problem right away."

"What?"

"Your well. It's quite new and would be in the middle of the addition. How will you service the well when a problem comes up, and one will?"

"I talked about the possible enclosure of the well with the guy who drilled it for me. He says it's not impossible, but a bit difficult. When I bought the place the old well was about shot so I replaced it with a new four inch well. What we would need to do is provide access with a trap door—the floor of a closet or store room like what is shown on the plans."

"I like the idea of being able to go to the garage without going outside in bad weather."

"Problem is, the front door is on the north side of the house and everything usually goes out front between the house and garage. Blocking the path to the front yard creates a lot of problems. That's why I set that aside and concentrated on adding a second floor."

They spent the rest of the afternoon revising the plans and walking around and through the place visualizing the changes.

✳ 7:00 pm ✳

"Aren't you getting hungry?" Ragan asked. "I'm starved and with no food in the house other than a few cans and some pasta, we must go out to eat."

"Where can we go?"

"Why don't we try the new restaurant in Webster?"

"Okay, let's."

We walked into a place packed with diners.

A young lady told us, "There will be a forty minute wait for a table."

Ragan turned to Marci. "What do you think?"

Marci asked the lady who greeted us, "Do you have any place we can sit while waiting?"

"Several benches outside by the door."

"Okay, we'll wait."

They only had to wait half an hour. After a leisurely dinner they drove back to Ragan's.

"Let's build a bonfire on the beach," Ragan said as they walked into the house.

He went to the front door and turned on the outside lights. A faint bit of light lingered in the western sky. The evening was clear and quite warm for October.

"You'll find a couple of jackets in the hall closet, he said, pointing. One of them will probably fit you. The air cools down quickly after dark this time of year."

"I'm way ahead of you. I put a sweater and jacket in the case I packed before we left. I figured we might stay here tonight so I brought a number of necessities in my case to be prepared. Why don't you go start a fire while I take the things out of my case and put them in the bathroom."

"All right. Good idea."

It wasn't long before they were snuggled up together on the bench with a roaring fire right in front of them. Ragan had a flashlight to use after he turned the lights off. They noticed several other bon fires across the lake. The night was moonless and the Milky Way brilliant with countless stars in the rest of the sky. They watched for and saw several meteorites as the fire slowly burned down into glowing embers. Marci noticed a faint glow reflected in the mirrored surface of the lake.

"How can I see the lake surface?" she asked. "It looks almost like it is lighted. I can see the reflection of the lights in the houses across the lake. You can even see reflections of the stars in the water. Why isn't it completely dark?"

"The glow in the sky to the southwest is from the lights of Warsaw. And the faint glow to the north—right on the horizon—where I'm pointing?"

"Yes, but I didn't see it until you showed me."

"That's light from South Bend. We'd see a lot more light if the sky was cloudy, but even on clear nights like this one you can see a faint glow above every nearby city. I think it's light reflected by tiny dust particles in the air above the cities."

"Why is it we can see the light here? I've never noticed it before, even from the farm."

"I think it's because of the lake. The horizon across the lake is so much lower than even on your farm. You can discern details much farther away. In the northwest, where I am pointing, right above those treetops. See those tiny flashing lights?"

"No, I don't."

"Actually, you should focus on the treetops. Faint lights are better seen if you don't look directly at them, but slightly away from what you are trying to see."

"Now I see them, a row of white lights slowly moving down toward the horizon. Some tiny red flashing lights are visible also. Are those lights from planes landing at O'Hare? that's impossible."

"Not impossible. Those lights are planes landing at O'hare field or possibly Midway."

"That's more than a hundred miles away."

"You can only see those planes when they are above eight or ten thousand feet. Lower, they are below the horizon because of the curvature of the earth."

"That's amazing. I had no idea you could see so far. . . wait . . . what's swimming on the surface, right out . . . oops, the critter went under."

"It was probably a muskrat. Many of them live around here. They burrow under the banks to dig their nests, and feed on clams and mussels from the lake."

"There it is again, see?" she said pointing

"Yeah, but it's much too big for a muskrat, probably a beaver. I've never seen a beaver around here. The nearest built several big dens up in Grassy Creek. Didn't I show you one when we went through?"

"I remember, but that's miles from here."

"I bet he's scouting the territory for a new den. Keep quiet. Let's see where he goes. Don't move or make a peep. He's coming our way."

The animal swam up to the shore, crawled out on the beach, then jumped up on the timber sea wall. Next it walked south along the timber and climbed up onto the neighbor's stone sea wall. Dark as it was they could clearly observe it's shape silhouetted against the faint light from the lake surface. The animal's silhouette moved blocking light from houses on the opposite shore and the sky reflected by the mirror surface of the lake.

Ragan whispered, "Do you see? that clearly is an otter. No other animal has that shape or moves like that. I've never heard of otters being around here, never."

"Me neither. You're right. It can only be an otter."

Ragan stood up slowly as the otter retraced its steps to his beach. It dove into the water and swam away when Ragan moved again. The otter surfaced about twenty feet out, swam north and out of sight.

"I'm going to call the DNR Monday and report this sighting. Wow, what an unusual event. I'm sure glad you saw what I saw too. No one would believe me if I were alone. That was certainly no muskrat or beaver. The animal we saw could only be an otter."

They talked about the animal and the beautiful sky for some time before calling it a night. They went in at midnight.

Ragan closed the blinds on the huge picture window in the bedroom.

"At night with lights on, this room is like a fish bowl. Anyone passing in a boat can see the entire room clearly. After we're ready for bed, I'll turn the lights off and open the blinds. I love the view from the darkened room. It's almost like sleeping outside."

As soon as Marci climbed into bed he doused the lights and opened the blinds.

"See what I mean?" he asked as he snuggled down beside her.

"It's beautiful, almost like sleeping outside. The line of lights from the places across the lake and their reflections in the smooth surface of the lake are quite a spectacular sight."

"See the green light? A green light shows a boat moving down the lake to the north. If he were going the other way the light would be red."

They enjoyed the scene through the window, the silence, and each other for more than an hour before going to sleep.

THIRTY-FIVE

Ragan continued living with Marci while his house was being remodeled. He was working as part of Jacob's crew, mainly because he loved carpentry and his labor also helped keep the cost down. He and Marci were having breakfast and discussing the remodeling.

"I like the changes we made from the original plan. The new bathroom is coming along nicely. Should be finished before Thanksgiving. They already poured the footers for the new rooms and will start laying block for the foundation on Monday."

"When will they finish the whole project? Any idea yet?"

"Jacob says right after Christmas, before the New Year."

"Wonderful. I told you it would be better if you moved in here and they could do everything without having to deal with anyone living in the house."

"You were right, of course. Here's another question for you. Did you earn any vacation time you haven't taken?"

"The last time I took a vacation was 2009. Does that answer your question? What are you thinking about now?"

"How long a vacation could you take, starting some time in January?"

"I'd need to talk with my boss, but January and February are usually our quietest times so the timing would be good."

"Could you take four weeks?"

"My goodness. Where were you thinking of going?"

"The Caribbean and up the Amazon. I'd like to try to locate Jake or Jerry Reese as he's known in Manaus. The Sheriff has no money to fund such an endeavor, but I do. The settlement I received from the accident was

194

substantial as you know. The settlement will pay for the remodeling and more. I would also like to use some to catch Ramsey."

"That wouldn't be a vacation . You'd be spending all your time trying to catch him."

"Dear heart, I would only need a couple of days total, even a few hours to find Reese. I'd hate to travel to such an exotic place on my own. I already checked out one cruise. It will leave from Port Everglades in Ft. Lauderdale and stop at Jost van Dyke, St. Barts, Terre-de-Haut, Barbados, and Devil's Island, before entering the Amazon. On the Amazon we stop at Santarem, Parintins, and end up at Manaus two weeks after we leave the U. S. We'd stay as long as we want in Manaus and fly back to the States, either to Miami, Ft. Lauderdale, or Chicago. Everything is on a first class cruise ship, a small one, but first class. I found two highly rated hotels in Manaus. You may pick the hotel and even change it after we arrive. The only time I will be working on the case will be while we are in Manaus and that won't be much. I'll be laying all of the ground work and making most of my contacts from here before we leave."

"Gotcha! Of course I'll be delighted to go with you. I was just tugging on your leg. I might even be able to help you catch the bum. It will be a marvelous vacation and I love the whole idea."

"I sure bit, didn't I? Okay, if you will find the best time to be on vacation, I'll make the necessary travel arrangements. I've a good friend in Chicago who specializes in unusual travel and cruise arrangements. Last week I called and told him what I wanted and the approximate dates. He said he'd be back to me this week. I said the time would not be set until we had your schedule. Find out as soon as you can, will you?"

"Tomorrow morning I'll talk to my boss. He will need a few days to find out. Surely I'll have the dates by the end of the week."

"I'd like to start the ball rolling as soon as possible."

"Look at the clock. It's nearly eight-thirty. Are you going to church with me?" I haven't gone since you moved in and I'd like to return to going regularly like I did the last few years."

"It's been a long time since I've set foot in a church. The last time was right after Rita died. Won't some of your church members look down their noses at us since I'm living with you?"

"Who's going to tell them. Certainly not me."

"I'm game, but we could face some embarrassing questions. I do remember how nosey some church women can be."

"Let's play this by ear. If anyone is nosey, let me handle it, OK?"

"My pleasure for sure. I'll follow your lead."

✳ 11:00 am ✳

After the service, Pastor Levi Garner made a point of greeting us as we left.

"Marci, I do believe this is the first time I have ever seen you at church with a gentleman friend. You're usually with Doc Miller and Doris. Welcome mister . . . "

"Yoder, Ragan Yoder," Ragan said as they shook hands.

"Aren't you the man Marci rescued in that terrible boating accident on Tippy a few weeks back?"

"That I am. And extremely grateful to Marci for what she did."

"I understand you live on the lake near where the accident happened."

"That he does, Pastor," Marci said. "He has a lovely home right on the lake about a mile from the Country Club. You've probably driven past many times on your way to Epworth Forrest or North Webster."

"You seem to be recovered from the accident. The paper reported you were seriously injured and required major surgery."

"Thanks to Marci and the rest of the trauma team at Goshen Hospital, I'm about back to normal."

"The paper also said you are a retired Chicago police detective. What brought you down to rural Indiana?"

"I grew up in Warsaw and love the lakes area. Left here to attend the Chicago Police Academy. When I retired, I moved back and bought the house on Tippy. I Stayed in touch with many friends in Kosciusko County while I lived in Chicago."

By this time several ladies were gathered and listening. Doc and Doris were among the gathering. Doc jumped right in to the conversation.

"I brought Ragan into the world, Pastor. I've known him his entire life. He's much more a friend than an ex-patient. His folks were also long time friends as well as patients. He's like family."

"Ragan, it's good for you to be here. Do come back. Now I must go back to greeting people. If you're still here when things quiet down I'd like to talk to you and learn more about you."

One of the ladies said to Marci, "Are you going to introduce us to your friend?"

Marci introduced Ragan to the ladies and their husbands who were in the group who stayed with them. The lady who first spoke was obviously interested and wanted to talk more.

"Marci, this is the first time in my memory you ever brought a gentleman to church."

"When you meet someone because two men died in an accident on your own property and rescue them from being pinned under water, I'm sure you understand how those experiences make for a rather sudden comradeship."

Ragan said, "As the one who's life was saved by this young lady, I will be eternally grateful. How can you pay back such a debt to anyone? We will always be in a special relationship."

Doc spoke up. "Now folks we have an important dinner some distance away so we must leave. I'm sure Ragan will be here again. Bye."

As he spoke, Doc and Doris hurried them away to the parking lot.

"When you leave, follow close behind me," Doc said. "I had to save you from Abbie. She's the biggest and nosiest gossip in the church. I'm heading for US 6 and turning west to make sure no one is following us. Quick now before she can go to her car."

They were off before Ragan could say a thing. As soon as they were in Marci's Mustang she explained things to Ragan.

"Abbie Schum is a real pain. Now she'll be nosing around asking everyone questions. She'll probably drive past my house late tonight to see if a strange vehicle like your truck is parked in my drive. She can be no end of trouble if she decides to be. The first person she'll go to if she learns anything will be pastor Levi."

"It's no skin off my teeth, but you, you're a different story. People like Abbie are the real sick ones. What can we do?"

"Doc's pulling into a restaurant. I'll do the same and we can go on home after we talk to them."

Doc walked up to the car. "I'm sorry if I rushed you, but that nosy gossip was about to pull one of her acts. I could smell it coming."

Marci laughed. "Doc, you did a clever job of rescuing us. Now I must take action before she makes a mess. She can't hurt me or Ragan, but she can upset a lot of people and do some damage at church. I'm going to cut her off at the pass, disarm her, pull all of the teeth of her gossip before she starts. Pastor always goes home after the last people leave and they close up the church. I plan to tell him the whole story. Levi's quite savvy and he hates gossip. He'll understand and he's the first person Abbie will go to if she learns or can invent anything."

"Great idea," Doc says with a smile. "I can just hear pastor's reply when she starts, 'Yes, Abbie, I know. Isn't it wonderful. Two people finding each other after such tragedies?' or something of the sort. Go do it."

As they drove off to go back to Milford Ragan said, "Why don't we go by your place on the way, leave your car in the garage and use my pickup. If she happens to see the pickup, she won't think it's us, just in case."

"Let me call pastor and find out if he's available."

After a short phone conversation she smiled. "He says he'll be home and will be glad to talk to us."

✳ Noon ✳

They spent nearly an hour telling the pastor and his wife, Irene, they were living together, and Ragan was remodeling his house so they could live comfortably in it when she had to move out of her home. They even told him about their planned 'honeymoon' in Brazil. Marci laughed as she told him how Ragan said he was going to ask her to marry him and what she said in return.

As they got up to leave pastor said, "I hear what most church people say about marriage, but I'm not too sure what you two are doing isn't equally moral. Things certainly changed in the last fifty years, some for the worst, but some for the better. I wish the best for you. I hope to be the one to administer your vows, if and when you take them."

"Ragan said, "I'm sure you will."

"Out the door," pastor said, pointing. "Speak of the devil."

Abbie Schum was walking up the steps.

Pastor grinned and said, "Let me handle this, please. I shall relish spiking her guns."

He opened the door at her knock. "Hello Abbie. Come in. You of course know Marci and Ragan. We've finished making some of their wedding arrangements. They even told me about the honeymoon they planned, a cruise through the Caribbean and all the way up the Amazon to Manaus. Isn't that exciting?"

"Marci spoke up. "We'd like to keep this a secret for a while Abbie. I'm sure you understand. We want to make the announcement ourselves. So please don't breathe a word of this to anyone, OK?"

Abbie was visibly shaken and speechless for a moment. Finally she shook her head and said, "I won't tell a soul. You can count on me."

They said good bye and walked to the truck leaving Pastor with a dazed and confused gossip.

As soon as they were in the truck and driving Marci burst out laughing. "I can't believe what happened. That poor soul hasn't a clue what to do about the situation. When Pastor told her we were planning a wedding she almost passed out."

"Yeah, and when you asked her not to say anything was the clincher," Ragan said through a huge grin. "Can you imagine the conflicts going through her mind?"

"Once she is over the initial shock, she may still cook up some nastiness," Marci said. "I wonder if we should avoid going to church for a while?"

"Nah! I'd rather enjoy going to church with you now."

"That would be for the wrong reason you know."

"All I would be doing is checking to find out if she kept our secret. What's wrong with that?"

"Okay, but please don't stir up a hornet's nest. She's not stupid and we've cut this whole thing out from under her. I can almost guarantee she's trying to come up with some nastiness."

"Don't worry, I'll be my old loveable self."

"That's what I'm afraid of."

"Don't worry. I'll behave. I promise."

"How about we go out for Sunday dinner? Why don't we go back to the place in North Webster? The food was quite good and we can stop by your house after dinner and see how it's coming along."

"Sounds like a plan."

THIRTY-SIX

Ragan meets with Sheriff Rabb and Gordy in the Sheriff's office.

"Ragan, I respect your abilities and your integrity, but we can't spare any funds to pay for you gallivanting all around South America no matter who you're after. You may not even be able to bring him back here if you do find him."

"Sheriff, I'm not asking for any funds, not a penny. All I want is an international warrant or any kind of document I can use to inform the local police I have official backing, and a legal reason to bring him back to the states. I had such documents issued by the Illinois Attorney General's office twice before when I went after a fugitive in Mexico. The Chicago Chief of Police requested them. He had some legal hoops to jump through, and the process required about three weeks each time to get those documents. I'm sure the procedure in Indiana is somewhat the same. The County Attorney will be able to answer your questions. Check with him. Everything is detailed in my proposal."

"I'm sorry, Ragan, I missed the part when you said no county funds would be required. That puts a whole new light on things. Let me go over your proposal again and talk the idea over with the County Attorney. Steve may have some ideas to help. If he can't procure those documents for you, I'm sure he knows who can. I would definitely like the bum to be behind bars."

"Now you're talking. I wondered if you had read the entire proposal. Before you ask, yes, I can pay to go on such a trip. I received a generous settlement from my accident. The money will pay for the entire trip and more. As a matter of fact, I'm planning on taking Marci with me. The cruise will be a vacation for us both. If I can round up that scoundrel as well it would be a bonus. The insurance company is offering a large reward for his return to the states and prosecution. Andy told me at our last meeting."

"So you'll be a bounty hunter now."

This upset Gordy. "Don't use that term, Sheriff. It has a bad connotation, and Ragan most certainly does not deserve it. The reward is not nearly enough to cover the cost of the trip."

"I'm sorry for my poor choice of words. I certainly wouldn't say so in public. I meant it as a joke—not funny."

Ragan laughed. "Sheriff, I took the comment as a joke and wasn't offended. I would request we keep the knowledge of what I am doing to as few people as possible, all the way down the line. The knowledge should be strictly on a need-to-know basis. I hope any attorney you contact will cooperate. Everything should be under the umbrella of attorney - client confidence."

Sheriff Rabb said, "In fact, the warrant does not need to mention your name. The other documents and authorizations will, but I can request everyone involved keep silent. That's no guarantee, but usually does the job. The main thing is not to let the media get wind of anything. We can be fairly sure of that. State's Attorneys especially are wary of sensitive information reaching anyone in the media. You know, don't you, those other documents carry little authority. They will merely be requests for cooperation. If Reese owns any of the local police, they may do more harm than good."

Ragan smiled. "Sheriff, I am well aware of that. When I went to Mexico, I spent a lot of effort finding out who was being paid off by whom before I ever told anyone I was a cop. That really helped. Kept me from making some serious mistakes. I plan to follow the same procedure here. No one will think I am anything other than a tourist. For cover, I will tell anyone I become friendly with I am an insurance investigator. I should be safe until I am thoroughly acquainted with who owns whom. My scalp will depend on my doing so."

"Sometimes I forget about your thirty years as a Chicago cop. I'm sure you could teach me quite a bit about undercover surveillance and how not to be caught."

"Sheriff, one important thing I learned is to err on the side of caution. Too much caution may be a waste of time, but too little and you're dead."

"Well said, Ragan. Gordy, are you paying attention?"

"Sheriff, I pay attention whenever you or Ragan speaks. I'm still learning and both of you are good sources of knowledge."

Ragan walked over and put his arms around Gordy. "I'll say one thing about you. You are certainly your father's son. I remember similar words coming from Greg more than once when coach Lessig was talking to us. You'll do quite well, young man."

"I'll echo Ragan's words," sheriff Rabb said. "And you've already earned the reputation as a good and dependable sheriff's deputy. The whole department thinks so. Now, I think we're finished here and quite a bit of work has piled up so I'd better start. Ragan, I'll keep you informed on the progress of our requests. Tell me the details of your planned trip and when you hope to leave."

"I just remembered something," Ragan said. "What happened to the Fuzario kid with the skull fracture? I was planning to talk to him when he was able, but my accident interfered."

Gordy answered. "You told Eric you were going to talk to him so he took over for you. He spent a lot of time with him during his long hospital stay. Impressed him with how close he came to dying, then visited him a number of times after he went home. He became a great male role model for the kid, something he never had before. He just may have turned him around. Only time will tell for sure. Eric told me Fred is working on his grades so he can apply to the police academy. That's an amazing turn around if it sticks. Eric should be credited with some marvelous inspiration and get an award."

"What did the county do with the money he had in his pocket?" Ragan asked.

"After much discussion it was put in an account for his education. He gets it only if he earns it by staying out of trouble and finishing his education. A funny thing, the local TV station did a short thing on Eric and the kid, a human interest story. That brought a number of donations to his education fund which is now more than eleven thousand dollars, and is still growing. He won't get a penny if he doesn't stay on the straight and narrow. I hope he makes it. Turning a single delinquent around is a very worthwhile goal."

"Well, one thing's for sure. Eric's an excellent role model for any young man to follow." "Now he's trying to start a mentoring program for mildly troubled youths to try to turn them around before they get in too much trouble. He just started trying to interest teachers and those in law enforcement to take part in the program. I hope he succeeds. Only time will tell."

Ragan said. "I hadn't heard that yet. I'll have to speak to him and find out if I can help."

"I'm sure Eric would be pleased. Now I must be going," Gordy said.

"Me too," Ragan said. I'm finished for now."

All three stood up and went their separate ways.

✳ Saturday, December 8, 2012, 9:00 am ✳

As soon as they had finished breakfast, Marci spread out on the table the tentative itinerary and brochures provide by Carl Smith, Ragan's travel agent friend from Chicago.

"The closest he came to fitting your schedule is a cruise departing from Port Everglades on January 6 and arriving in Manaus on the 20th. In case we want to arrive sooner, he found two flights to Manaus. Copa Airlines leaves Chicago at 8:00 am, stops at Panama City, Panama, and arrives in Manaus at 8:45 pm. USAir leaves Chicago at 7:20 am, stops at Charlotte, NC and Miami, FL, and arrives in Manaus at 10:18 pm. He suggests the Hotel Adrianopolis for our stay. It's a fairly central location to stay and it's five star rated."

"I wonder about Copa Airlines. Never heard of them before. I still think we should go by cruise ship. We'll be a lot more like tourists if we do. We can fly home when we want to. I would like this to be sort of a honeymoon for us. That's why I would like for us to go there on a cruise. We'll do nothing but enjoy ourselves. And who knows, we may like Manaus and want to stay for awhile. I don't want to merely fly there and come back. Besides, the hospital said you had accumulated even more vacation time than you asked for."

"Isn't this going to cost you a bundle? I can chip in with some of the money I saved up for the new house on the farm. The cruise alone costs about twelve thousand, and that's without any side trips or excursions"

Ragan laughed. "The settlement from the insurance company is a lot more than this trip will cost. I can't think of a better way to spend it."

"Yes, but weren't you going to use that to pay for the addition to your house?"

"It will leave plenty for **our** house. And don't forget about the reward money from the insurance company when I catch Jake Ramsey and he is prosecuted."

"That's iffy, is it not? You must catch him first and bring him back to the States. That's far from a sure thing. What will you do for money if you don't catch him?"

"If all else fails I've always got my substantial police pension to fall back on."

"Come on, Ragan, I'm being realistic. If we put our lives together, and it sure seems like we will, I can help with finances. I saved enough money to build a new house on the farm. If we live in your remodeled house I won't need my house money, plus I'll feel more of a valuable part if I invest some money in the house. Sooner or later we will need to deal with the financial part of putting our lives together. Might as well be now."

"Okay, but I do owe you a big apology."

"Why?"

"I've not been revealing with you about my financial condition. I should have explained earlier, but now's as good a time as any."

"My goodness, what should you explain?"

"You couldn't know, but I'm actually quite well fixed. I don't talk about it, in fact, I work quite hard to keep the truth from being known. When my parents died in a terrible accident in 1977, my sister and I were left with a fair sized portfolio of stocks he had collected for their retirement. In their portfolio were several thousand shares of Microsoft. Need I say more?"

"My God. What are they worth now? Don't answer. I really don't want to know."

"My dad always stressed to me that I make investments and never touch the principal. 'Use the interest and dividends' he drummed into me. 'Never touch the principal and you will build a fat nest egg for your retirement,' he always said. It's so sad he and my mom never got to use their nest egg. They were killed the same year I graduated from the Police Academy. My sis and I both felt guilty about the inheritance for some years. We got over that, but neither one of us ever touched the principal. We both let our dad's accountant manage our accounts for years. When he retired, his two sons took over the business. The only time I realize how much that nest egg has grown is when I sign my income tax forms. In recent years that has become almost scary. My accountants—actually they are now investment managers—reinvest what I don't need from the interest and dividends."

"Ragan, I am certainly glad I did not know this before."

"I'm quite sure I understand why, and I too am glad. I'm also sure you will keep my secret."

"Had I known this when we met, I'd have avoided you like the plague."

"I hope it won't make any difference now. I'd sure hate to lose you for no good reason."

"We're way past that now. You and me come what may is the way, good or bad. We already have one problem."

"Oh? What?"

"You've already told me you plan on asking me to marry you. Now that really scares me."

"Why? We're still the same two people. We're still very much in love. I got used to forgetting about the money, and it worked for me. You can do the same, I guarantee. We certainly won't tell anyone about it. I wouldn't even tell you now if I wasn't sure about who you were. Don't fail me now sweetheart, please."

"I can think of a million questions I don't know how to ask."

"Ask away during our honeymoon. We'll have plenty of time together to talk. It shouldn't make a bit of difference."

"I'm glad I found out the kind of man you are before you told me. I will always love you for who you are. I promise."

"That's my lady. Now lets continue planning our honeymoon."

"There's one good thing."

"Oh, what?"

"I can enjoy the trip without feeling any guilt having you spend your money taking me with you. That was actually beginning to bug me."

Ragan laughed. "And I won't feel the guilt I did before with you not knowing. We both win."

"Okay, Mr. Microsoft tycoon, let's plan and order this trip."

"You really know how to hurt a guy, don't you?"

"Just keeping you on your toes, I like keeping you on your toes."

THIRTY-SEVEN

Marci had swapped days off with another nurse at the hospital so she could stay home and work with Ragan on their trip. They would go over the lists they had prepared over the weekend for their trip, lists of things they needed to take and to do. After an early breakfast, they went to work.

"I'm placing a red circle on each item we will order from the Internet," Marci said. "If we find an item locally, we can mark it off. I'll also mark each item I can take care of, OK? Why don't you do the same? That way we will not duplicate efforts."

"Sure," Ragan answered. "One thing we didn't discuss or list is satellite phone service. I'll take care of adding a phone for you to the service I already use. Cell service is so lousy at my house I finally bit the bullet and got a satellite phone almost a year ago. That cuts out all the crap of arranging for overseas cell service. I'll also bring a battery-based charger for those phones."

"Isn't that terribly expensive?"

"It used to be, but I rely on a new service from TeleCom. The phones switch automatically between cellular service and satellite. If no cellular service is available, a pleasant voice says, 'Do you wish to make this call by satellite?' You say yes or no and the phone does what you tell it to do. Texting is handled the same way."

"Amazing! How can you expect this little farm girl to understand all the technical stuff?"

"Yeah, I'll bet. Don't hand me that malarkey. I know you, remember?"

"Okay, back to work. Let's try not to take more than we must. I hate to wrestle heavy suitcases around."

"We can ship some things to the hotel. I will ship some special items, things we can't take on a plane."

"What are those special items? Or do I not want to know?"

"The usual weapons a cop carries, two 9 mm Glock automatics, a Glock 26, mini in an ankle holster and a full size Glock 17 with night sights. The night sights are only mounted when we will be in low light or darkness. I can't take them on ship or plane without authorization, even broken down and in my luggage. Doing so would signal that I'm a cop and we don't want that known. I ordered a special, lead-lined box for sensitive film. Both guns fit neatly in the lead walls of the box and can't be seen by x-rays or other examination. The walls also hold 100 rounds of 9 mm ammo and a spare magazine for each gun. The box may be opened without revealing guns or ammo. I can safely ship it almost anywhere. The box is quite heavy and has a warning on the lid saying 'Highly sensitive film inside. X-ray proof box. Open only in a dark room or greatly reduced light. Keep away from radioactive materials.' A substantial combination lock will defy all but destructive efforts to open. My box has never been questioned during shipping and should be delivered to the hotel in Manaus with no problem. I planned for the shipment to arrive the day after we do. I've never had a problem shipping my guns."

"That's a little bit scary. I've hunted with both rifle and shotgun, deer, squirrels, rabbits and ducks, but I've never handled a hand gun."

"We will go to the local pistol range and I'll show you how to handle and shoot these babies, a little bit of insurance."

"I don't know if I could pull the trigger of a gun aimed at another human."

"Honey, if the other human was threatening your life or the life of someone you know, you'd pull the trigger. I've seen you in action in an emergency. You'd shoot."

"You're probably right."

"This afternoon I'll bring both guns and give you your first lesson in handling them. Unless you are planning to shoot a handgun, the first thing you do is make sure the chamber is empty and the magazine is removed. That's one of the first rules we learned at the academy. The second is that you never point a gun at another person unless you intend to shoot them. Accidental shootings are a major cause of gunshot deaths in America."

"I took a gun safety course before my dad would ever let me go hunting. I wasn't more than eleven when I took that course. Those were some of our first instructions as well. We always unloaded our guns as soon as we were done hunting. Of course, I was taught you never point a gun at another person, ever."

Ragan called the travel agent and confirmed their trip. The agent took nearly two hours to arrange everything. He called back at noon and gave them their confirmation numbers.

"I'll send all the papers for you to sign and a list of the proofs of vaccinations you will need. By the way, you'll be staying in the honeymoon suite at the Adrianopolis. It was the only suite available that met your request. I hope you don't mind."

Ragan had a hearty laugh. "That's quite appropriate. I won't tell Marci until we arrive."

"You have plenty of time, but sign those papers and send them back to me as quickly as you can. You never know when some official will hold things up. No problem on the cruise, but in Manaus you'll be on your own. Neither of us wants any glitches. I'm still having a problem with your request for an older car that will meet your requirements. The two leads I chased down so far went nowhere. I found a well-run garage that builds and maintains race cars, some that run international. Their reputation is excellent, but the owner has yet to return my call. I'll keep after them."

"I want something that is powerful and handles well but will not stand out, one that is common-looking around town."

"I got the message, but that's not an easy task. I hope I can arrange for such a vehicle before you arrive."

"If all else fails, find me a truck with a big engine."

"You're the boss. I should be able to scrape one up before you go. I'll keep you posted."

"Okay, Carl. I can count on you. Now I need to return to Marci. Bye."

That afternoon they spent nearly two hours at the gun range.

As they left Ragan said, "You caught on quickly. Of course, hunting with a rifle taught you more than just the basics of aiming. Once you were accustomed to the kickback, you were quite accurate. You are already a good pistol marksman, at the pistol range."

"I was surprised at how quickly I caught on. Of course, the game I hunted never shot back at me. I hope I am never in that kind of situation. How do you handle that?"

"I'll say one thing. It's always scary, unless you're an idiot. Anyone who says they aren't frightened when facing a gun in the hands of someone who wants to shoot them is either lying or a complete idiot. I only faced that situation a couple of dozen times in my 25 years. I can remember each one as if it happened yesterday."

Marci was serious. "Hopefully that won't happen to us on this trip. I have no idea how I would react."

"I certainly agree. I wouldn't worry about you. I'm betting you'd react well. Your actions in an emergency were demonstrated quite well in that boat accident. You certainly reacted quickly then, thank you."

Marci chuckled. "And I remember clearly I was scared to death and worried about you."

"Maybe so, but you thought clearly and quickly. If that boy hadn't been killed by the impact, you would have saved two lives that day. Didn't you realize all those people in boats did nothing but watch? Like so many in emergencies they were paralyzed. They only acted when you told them what to do. That's often the situation at times like that, mostly because of fear and human nature. I learned never to fault people who act like that. They have no idea what to do unless someone tells them. I've seen people like that do amazingly brave things when asked or told. That's why I don't criticize anyone in crisis situations."

"Ragan, you're a good and wise man. I realized that almost from the moment we met. I never had to think twice about inviting you into my house. What has happened since has been amazing to me while at the same time I'm not terribly surprised. Everything has been as natural as breathing and quite beautiful."

"I feel the same. Our being together seems natural, like we've always been together. That's a warm and comfortable feeling."

They stood looking at each other and smiling, a quiet, loving moment. They walked to the truck, hand in hand, like two kids in love, a quiet moment that spoke volumes in their shared feelings.

✳ 4:00 pm ✳

Once they returned to Marci's they resumed their trip planning. During the rest of the day they completed their lists of clothing and other items. After a break for dinner, they worked on crossing the less essential items off the list. They decided to mark a number of maybes to be decided when they were packing.

Finally Marci said, "I think that's everything. We'll see how the packing goes and add things in order of importance according to whatever room is left in our suitcases."

Ragan said, "We kept a list of things we want in Manaus but don't need on the cruise. We can ship them with the other stuff to go to the hotel. I don't know about you, but I'm about ready for bedtime."

✳ Saturday, December 22, 2012, 9:00 am ✳

Ragan received a call from Carl, his travel agent. "Good news, Ragan, I arranged for the vehicle you wanted. The rental is a 1997 BMW 540i with a stick shift. The car belongs to the owner of the shop I was telling you about. He uses it to run stuff around Manaus. He says it's not very pretty, about like most cars that age in Manaus. He keeps the engine and running gear in top notch shape. The tires are almost new. It's one of three delivery vehicles he uses. They just added a fourth so he's pleased to rent this one to you. I told him you were a VIP and appreciated nondescript vehicles that ran and handled well."

"Sounds like a winner, exactly what I need. How will I get it?"

"He'll deliver the BMW personally to your hotel when you arrive. Says he wants to meet you. I told him when you'd be checking in."

"Okay, Carl, what did you tell him that made him so interested?"

"Just what you told me, that you were thinking of buying a business in Manaus."

"Damn, Carl, that is my cover story. I didn't want any publicity."

"I told him you did not want that spread around and not to tell anyone else. That you did not want to be inundated with offers of businesses for sale. He'll keep the info under his hat."

"Whatever damage was done will need to be dealt with. Now that I think about it, that information could be used to my advantage. I'll handle that with him when he delivers the car. Thanks for making the arrangements. Oh, and I received the papers on the twelfth, signed them, and sent them off to you in two days. Did you receive them yet?"

"They're off to those who need them so everything's copacetic. Your tickets and confirmations should be in your hands by Monday, Thursday the latest. Call me if they aren't delivered by then."

"I will, Carl. Thanks again and good bye."

THIRTY-EIGHT

Marci and Ragan had breakfast and exchanged their gifts. Ragan received a new digital camera to take on their trip.

"It's perfect," he said when he opened it. "Now here's yours."

He handed Marci a small box wrapped in silver paper with red and green ribbons. Marci looked softly at him as she took the box. Ragan was frantically loading the camera with batteries and preparing to take a photo of Marci as she opened her gift.

"Hold it up so I can take one and find out if I'm doing things right."

Marci held the box up by her face as Ragan snapped several photos and looked at them.

"Your gift works perfectly. Check these out," he said, holding out the camera.

"Wow, those are beautiful photos, so clear and bright. Can I open now?"

"Absolutely!"

"Oh my goodness, Ragan, they're beautiful. I've never seen anything like them. How did you ever find them?"

Marcy held up a pair of drop earrings. They were in the shape of a stylized G clef with a single diamond in the center and a pearl on the projection at the bottom.

"I didn't find them. I had them made just for you. Jeweler, Fred Bell, was a classmate in Warsaw High and on the basketball team with me. We sat down together and he worked up several designs. We both decided this one was the best. Another piece is still in the box."

"Oh, wow!" Marci said as she pulled out a fine gold chain with a pendant exactly like the earrings. "That is a spectacular set. I'll be especially proud to wear them and brag about the gift from my man. How can I ever thank you?"

"Wear them. That's all the thanks I'll need. I'm overjoyed that you like them sweetheart. You are especially beautiful in them. Let me take your picture."

"I never dreamed . . . I'm going to kiss you for an hour," she said as she ran and threw her arms around him. "I'll show them off today at the dinner at Doc's. I'll wear them with the perfect outfit to show them off, my simple little red dress. I've never worn the dress for you. I'll wear my red sling pumps. Now, if I only had a mink . . . scratch that. And don't you dare go and buy me one. We don't want people to suspect you are wealthy, remember."

"I promise I will not buy expensive gifts without your knowledge and permission. Actually, that set was not terribly expensive. They just look that way. I've owned those one carat diamonds for years. All I had to buy was the settings and those took careful planning and a master jeweler to design and make them. He finished them just a few days ago. I am so proud to be able to give them to you and pleased that you like them."

Around noon Marci's son, Bruce and his wife, Miriam, arrived from Chicago for Christmas. After Marci introduced them to Ragan she showed them her Christmas jewelry.

"Look what my man gave me for Christmas. Aren't they spectacular?"

Bruce said, "Mom, you are positively radiant. Having Ragan in your life seems to agree with you.

Miriam said, "Ragan, I've never seen Marci so happy, and those earrings, they are spectacular. How did you ever find them?"

Marci launched into how Ragan had them made and how pleased she was with them. She went on and on about how happy she and Ragan were until Bruce interrupted.

"Mom, you've been running off at the mouth with enthusiasm and excitement since we walked in. I heard not a word from Ragan and I'd like to get to know the man who has made you so happy. What do you say, Ragan?"

"I stand here in awe of your mother's enthusiasm. I wouldn't think of stopping her. I'm happy just to listen. I am so proud to be her man. When things calm down after dinner we can talk. You're going to be here for few days I understand."

"Till Sunday."

"We will take the time to learn about each other when things calm down a bit. OK?"

"Ragan, I am beginning to understand why Mom is so happy to be with you. You and she are a fine match. Christmas is a day to be with family. I'm beginning to think of you as family already. You sure fit in."

"Thank you, Bruce. This will be a Christmas to remember, and has barely started."

Around one Marci announced she was going upstairs to dress for dinner. Ragan went with her to put on his Christmas duds. He was the first one down and ready with his red Christmas tie and blue suit. Every one oohed and ahed as Marci pranced down the stairs in her simple, slinky red dress and pumps set off by her new jewelry.

Ragan stood. "Marci, you are the most beautiful woman I ever met. Gawd, you are gorgeous!"

"Thank you, dear man. You are quite handsome yourself. Now, if you'll help me into my coat and put yours on we can head to Doc's, over the river and through the woods."

✳ Christmas Day, 2:00 pm ✳

On the way to Doc's they drove through blowing snow with the temperature in the teens. Marci had on her good winter coat with a fur collar and furry boots over her pumps. They walked up the walk and into Doc's. Marci kept the coat wrapped tightly about her neck. She planned on making a grand entrance. They were the last to arrive. They were greeted by Doc and Doris, Terry, Marci's brother and his wife, Carey. Even the minister, Levi Garner and his wife, Irene were there. Marci stood clinging her coat about her.

"You may wonder why I kept my coat on. I wanted to be able to save the sight of the beautiful gift Ragan gave me this morning for the right moment . . . now. Ta Da!"

With that she opened and shed her coat. She was greeted with dead silence. Finally her brother, Terry spoke.

"Marci, you are positively breath taking. I assume the gift is the earrings and pendant. They are indeed beautiful, but that's gilding the lily. I have never seen you so vibrant, so beautiful. I'm thinking Ragan has had a lot to do with you being so . . . happy . . . a blessing for us all."

Irene, the pastor's wife spoke. "I couldn't agree more. God has blessed you with beauty which you share with us. I think the beauty from within makes you so radiant. God must be quite pleased with you."

Doris said, "Marci, I've known you your entire life, and that's quite a few years. You were always beautiful, but today, right here, you are the most beautiful. I think Irene is right. God must be pleased with you and with Ragan."

Marci looked a bit shocked. "I can't think of what to say. I do want to thank my man. He has made me the happiest ever, and I guess it shows. Now lets all enjoy a merry Christmas and . . . I understand from Doris that the food is ready. Let's eat."

Marci's words broke the paralyzing magic of the moment and everyone drifted into the dining room. The dinner was indeed a wonderful gathering of kindred souls . . . A Christmas celebration for all.

THIRTY-NINE

✳ Sunday, December 30, 2012, noon ✳

Marci sat on her couch surveying all the things they gathered to take on their cruise. She was wondering if they could put them all away by tomorrow in time for their New Years Eve party. Two piles were spread on the floor, one to go with them on the cruise, the other to be shipped to the hotel in Manaus. Ragan walked in with three boxes.

"You don't think you will pack everything in those three boxes, do you?"

"Of course not. One box contains packing. Everything will go in the two other boxes. We'll pack essentials first and whatever we can't pack will stay behind. I think you will be surprised at how much these two boxes will hold. If we can pack them today, I'll ship them off on Monday."

"What if we discover something we need after they are shipped?"

"We've already spent enough time agonizing over what we are taking. Anything else will not be needed. I'll pack the film/gun case first on the bottom."

Ragan placed some packing around the case to hold the item snugly in the box. He then sorted the other items in two piles.

"I think you did this before," Marci said. "What do you want me to do?"

"I'll show you how to wrap each of the hard items and place them in the boxes. We can use the clothes and raincoats as packing to minimize space requirements. The main thing is to pack everything tightly in place so nothing moves or bounces. Heavy things go on the bottom."

In less than thirty minutes everything was packed and they still had some room in one of the boxes.

"I cannot believe we did that so quickly or that one box still has some space."

"I'm going to seal the full box and leave the other for anything we find before I take them on Monday. We can stick them under the ping pong table where they'll be out of the way."

"What about the rest, the stuff that will go in our suitcases?"

"I picked up two long flat plastic storage boxes and placed them under the bed. Everything else will probably fit in just one of those boxes. I'll get it."

Another thirty minutes and everything was put away. Marci was amazed.

"We will pack our suitcases right before we leave for Miami. No point in packing till then so most of our clothes can stay where we always keep them. The only problem I found is what to do with our winter overclothes and boots after we are in Chicago. We certainly won't need them on the cruise or in Manaus."

Marci grinned. "I already arranged that for us. Bruce will meet us in the O'Hare terminal and hold them until we return."

"Did I ever tell you I can't get along without you? You are one clever and resourceful lady."

"Don't you forget either," She said with a big smile. "Now that our things for the trip are taken care of, we better start preparing for the party tomorrow. Unless I miscounted, between the Sheriff's department, the hospital, friends, and relatives, around forty guests will be here. Nearly all of those we invited responded that they are coming. My house will be packed with celebrants."

"Yes, and with the hospital people providing the food and the Sheriff's department providing the beverages, all we do is make sure to have enough places to sit and hold plates and glasses. Such good and helpful friends are wonderful."

Marci sat down to relax for a few minutes.

"Ragan . . . only three months passed since we met. I can hardly believe how much my life has changed in those three short months. Labor day we had a cook out at my brother's place on Dewart Lake. I remember sitting with him and Carey discussing the future, my building a house on the farm and moving in. We even talked about what my plans might be for retirement. In my wildest dreams I couldn't imagine what was going to start in just three days when I met you. If anyone mentioned such a wild possibility I'd have laughed and called them a crackpot. Boy, did that ever change my life."

"No more than mine, sweetheart. Look at us now. We're going on a cruise a thousand miles up the Amazon among other things. What an amazing turn of events. I cannot imagine life without you. You may not think this is a good time for me to do so, but I'm doing it anyway because a best time might never be. I said I was going to ask you to marry me, and I am doing so here and now. Consider my question an open proposal without a time limit. When and if you can answer, let me know. I will not press you nor will I ask you again. The papers for the cruise got me to thinking. You haven't seen them, but the people that processed them saw that we were both named Yoder and assumed we were man and wife. All of our reservations and even the name listing for tables on the cruise ship has us as Mr. and Mrs. Ragan Yoder. The card to be placed on our cabin door says the same. I was quite surprised, but frankly, I was rather pleased. I can ask them to change them if you want."

Marci smiled sweetly. "I understand and adore the way you proposed. I will consider your proposal exactly the way you said you meant. I wouldn't change those name cards or reservations for the world. I will be quite proud to be referred to as Mrs. Ragan Yoder. I might like the name so much I'll want to make things official. Thank goodness neither of us is pressing the issue. That makes life so much easier. You are my man, and I do love you very much. At that Labor Day cook out I told Terry and Carey that I was certain I would never need or have a man in my life. Starting just three days later I'd reverse that and eat those words. I love the way things have gone."

With that she plopped down in his lap and gave him a big kiss. They stayed in each other's arms for the next half an hour, like two kids in love. Then Marci jumped up.

"I hate to bring us back down to Earth, but we've a party to prepare for. Let's try to be ready tonight so we can relax and enjoy ourselves tomorrow."

"Right on, sweetie, right on."

It was nearly midnight when they went up to bed.

FORTY

Ragan opened the door for Celia and Elisha, two nurses from Goshen Hospital. Their husbands were behind them carrying a large, heavy box.

"Come on in. Can I help you with that."

"With one of us on each end this is manageable. I think another pair of hands would be in the way, but thanks anyway."

"It should go in the kitchen. Here, I'll hold the door."

They opened the box down on the floor. Inside were three electric roaster ovens full of hot appetizers.

"Celia said your kitchen had a large island with electric outlets," One of the men said. "She was right. They are warm, not hot so can we put them out now? Another box with three more is right behind us, and the cold stuff is right behind them."

Ragan said, "That's a granite top so heat won't cause any damage and they won't scratch the surface."

Soon eight or ten nurses and their husbands were scurrying about placing the roasters and the plates of cold hors d'oeuvres on the kitchen counters. Marci walked into the kitchen.

"My goodness, gang, everything smells and looks fantastic. That's enough food for an army," she said as she popped a rumaki into her mouth. "Mmmm, delicious."

Celia came over. "Forty people for six hours? You'll be surprised, Marci, how much a gang like that can consume, especially if they wash everything down with beer, wine and other drinks. The Sheriff's department is parking coolers out on the porch. Must be a dozen or more on the porch and Gordy is setting up the bar."

"You know Gordy?"

"We dated when we were in high school, and I married his best friend. I sure do," she said, then stood back and stared at Marci. "Wait a minute. I just got a good look at your outfit. You look fantastic. Where did you find those earrings, and that matching pendant? They are gorgeous."

"Ragan had Fred Bell make them for me for Christmas."

"They had to cost a fortune, especially those diamonds. They must each be a carat. How'd he manage that on a retired cop's pension. The Sheriff's department doesn't pay him much. He must love the work."

Marci laughed. "Ragan told me he's had those diamonds for a long time. He would lose a lot if he sold them so he kept them and used them for me. He even helped Fred design the piece. He said the gold settings were not terribly expensive and that's all he had to pay for. He had Fred give him an appraisal for insurance but wouldn't tell me how much."

"Wow, I'll bet it's a fancy bundle. And now you're going on a cruise up the Amazon? I'm sure Ragan got a substantial settlement from the boat accident, but that's a lot of money he's spending in a short time. And that property he bought on Tippy, that wasn't cheap. I know I shouldn't be nosy, but some of the nurses at the hospital were speculating about his wealth and not always in a good way. I stay out of that gossip, but that's why I'm asking you. You must have a good explanation."

"Celia, you've been a good friend, and you're no gossip. Why don't we go in the study and I'll tell you where the money comes from so you won't wonder."

After they walked into the study, Marci closed the door.

"Ragan doesn't talk much about his finances, but he finally explained to me exactly what and why. He said he should have told me earlier. Do you know why we're going on this cruise?"

"No, not really. To take a cruise I suppose."

"Please don't say anything, but Ragan is going to try to bring a criminal back to the states for prosecution. If he succeeds he will earn a substantial reward."

"Oh my God. That's wonderful. I wish him and you luck. Is this dangerous?"

"That's the problem, but Ragan is quite sure he has that handled. Over the years he was in Chicago, he split a number of rewards with others under some arrangement with the Chicago police department that I do not understand. Something to do with hazardous action bonuses. He assures me everything was legal. He's a stickler on being legal. Anyway, he never spent a penny of that money. He invested and did so wisely through an attorney he worked with who was also an investment counselor. Twenty years doing that and never touching the money paid off. As a result, he's quite well situated financially. He does live comfortably. The house on Tippy was his first use of that money as an investment. I'm sure you can understand that. Your husband's a banker, I know. He would understand how even small contributions invested wisely over twenty years can add up to a sizeable nest egg. And don't forget, his pension from the Chicago Police is quite generous and covers all of his usual living expenses and more."

"Why are you telling me all of this?"

"Because I can trust you and your judgement. Should you hear any destructive gossip, you will know how to prevent the story from going in the wrong direction. One more thing. We will certainly put our lives together in the next year or so. You know about the farm I own south of here and probably that I saved money to build a new house when I must leave this one next June. I've talked about that enough."

"Yes, you did tell me about that. Because of your divorce settlement, right?"

"Right. Well now I will not build that house and will probably put my savings into expanding and remodeling Ragan's house on Tippy. We will be joint owners. We're already working on remodeling plans. To add to the situation, a few days ago he asked me to marry him."

"My God, Marci, you did say yes didn't you?"

"My instincts said to say yes, but I told him I wanted to wait until after our cruise. He understands and agreed. Can you believe we met less than four months ago? I think I knew by the end of the first week he would play a part in my life. I didn't realize how big a part."

"I think you both are fantastically fortunate. You experienced more excitement in those four months than lots of folks do in a lifetime. Now you are about to go off on another major adventure. I pray for your safety and God bless you."

"Thanks! Now we'd better go back with the partiers. I can hear the revelry outside the door."

The party was an outstanding success. Marci's bright red outfit and new jewelry were the talk of the evening. Everyone had a good time, and no one got drunk. The guests stayed and helped clean up and put things in order. Around three the last guest left, and they collapsed on the couch.

"Our friends were unbelievable," Ragan said. "The place is as clean and orderly as it was this morning. Nothing for us to clean up so let's go to bed before we go to sleep on the couch. We are looking forward to a busy week."

They both went to sleep the minute their heads hit their pillows.

✳ Saturday, January 5, 2013, 9 pm ✳

The six days until their departure passed quickly, and long before their deadline, everything was prepared, packed, and ready to drive to Chicago in the morning.

FORTY-ONE

They left home for O'Hare Airport with time to spare considering the traffic on the Borman and around the city on I-294. On the way, they called Bruce and Miriam who would meet them at the terminal to pick up the truck and their winter clothes.

The usual hectic traffic mess greeted them as they drove to drop their luggage. Miraculously, Bruce was right behind them when they pulled to the curb. After dropping their luggage at the pickup station, they quickly said their good byes. After Miriam left in her car, they stepped inside out of the slush and removed their winter coats and boots. Bruce grabbed them, hurried out to the pickup, and left for home.

"Well, here we are with nearly two hours to go through the TSA search and delete," Marci said as they wheeled their carry-ons toward security. "Look at the crowd. I wonder how long we will be held up here?"

"I'll bet we'll be through and on our way to the gate in less than thirty minutes. They've improved and speeded things up considerably since they first started. Of course Sunday morning is one of their least busy times. Try Friday at six and you will take an hour and a half to go through. I tried never to fly during those busy hours."

"Did you fly often?"

"Only on police work and a couple of vacations. Mostly during the last five years before I retired. Security has become faster and I think better. That traffic mess at the drop off has always been hectic. No one has yet come up with a viable solution so you still fight your way in and fight your way out. Here's our gate. Thank goodness our gate is not out at the end of the concourse. That's a long walk."

The flight was uneventful as was the shuttle trip to the dock. Their ship, the Sea Explorer with seven decks, appeared small next to the huge 13 deck monster cruise ship docked nearby.

"That smaller ship is ours," Ragan announced. "It has seven decks and accommodations for around 1,200 passengers. The other ship probably has 15 decks and room for four or five thousand passengers. I much prefer cruising on a smaller ship like this one or the National Geographic ship."

"Having never been on a cruise, I must take your word."

It took more than an hour to check in, tag their luggage, and wait for the porters to pickup and take each piece to their cabin. They were on the second deck, the same level as the dining room.

✳ 2:00 pm ✳

When they entered their cabin Marci said, "Our cabin doesn't look as big as shown in the brochure. That doesn't surprise me though."

"To me it's bigger than I thought. Of course, I did not pay any attention to the brochure. We will be quite comfortable here. Our luggage is not here yet. Let's walk back to the dining room and wander about to see what we can find."

They explored for an hour. When they returned they found their luggage had been delivered to their door. On the desk was a book with information about the ship and all of their assignments. Marci wanted to go through the book before unpacking their suitcases.

"Okay, **Mrs.** Yoder," Ragan said. "I guess I'll become used to being the browbeaten husband."

Marci punched him in the arm playfully and pushed him down on the bed. "How right you are. Now let's check out that book."

It took more than twenty minutes for them to read through all the instructions and advertisements.

"I don't know," Marci said. "I didn't realize how many rules and regulations they would have. Oh, here's our table assignment for the formal dinners. 'Coats and ties and dinner dresses required.' Here! Look! Our table is clear at the back of the ship."

"That's the stern, Marci, the stern."

"Okay, Mr. Seaman. We're at a table for ten. They have tables for eight and some for six. I'm glad we're at a big table, more people to meet and talk to."

"Yes, and here's a listing of those seated with us at the table. Here's their names and where they are from. That's thoughtful of the cruise people."

"Four are from Manaus. They surely can give us some tips on the city. The guests at our table include a couple from New York and another from St. Augustine. Little old Milford, Indiana doesn't seem exciting next to the other places. That should be an interesting group to dine with. Here's a note that says we can ask to be seated at another table with other people after either of the first two dinners."

"I suppose that's in case we don't fare well with someone."

"Are you finished with the book? We'd better continue our unpacking. They are holding a get-acquainted cocktail party in the lounge starting at five. That's a little more than an hour from now."

"Should we take this list of names so we can look for them at the cocktail party?"

"Sure, stick it in your purse. Dinner is at seven-thirty. I suppose that's to give the clothes horses time to change from cocktail outfits to dinner dress. I'll bet some of these women will never wear the same outfit twice."

"Careful there mister. Using mix and match, I'm prepared to never wear the same combination twice myself."

"Sweetheart, whatever you wear you'll without a doubt be the most gorgeous lady on the ship. I guarantee."

"Thank you, Ragan, but that will only be because I will be with the most handsome man."

"Enough of this praise party. Let's unpack so we can clean up. Otherwise, we could be the most bedraggled couple at the party."

✳ 4:30 pm ✳

Marci put on her little red dress, the same outfit she wore New Year's eve.

"I thought you'd be saving that for the Captain's formal dinner party near the end of the cruise."

"It's a cocktail dress, Ragan, not a formal. I will surprise you at that dinner party, wait and see. Besides, I want to make a good first impression and tonight is a good time to do that."

"Marci, you will do that in spades. That outfit always takes my breath away. I can't imagine what you will wear to the formal dinner. However, I'm quite sure you will be spectacular. Grab our name tags. I've got the door key-cards. Let's go down to the party and meet people."

＊ 5:20 pm ＊

An introductory reception line stood inside the door. The line consisted of several heads of the ship's service groups, the entertainment director and activities leader, and Captain Vladimir Medvedev and his wife, Katerina. They chatted a bit with each one as they introduced themselves. Captain Medvedev was of medium height, of obvious Scandinavian ancestry, and had blonde, curly hair. He was somewhat taken by Marci and spoke to her for several minutes. After she spoke to Katerina, she started walking into the room. Katerina was quite a beauty, blonde and tiny. As she spoke to Ragan, she pulled him aside.

"Mr. Yoder, you and your wife make a striking couple. Vladimir was impressed by your wife's beauty and friendliness. I expect, no, I know he will be sending you an invitation to join us at our table for one or more of the formal dinners. Please come. I would like to better know you and your lovely wife."

"Thank you. I can speak for Marci and say we would be honored and of course will accept. You and your husband are also an attractive and gracious couple."

When he caught up to Marci, Ragan told her what Katerina said to him and his response.

"Wow, the Captain's table. That's quite a move for this little Indiana farm girl. I hope I'll how to act."

Ragan laughed. "I'm quite certain you can hold your own at that table or any place else you go. I hope you keep the little farm girl act between us. You're as sophisticated as any woman on this ship and twice as beautiful."

"Thank you, dear heart. Now let's mingle and try to find some of our dinner group."

It wasn't long before the Fittipaldis walked up and introduced themselves. They were soon joined by Dr. Fernanda Calmon and her husband Lucio. They were all from Manaus and traveling together.

Lucio explained, "My wife attended the recent medical convention in Miami along with Bráulio who is a medical technician. Adriana and I came along and the four of us decided to take advantage of this cruise back to our home. We've been close friends for many years."

Ragan said, "We saw you were from Manaus and immediately decided to try to pick your brains about the city, if that's okay with you of course. We've never even been to South America, so everything is new to us."

Fernanda said, "We'd be delighted. We can tell you many good places to go and also warn you of those that are not so good, We'll enjoy lots of conversation since we will be dining together."

"How long will you be in Manaus?" Bráulio asked. "Most people on this cruise will fly home the day after arriving."

"Marci and I will be in Manaus for at least two weeks. We left our return plans open so we could stay as long as we want to. Fortunately we are in no hurry to return. Well that's not actually true. Marci is a trauma nurse who has taken a leave of up to six weeks. We do face that deadline."

"A trauma nurse you say?" Fernanda was quite interested. "We'll take the time to share experiences some time on the cruise, or even in Manaus. I'm always eager to share ideas with fellow medical professionals."

"Yes, definitely," Marci said. "I think the same, a good way to expand one's knowledge in any field."

"You all speak English fluently," Ragan said. We were afraid of communication problems since neither of us speaks Portuguese."

"You will find that almost all professionals and many others in Manaus speak two languages fluently, some three," Lucio explained. "Portuguese is the primary one and English is the second. A number of native languages are also spoken. Most of the natives in Manaus are of the Dessana tribe. Fernanda's mother is one of them. We kid her a lot about her eyes. They are quite green like Fernanda's, not dark brown like all her relatives."

Another couple, quite elderly, joined them.

"We're Carlos and June Miranda," Carlos said. "I believe we will be dining with all of you."

"You're from St. Augustine, right?" Marci asked. "Welcome to our little group."

After introductions all around, Carlos asked, "Have any of you ever been to St. Augustine? June and I lived in a house on the ocean for fifty-one years and still love it."

After a chorus of nos Carlos continued. "Have any of you seen the Murphys? They're the only ones from our table we've not met."

More nos. They talked for a while, then decided to mingle and meet other people. By six they had met a number of other folks. Ragan spotted an empty table for four and sat down.

"Let's sit for a while," Ragan said. "I'd like to relax and people watch, and that pianist is quite good and versatile. I'll grab some fresh drinks. What would you like?"

"Vodka and tonic like always. That's pretty much all I care for in hot weather."

"I'll order two and be right back."

When Ragan returned with the drinks, the pianist was sitting with Marci. He smiled and stood up to introduce himself.

"I'm Oscar Dafoe. I hope you don't mind, sir, but I saw this stunning lady sitting here alone and came to ask if she had any requests, any numbers she'd like me to play for her."

"I don't mind at all. Might I make a request as well?"

"Certainly! What would you like to hear?"

"On second thought, play whatever Marci requested."

"Gladly. And sir?"

"Yes?"

"I must say your wife is one of the most beautiful ladies whose requests I've had the pleasure to play."

Ragan smiled. "Yes she is lovely. I couldn't agree more. I am one lucky man."

They listened to Marci's three requests while holding hands and enjoying being together—it was another magical moment.

The bartender's "Last call before dinner!" took them out of their reverie.

"I guess we'd better head for the dining room," Ragan said. "Are you as hungry as I am?"

"Ravenous! We missed lunch if you recall."

"We did, didn't we? I didn't realize until you told me. No wonder I'm so hungry."

FORTY-TWO

Ragan and Marci were the first ones at the table. The rest of the group who met at the cocktail party soon came in and sat down.

Quite some time later Ragan began looking around. "I wonder if the Murphys missed the boat? Most diners are already seated."

The waiters were beginning to pick up the guests' dinner selections when a young couple hurried to the table and took the two remaining seats.

"I'm Cotner Murphy and this is my wife, Joyce. I'm sorry we're so late, but our luggage got messed up and . . . well . . . we're here."

After introductions the waiter picked up the lists with our selections.

Carlos said, "You two don't happen to be on your honeymoon do you? You seem like a couple of newlyweds."

The two looked at each other, then Joyce said, "I guess you could say that. We decided yesterday on our way to the ship that we would be married when we returned home. We've been living together since we were nineteen. I guess we could call this a honeymoon."

"That's what I told her when we were planning our trip, a honeymoon. Remember, doll?"

Ragan and Marci looked at each other and couldn't hide their grins.

Adriana said, "Wonderful, that means we're a table of old married folks on a cruise. Why don't we start off by each standing, giving our full names, where we're from, and what our job or profession is. I'll start off. I'm Adriana Fittipaldi from Manaus, a buyer for the Manaus Airport Terminal Company."

"I'm her husband, Bráulio and I'm an X-Ray technician at the Lutheran hospital in Manaus."

"Fittipaldi, that's a famous name in auto racing," Carlos said. "Is Emerson Fittipaldi any relation? I'm a big fan of his."

Adriana said, "He's actually Bráulio's cousin. Their fathers are brothers."

This led to some discussion of auto racing and famous people before getting back to individual descriptions.

When Ragan's turn came he said, "I'm Ragan Yoder from Leesburg, Indiana and I'm an insurance fraud investigator."

Marci immediately got up and said, "I'm Marci Yoder from Milford, Indiana and I'm a trauma nurse."

Apparently no one caught their mention of different towns and the introductions continued. The Murphys were the last.

Cotner stood. "I'm Cotner Murphy from Elizabeth, New Jersey, and I'm a Wall Street clerk hoping to some day become a banker."

Joyce stood. "I'm Joyce Carrier, soon to be Murphy, and I'm a student at NYU working toward a computer engineering degree."

By this time dinner was being served and the conversation dwindled. Everyone was hungry.

When conversation resumed, June directed a request to the four from Manaus. "Can any of you suggest things we might do in Manaus? Carlos and I plan on staying a week before we fly home. We read lots of travel propaganda but we've never even met anyone who's been to Manaus."

Several of the others said they were in the same situation.

Dr. Calmon said, "I think we can help you out. Why don't we all meet in the lounge after dinner, all of you who are interested, of course. We can probably give you some suggestions."

All but the Murphys sat in the lounge listening to the four from Manaus explain about their favorite places. The Opera House and the market were the only must see places touted in the promotional literature. By ten-thirty they had covered most of the other places suggested and settled down to listen to the piano player.

Yoder asked the four from Manaus, "If any of you can tell me anything about a man named Jerry Reese, I'd like to talk to you sometime. Not now of course but when we can spend some time during the day."

All four reacted visibly and unfavorably with frowns and negative head shaking..

Dr. Calmon spoke up, "Jerry Reese is an evil man. We could tell you much of him and his actions. I don't think any of us would say anything good about him."

"I hope I didn't upset anyone. I failed to realize I was dealing with such an unpopular subject."

Lucio replied, "He's certainly an unpopular subject, someone I think we would all prefer to discuss at another time. Without going into any detail, what interests you about this louse?"

"I'm sorry. I will definitely wait until a better time when we can discuss him. One important bit of information and I'll quit until later. He is a suspect in a huge fraud case back in Indiana. That's one of the reasons we're going to Manaus, to work on the case and learn more about him and his whereabouts. Now lets return to more pleasant subjects."

"Good idea." Bráulio said. "I'm sure we would love to help if we can, later of course. Call me tomorrow and we can set up a time. I'm sure each of us would love to be able to help nail that villain for something. He's paid off most of the officials and quite a few of the police so whatever you are planning won't be easy."

Adriana was sitting next to Ragan. She leaned toward him and said, "Your wife is without doubt the most gorgeous woman on this ship. That simple red dress and matching shoes set off by her jewelry is a stunning outfit. Not many women could wear an outfit like that so well."

"Yes, that and for lots of other reasons I am a lucky man. I tell her so every chance I find."

"Good for you. Those earrings and that pendant are quite unusual, simple, and quite elegant. Wherever did you find them?"

"Actually, a jeweler friend of mine designed and made them for me. I gave them to her for Christmas."

"Well, your jeweler friend is quite an artist. So much modern jewelry is so gaudy it's actually ugly. I love simple designs. They are so much more tasteful. See, my husband thinks so too. He's heading for the dance floor with her. You're not jealous, are you?"

"Not at all. Marci and I are quite secure in our relationship."

"I know what you mean. Bráulio and I are the same way. We've been married for thirty years. He's a good man and a wonderful father. You have children?"

"Marci has two, a young engineer and a college senior, but I have none. Sadly my late wife could not bear children. We both wanted them, but finally found out she could not conceive. That was a sad day for both of us."

"Your late wife? So Marci's not your first? How long have you been married?"

Ragan had no idea what to say, so he told the truth. "We don't advertise, but we're not married. We will probably tie the knot when we return home, but no date has even been considered."

Adriana chuckled. "So her name is not Yoder?"

"Oh, her name is Yoder all right. Her ex husband may be a distant relative of mine. Many Yoders live in northern Indiana, especially among the Amish and Mennonites. Yoder is an old German name. Both our names being Yoder is a coincidence."

"I should quit asking questions. I don't want to make you uncomfortable, and I won't mention this to the others, except for my husband of course."

Ragan laughed. "No, I am not uncomfortable in the least. We've never hidden our relationship from anyone. We've only been together since September, but lived a lifetime during those few months. She even risked her life to save mine in a boating accident. But for her bravery and quick action, I would be dead. No kidding."

"That's quite a story. Can you tell me how the accident happened?"

Ragan described the accident.

"That's an amazing story. I now respect your lady even more. She's quite a talented and brave woman in addition to being beautiful. You are indeed a lucky man. If I may ask, have you known her for a long time? How did you meet?"

Ragan laughed and shook his head. "That's another improbable story of circumstance."

He told of their meeting because of the accident but not that he was a cop. He edited the reality saying that he happened to be at the intersection when the accident occurred and he rushed over to help. He related most of the happenings, the coffee, and the dinner leaving out significant details.

"Simply stated, the time was magic for both of us," Ragan said. "We were in love and committed so fast we had no time to think. Marci said she felt like we had known each other forever."

"Destiny. That was destiny. You two were destined to be together. What a wonderfully romantic story, beautiful. I'm dying to share with the others, but would rather you told. I've never heard of such a wonderful happening, and look where you are now. Will you tell? I certainly won't if you don't want me to. The story is right out of a movie script, only better because it's true."

"It's rather late. Should we do that another time?"

"It's only eleven. We'll be here until midnight. Please!"

"Let me check this out with Marci first. If she says Okay, it's Okay. She can tell much of the story and is a better story teller than I am. I'll ask her quietly when she comes off the dance floor. Then, if you want, you can introduce the story."

"I would love that."

A soon as Marci sat down I drew her aside and asked. She was a bit surprised and thought for a few minutes.

"What the hell," she said with a sly smile. "We might as well. It is a rather intriguing story, romantic. I'd rather like to share."

"Don't forget to leave out any references to the police or that I am a cop. Let me tell the story of the accident and why I was in your yard to be sure."

Ragan walked over to Adriana and said, "It's a go. Marci said Okay."

Adriana stood up and said to our group. "Attention everyone. I heard an unbelievable and amazing story from Ragan about how he and Marci came to be together. It's beautiful, will warm your hearts, and blow you away at the same time."

Marci and Ragan told the entire story to the rapt attention of all. They left out his part as a cop of course. They all retired to their cabins soon after midnight.

FORTY-THREE

Ragan met with Fernanda and Bráulio the next morning to talk about Jerry Reese. They sat in a booth in the forward lounge.

After morning greetings, Bráulio said, "The two of us should be able to answer all your questions about Reese. We know a lot more about him than our spouses do. Why don't we each give a short rundown of his operations and then answer specific questions?"

"Sounds good to me," Ragan said. "I brought a listing of his businesses and homes and their approximate value along with his debts from research we did earlier. That's about all."

"His house here is a fortress, thick high walls surround the entire compound, and armed guards man the gate. The place was an old estate built long ago by one of the rubber barons. He's been the owner for quite a few years. Incidentally, his mortgage and probably all of his loans are with a local bank with suspected criminal connections. His interest rate on all the loans is zero. Can't be much better than that."

"No wonder he has his houses mortgaged to the max," Ragan said. "He owns another house on Dominica and one in Indiana. The one in Indiana is the location and subject of the fraud charges. The house has been seized by the courts."

"That sounds like him," Bráulio said. "His hotel services company controls all the laundry services for every hotel and flophouse in Manaus. He uses strong arm tactics to keep out competitors. That also gives his people access to every visiting business person doing business in this area of Brazil. His thugs will be able to access many things about you and your belongings wherever you stay, so be forewarned."

"That's good to know. What about his river freighters? I understand one of his companies operates a small fleet."

Bráulio laughed. "Rumor is his freighters run drugs and other contraband in most of the navigable waters in the Amazon basin. They go down river to Santarem and up river all the way into Columbia. Crates of automatic weapons were reported seen being loaded on his ships and off loaded to other ships. That's only rumor, but probably true. Fernanda will tell you about his gold mining operation. She is involved with one of the tribes that work the mines with terrible health consequences."

Fernanda said, "The tribe of indigenous people my mother is from, the Dessana, are related to the Yanomamo on whose land Reese's gold miners are working. The Yanomamo keep fighting with the miners trying to evict them from their tribal lands with modest success. The mines decimate the land and poison the waters with mercury. Dangerous amounts of methyl mercury are found in many fish the Indians harvest for food downstream from the mines. This chemical is dangerous for the nervous system of adults and devastating to foetuses. Gold mining poses a serious threat to the health of these natives. The government is trying to control this, but the remoteness and isolation of the area being mined makes this extremely difficult. Greedy men like Reese don't care how many sicken or die, mostly children, as long as they can mine gold profitably. Now, does that tell you why we would like him taken down?"

Ragan shook his head. "He really is an evil character. Frankly, I doubt we will be able to extradite him. The process is underway, but in the best circumstances is quite difficult and time consuming. My trip is primarily to help the process and speed it up if possible. I need to meet with the politicians who will decide about the extradition. That will not be easy. Still, it's worth a try. One of my other efforts will be to try to find a way to lure him onto American soil so he can be arrested. Any information or help would be appreciated."

Bráulio smiled at Ragan. "Here's a bit of information that might be of help. He flies to Dominica and uses the house he has for some reason. Rumor says that is where he meets with members of the drug cartel. Dominica is a safe place for them to meet. Here's what you want most to know. He usually flies commercial. Only once in a while does he use a charter. Too much risk. A charter could be dangerous for a man like him.

The flights he takes involve a plane change in San Juan, Puerto Rico - American soil. Perhaps you can use the information."

"Fabulous! that may be our best chance to nab him. How could we learn if and when he is planning a flight, or for that matter, any critical information about him?"

"I don't know, but Adriana might be able to check for his next flight reservation and notify you. I'll ask her. I know she'd love to help catch that miserable excuse for a human being."

✳ January 8 through January 20, 2013 ✳

They enjoyed the rest of the cruise, meeting and sometimes traveling ashore with the friends made at the dinner table and elsewhere. After the second night, the Murphys opted to find another table. When the Mirandas learned of this, they replaced them with the two friends from St. Augustine they were traveling with. The Clarendons, Mark and Lois, fit right in. Both had retired from Grumman, him as a mechanic and her as a secretary. The entire group did many things together. They had a rather sad parting when they reached Manaus. They exchanged addresses and agreed to keep in touch.

✳ Monday, January 21, 2013, 8:00 am ✳

Marci and Ragan went to their hotel but would not be able to check in until eleven. Ragan checked and found the boxes he had shipped were not at the hotel yet.

"That's Okay, Marci," he said. "They were shipped to arrive after today. The hotel will notify me when they are here. Let's walk around and spot some places to eat or shop nearby."

They walked around and Marci found several interesting shops.

"I won't buy anything now. I'll just look. I can always come back later if I find anything I like. You stopped at that sporting goods store with all the fishing regalia in the window. Are you planning on doing some fishing?"

"You never know. I might. I understand some monster fish live in Amazon waters. I'll inquire around and see what I can discover. The river is certainly much bigger, deeper and quite different from Tippy. Right now we'd better head for the hotel. It's almost noon."

As they walked up the hill toward their hotel, Marci saw a small restaurant as they passed by.

"Let's eat lunch here. We can check in later, after the rush."

Lunch was excellent so they decided to come back during their stay. At one o'clock they checked in. Luggage emptied into the drawers and closet, empty luggage stored away, they sat across from each other at a small table and relaxed. They sat in silence for about ten minutes. Marci stood up, walked over to Ragan, put her arms around him, and whispered in his ear.

"Let's talk about being married."

"This is so sudden," he said. "Whatever gave you the idea I would consider marriage?"

"Come on, Ragan, can you be just a little serious for a moment or two. We can now take the time to talk about it, and we're still on our honeymoon if you remember."

"Yes, I completely forgot about that."

"I'll bet you forgot. Earlier, while we were cruising, I though about getting married aboard ship. Then I decided I wanted to be married in the church in Milford with our dear friends and family. I'm a rather conventional thinker when it comes to marriage. I'd like some flowers, a reception and a wedding cake. Is that too much to ask for?"

"My dearest Marci. Nothing would make me happier than for your wishes to be granted. I love you very much and will do whatever is necessary so our wedding will be a wonderful celebration. What you described is exactly what I would like for the two of us, a small church wedding with all the traditional trimmings. We can start listing things we would like in our wedding right now. By the time we are home most of the details could be all planned.

FORTY-FOUR

Marci was walking down the street from their hotel to Meet Ragan for lunch. She hadn't walked a full block when a van and a car pulled quickly to the curb beside her. Four men jumped out of the vehicles, grabbed her, threw her in the back of the van, and drove off. The inside back of the van was a wire cage with no possible way of escape. Thinking to protect herself she took the tiny Glock out of her purse and palmed it so her abductors wouldn't find her gun without a thorough search. It was still sealed in the zip lock bag. Strangely she was not badly frightened, but angry at herself for not being more cautious.

Her mind raced, *what should I do? I could shoot them through the seats, but the seats could stop the bullets. If I do shoot them, I still can't escape this cage and another two are in the other car. What about the Glock? No place to hide it. They're bound to search me. Wait, I know. It's in a sealed plastic bag. I can stick it where they're not likely to search. It's uncomfortable, but well hidden. What else?*

Marci examined her prison carefully. She looked for the wiring for the lights but she could not reach it through the cage wire. Obviously the van had been constructed to hold prisoners. With no windows in the back she could only see outside around the end of the bulkhead separating the drivers from the cage. All she could see was buildings close to the van on the right and water on the left. The van turned left, went down a ramp of some sort, and stopped. The cage was opened and she was ordered out.

One of the men grabbed her purse and flung it back in the van. "You won't need that." he said, taking her arm and pulling her onto a narrow gangplank that went to a small freighter moored to the dock they were on. She thought about jumping into the water but decided that could be even worse. The man behind her pushed her up to the ship.

242

"Don't give us any trouble." he said. "Follow orders and you won't be hurt. You wouldn't want that pretty face smashed in."

They pushed her into a small cabin with a bunk, closed and locked the door from outside. They hadn't bothered to search her probably because her light summer dress provided no place to hide anything. For half an hour the cabin was pitch black. The cabin had no window or opening for light. She felt her way onto the bunk and stretched out. She removed the Glock and was much more comfortable. She took it out of the ziplock, turned the safety off and stuck it under the pillow on the bunk. She would be ready for whatever came next. The ship's engines started and she could feel the boat moving. The overhead light came on and someone was unlocking the door. She sat up, slipped her hand under the pillow and grabbed the gun. Two men were standing in the doorway.

"Feel free to walk about the ship," one said. "I wouldn't try jumping off and swimming to shore. Piranhas would cut you to pieces long before you could reach any land. You'll be dropped off at a Dessana Indian village about a hundred miles upstream for safe keeping. The Dessana speak no English and little Portuguese. You'll stay in the village till Reese doesn't need you anymore. If you're lucky, someone will come and take you back to Manaus."

They turned and walked away. Marci took the gun, set the safety on and tucked it into her bra. The frilly collar on her dress hid the lump the gun made. She walked slowly about the deck of the freighter checking to find out how many crew were on board and where they were. She counted five plus the Captain. Several had holstered weapons. She realized she would probably lose any gun battle. She was outgunned. She would wait it out. As the ship moved upriver, she developed a plan of action for when she reached the village.

✳ Friday, January 25, 2013, noon ✳

Ragan walked to the doorway of the restaurant and looked up the street for Marci. *She should be here by now. She's never late.* He thought. *I'd better walk back to the hotel and check.*

Back at the hotel he checked their room. *Her purse is gone so she obviously left. Where could she go without his knowledge?* He called her cell phone . . . no answer. He went to the desk and asked for any messages . . . none. He went outside and checked with the doorman.

"Sir, I'm wondering if my wife left the hotel say about half an hour ago? She was wearing a dress with red and blue flowers."

"A pretty lady in a dress like you described left about half an hour ago."

"That's her. Thank you. Did you notice which way she went?"

"To the right down that street," he said pointing toward the restaurant.

Ragan was quite concerned and at a loss as to what to do. He walked down to the restaurant and back to the hotel. It was twelve thirty when he walked up to the desk in the hotel.

"Are you sure you have no message for Ragan Yoder?"

"No, but a man dropped off a package for you. Here. Take this."

It was a brown paper bag stapled shut with no writing on it. "Are you sure this is for me? There's no name on it."

"The man who dropped it off said clearly, 'This is for Mr. Ragan Yoder.' Then he left. You probably passed him on your way in. I didn't even get a chance to put it in your box."

"Thank you." Ragan said as he headed for a chair to sit while he opened it. He was worried when he saw it contained Marci's purse. A quick check and he found everything including her cell phone, but no gun. That really worried him. He opened the thick envelope that was also in the package. It was some specific instructions. They follow:

Mr. Yoder, Your wife has been taken to a safe place where she will remain until these instructions are carried out exactly. Should they not be carried out precisely as described, you will never see her again.

1) Do not contact any local authorities about this. We will know if you do and your wife will suffer but not for long.

2) You will board the ten o'clock plane to Miami tomorrow taking all of your luggage with you. You will not return to Manaus.

3) When you reach Indiana you will cancel the extradition order and all outstanding arrest warrants for Jake Ramsey and Jerry Reese.

Once we confirm these instructions were carried out, your wife will be returned to Manaus good as new. She can make her way home any way she wishes.

Cross me in any way or fail to follow all of these instructions and she will never come out of the jungle.

Ragan sat for several minutes considering his options. He had few. He got up and headed for his room where he began packing his things and Marci's. He pulled the film case out from under the bed, went into the bath room, and closed the door. He removed both guns and packed them in their places in the film case. He was taking no chances on spying hidden cameras. He started to pack the film case in one of the shipping boxes but stopped. The rest of the items he had shipped were packed in his suitcase along with several items Marci had purchased. He packed all of the things Marci might need into the other packing box. The rest of her things were packed in her suitcase. He had a plan that involved help from Adriana. He called the Fittipaldis and arranged to meet them that evening. On the way to their house he stopped at a luggage store and bought another suitcase.

After greeting him Adriana said, "Come in. What's this all about, Ragan? You sounded upset and quite serious over the phone."

"That's because this is quite serious. Reese has kidnaped Marci and threatened to kill her if I don't follow his instructions exactly."

"Oh my God, Ragan. That's terrible. What can we do to help, anything? How did this happen?"

"Yes, you can do several things to help. I'm taking a big chance that you are not the ones who tipped Reese to what I am doing and where Marci and I were staying. Someone did and I trust you are not the ones."

"Well, it certainly wasn't either of us. Who would do such a terrible thing?"

"I don't know and right now I don't care as long as you weren't the ones. You can help as I will not even consider leaving Manaus without Marci. I made a reservation on the ten o'clock flight to Miami tomorrow morning as I was ordered to do. They will be watching to make sure I board that plane. If you can help me, I'll go on in plain sight and then get off without their knowing. Here's my plan."

Ragan outlined his plan and showed them the note from Reese. Adriana thought the plan would work and agreed to make the arrangements for Ragan to get off the plane unobserved. They talked for several hours and invited Ragan to use their guest bedroom.

"Are you sure? That bastard could cause you big problems if he finds out. I hate to put you to such a risk."

Bráulio smiled. "I'd love doing anything to damage that rat. It's worth the risk. Our guest bedroom is in back over the garage. Not only that, but the garage has a double rear door so a vehicle can go into the garage from the alleyway and need not go down the street. A stairway goes up to the bedroom from inside the garage. That room is the same now as when we bought the place. We'd love for you to use it."

"If you're sure. The place sounds perfect for me."

Adriana said, "I'm sure I can arrange to put you on and off the plane. I'll make the necessary calls tomorrow morning, first thing."

Ragan returned to his hotel room and prepared for the morning's activities. He packed all his clothes and things that he would need into the new suitcase, took the suitcase down to the garage and put it into the rental car. He returned to the room and went to bed.

✳ 10:00 pm ✳

Marci realized the boat was docking. The night was pitch black with no lights on the shore. Only the lights of the ship pierced the darkness. Someone opened the door.

"You can sleep on the bunk tonight. It's too dark to walk ashore," the man said, then closed the door which he did not lock.

FORTY-FIVE

✳ Saturday, January 26, 2013, 6 am ✳

Ragan got up and called for a bellman to pick up his luggage. When the luggage was taken, he went down to the front desk and checked out. He had them bring his rental car around to pick up his luggage. As they were loading his boxes, he asked the bellman where he could ship the boxes, the location of a UPS or FEDEX store or the like. He made a big deal out of shipping those boxes, knowing the bellman worked for Reese and would probably report what he said. *A bit of insurance*, he said to himself.

By seven he was at the airport with his rental car. He was sure someone was following him so he drove to one of the car rental agencies, parked, and went inside. He told the man at the desk he wanted to park there for a while so he could take his luggage and check in for his flight. He needed to run some errands before turning in his rental car and going through security.

I hope he's not one of Reese's men, he thought to himself as he stood with his luggage waiting for the shuttle.

In the airport he paid for his reservation to Miami and checked both bags. Boarding pass in hand he headed for the gate going through security on the way. When he was called to board, he took his carry on and entered the plane. Knowing one of Reese's men was undoubtedly observing, he turned and headed toward the seats. As soon as he was out of sight through the entrance, he donned a white smock handed to him by an attendant and picked up his carry on. The smock was one of those worn by the food service people. He exited the other side of the plane onto the service platform after they finished unloading food for the galley. As soon as he was aboard, the platform was lowered to where he could step to the ground. Still wearing the white smock, he followed several similarly dressed workers back into the terminal. Adriana's help and plan had worked perfectly.

247

After the shuttle ride back to the rental car office, he put his carry on into the car and headed back to Manaus and the Fittipaldi's house. About ten-forty-five he decided to head for the American Consular Agency instead. He was glad his guns were still hidden in the film case as he would not be able to carry them into the agency. He identified himself and showed his credentials as a law officer to the Marine guard at the parking lot and was granted permission to park in the lot.

Inside the receptionist informed him, "You must schedule an appointment unless you're situation is an extreme emergency."

"My wife has been kidnaped and her life threatened if I don't exit the country immediately, all because I am an officer of the law seeking information about a fugitive. Does that qualify as an emergency?"

Ragan was soon seated with the consular agent, Wesley Selkirk. The first question Selkirk asked after Ragan explained the situation was, "Did you notify the local police?"

Ragan smiled. "Since Mr. Reese seems to own a lot of local politicians as well as a number of the local police, I don't think that would be a prudent thing to do. Besides, if you will read this list of demands, Marci will be killed if they find out I contacted any official authority or did not leave the country as ordered."

Selkirk read the list of demands. "I don't know if we can do anything, but I will contact the embassy in Brasilia and look for ways they can help you."

"I'm beginning to think contacting you was a mistake. Suppose they intercept your communication with the embassy? I can't risk Marci's life."

"We maintain secure communications with the embassy. No one would hear about this except trusted embassy personnel. We must keep lots of information secret and confidential. Don't worry, no one other than qualified embassy personnel will ever see this information."

"Okay, I guess I must trust you. Here's my card with my satellite phone number. All communications through that number are secure and encrypted. Contact me if anyone comes up with anything. You should provide the embassy with my number. They can contact me directly if necessary."

"Good idea. I'll do that. We will do what we can to help and keep everything top secret so don't worry. Be assured only trusted US government personnel will learn any of this."

"Thank you. Now I'd best be on my way and figuring out how to rescue my wife. So long."

"Be extremely careful, Mr. Yoder. We do not want you or your wife to suffer any harm and will do what we can to prevent it. Oh, and good luck."

✳ 11:45 am ✳

Ragan drove to the Fittipaldi's, parked in the rear, and rang their doorbell. Adriana came to the door.

"I trust everything went well at the plane."

"Like clockwork. Your plan worked out beautifully. I'm certain Reese thinks I left on that plane. I checked all our unnecessary luggage to Miami where we can pick it up when we are back."

"Wonderful. I'll give you the key to those back doors. You can unload what you need in the garage and haul everything upstairs to our guest room."

When she came back, Bráulio was with her. "Would you like some help with your luggage?" he said. "Those stairs are fairly steep."

"For now I'm only taking my carry on up to the room. Everything else I will leave in the car in case I need to leave in a hurry, but thanks."

Adriana said, "Fernanda called a while ago. She sounded extremely upset. She asked if you were here yet and said that she must speak to you. I invited her to come late afternoon and stay for dinner. I hope that's all right with you."

"Of course. I wonder what has upset her. Did you tell her about Marci?"

"That could be what's bothering her. I told her early this morning when she called. Things seemed all right. She was upset hearing about Marci but not like she is now. Whatever happened must be serious," Adriana said. "She is not usually so upset about problems."

"We'll find out when she is here," Ragan said. "Right now I'd like to take my carry on up to the room and make a few calls. I'll need to quash those warrants and extradition requests so Reese will release Marci."

"Can you do that by phone?" Bráulio asked.

"Yes, but I'll only suspend them temporarily. As far as the public record is concerned, they will be gone. As soon as Marci is safe, I can reinstate them. Actually, after what I learned at the Consular Agency today, they may not do any good anyway. As you suggested, I'm working on a plan to lure him onto American soil where we can arrest him. That seems like our best course of action. But first and most important, I must rescue Marci."

Ragan put his car in the garage, took out the film case and retrieved his weapons. Then he grabbed his carry on and went up to the guest room. He dropped his case on the floor, took out his satellite phone and placed a call to the sheriff's office. He was soon talking to Sheriff Rabb.

"It's good to hear from you, Ragan. How are things going? How was the cruise and how is Marci?"

"Right now things are not going well."

That said he launched into what had happened and that Marci had been kidnaped. The sheriff agreed to withdraw the warrants and extradition order temporarily until Marci was safe. They talked for fifteen minutes.

"Damn, I hope your lady is back in a short time," the sheriff said. Everyone here will be sorry to hear your news."

"Please don't tell anyone yet, sheriff, especially her family. No need to bother people who can't do a thing but worry. I've got some good people here who are helping me arrange her return. It's too early for any new information to reach me. I'll let you know when I learn anything."

"Okay, Ragan. I'll keep this under wraps. Please keep me informed of your progress."

"I certainly will. So long."

FORTY-SIX

Saturday morning early Marci heard the door open. "Time to go ashore. Hurry, the Captain wants to head back to Manaus immediately."

Marci got up, straightened her dress, and headed off the boat. The Glock was still hidden in her bra. As soon as she was ashore the ship left. She walked slowly into the village. All eyes followed her but no one came near. She walked up to one of the huts that stood high above the ground on bamboo stalks. She saw no steps or ladders. She did notice a few women climbing up a single fat stalk of bamboo by hooking their big toes into holes cut at regular intervals. She decided she could do that if she had to. Most of the village was on a mound about thirty feet above the river level. Only the huts at the highest point were near ground level. Their floors were only about three feet above the ground. The huts lower nearer the river were as much as fifteen feet above the ground. In the center of the village stood a heavy table, solid wood with no legs. The table was obviously cut from a large tree nearly six feet across. As she neared the table, several women came up to her and stopped her from going any nearer. They did not touch her but used their hands to indicate she should not go closer.

As she stood, several children came up to her and touched her dress. They seemed fascinated by the flowers and by the filmy material of the collar and on the hem. No one was saying a word. There was absolute silence. Before long, a large group of small children gathered around her and touched her dress. She smiled at them and they returned her smile. Three elderly women appeared, walked up toward her and said three syllables. The children immediately scattered and ran into the nearby huts. The women came up to her slowly and cautiously. Soon they were touching her hair and the fabric of her dress. When one of the women started pulling on her collar she slapped her hand away and said NO! Loudly.

They paused, put their heads together and began mumbling. Marci decided to do what she had planned. Distinctly she said, "Calmon, doctor Fernanda Calmon, Manaus."

This she repeated a number of times, pointing down river. Then she pointed to herself and said slowly, "Marci Yoder."

The women seemed to be conferring among themselves. One of them stepped toward her and said, "Calmon." clearly.

Marci pointed down river again and repeated, "Calmon, doctor Fernanda Calmon, Manaus."

The other two women took off running to another part of the village. She realized a large number of women of all ages were standing around staring at her. None came closer than a few yards. Some of them were mumbling, but most were silent. They were wearing an odd assortment of jeans, T shirts, cloths and scarves wrapped around their bodies. Many of the women were bare breasted. None of them wore shoes. A sudden loud male shout from somewhere in the village and the women vanished, all but the one older woman of the first three. The other two were walking back with a man she guessed was a chief. He carried a large spear with red feathers, an elliptical shield also covered with feathers, and wore a huge headdress of red and blue feathers. He walked up and stopped about three feet in front of her. She noticed the women lowered their eyes and did not look directly at him.

Marci looked him straight in the eyes, pointed down river, and said firmly, "Calmon, Doctor Fernanda Calmon, Manaus."

Clearly he did not like her staring straight at him. She knew she must continue to do so or he would control the situation. She repeated in firm tones, "Calmon, doctor Fernanda Calmon, Manaus." while pointing down river. When the chief's eyes wavered, she realized she had won him over and was in control. He handed his spear and shield to one of the women, walked directly up to Marci, took both of her shoulders in his hands pushed his cheeks against hers, once on each side. As soon as he stepped back there was a flurry of activity. Women brought out woven mats and spread them on the ground. The chief sat on one of the mats and seemed to indicate that Marci should sit also. As soon as she sat, a number of other men with painted faces and feather regalia came and sat on the mats. Obviously a feast was being prepared. A large fire was started off a ways from the mats. Women brought food in wooden bowls, on leaves, and on wooden platters. To Marci's surprise, drinks were served in plastic cups. Western civilization had intruded on this native gathering. Marci was quite hungry and had no idea what she was eating except for the fish and plantains. The fish was good. The beverage was slightly bitter and was probably fermented, a native beer of sorts.

At this point the chief stood, waved his arms, looked at Marci, pointed to himself and said, "Tribencoma eh Desanna." Apparently he was Tribencoma of the Desanna tribe. One by one the other men stood and introduced themselves as being of the Desanna tribe. The painted face of one man was quite different from all the rest. He stood last and introduced himself as being of the Yanomamo tribe. This was followed by what Marci perceived as some good natured razing as Americans would call it.

Marci stood, pointed to herself and said, "Marci Yoder, American."

This caused quiet a stir among the men. Several times Marci heard the word American clearly.

She pointed down river and said once more, "Calmon, doctor Fernanda Calmon, Manaus."

There was a noticeable pause and then a low rumble of conversation between the men. No anger was expressed in the rumbling, only what Marci took as respect. She thought to herself, *I must have struck a nerve. Now if I can only persuade them to contact her. How do I do that?* Then she had a stroke of genius.

She reached out and smoothed the dirt. She drew two wavy lines to represent the river. In the river she drew an arrow pointing east, down river. On the banks of the river she drew two rough circles. She pointed to the upriver circle and said, "Desanna." Next she pointed to the down river circle and said, "Manaus, doctor Calmon, Manaus."

Again she pointed to herself, said, "Marci," and pointed at the down river circle and said "Manaus, doctor Calmon, go."

The chief and his men seemed puzzled and talked among themselves while looking at the marks Marci made in the soil. She had no idea if they understood or not. Some time later, when the fire was only embers, one of the women came to Marci and indicated she should follow her. She was lead to a smallish hut and taken inside. Several young girls lay on mats and with light cloth covers. She assumed this was where she was to sleep. One of the girls indicated an empty mat so Marci lay down. Soon one of the girls covered her with one of the light cloths. Another handed her a rolled-up cloth to use as a pillow. She felt she was among friends so she did not take long to fall asleep.

FORTY-SEVEN

Bráulio came to the door of the guest room. "Ragan, you'd better hurry down. Fernanda is here and is distraught and in tears. She wants to see you immediately."

"I'll be right down."

When I reached the living room, Adriana was holding Fernanda who was sobbing uncontrollably. The minute she saw me she gathered her self together as best she could, choked back her sobbing and walked over to me.

"That bastard husband of mine sold you out to Reese for ten thousand dollars. I'm so sorry and ashamed. I threw him out of my house. I dragged that out of him after I discovered the money in his dresser when I was putting some of his clothes away which I almost never do. In recent years he has become increasingly resentful of my income. His art has sold less and less lately, and he has come to depend on me for money more and more. He sounded apologetic but rationalized his actions by saying Reese would know about this anyway. When Adriana told me Marci had been kidnaped I blew up. I never want to see that poor excuse for a human being again. I make plenty of money for both of us. I wonder why he couldn't continue as we were and be satisfied. I am so terribly sorry, Ragan."

"Don't be so upset. You didn't do anything. I've already given Reese what he demanded. At least he thinks so. We'll wait and learn if he returns Marci as he promised."

Fernanda was adamant. "That phoney Reese can't be trusted and certainly can't be counted on to keep his word. I am so terribly sorry. I'll do anything to bring her back. You could exchange me for her. I feel so terrible."

Adriana said, "Can I fix you a drink? It would relax you."

"I don't think so. I've already taken two Valium and that doesn't seem to help. Now I shouldn't take any alcohol. Talking and being here with you seems to help some. I'm calmer now than since I found out about Marci."

Adriana continued, "We're going to serve dinner in a little while, soup and a salad, light fare. Why don't you join us? Better yet, Why don't I run you over to your place so you can grab some things you need and then stay with us overnight. I don't think you should be alone."

"I couldn't put you out like that. I'll be all right at home."

Bráulio was not about to let her go home. "We would not be at all comfortable with you home alone under the circumstances. Adriana would be a basket case worrying. You'll stay with us until you are feeling much better. That's what friends are for. You've often said that yourself. No arguing, you're staying here."

"That's sweet of you. I do feel more comfortable being here with you. Thank you"

"Tell me what things you want from your house and I'll pick them up for you," Adriana said. I've been there so often I know where most everything is."

"I'm feeling much better now, thanks to all of you. Adriana, I can go with you to get what I need. What a relief I feel, telling you and talking with you. Now if I can only find a way to help bring Marci back I will feel much better.

After the women left, Bráulio spoke to me about Lucio. "I've been friends with Lucio since we were young, long before he even met Fernanda. He has always been into his art strongly even before he went to art school. When his paintings began to sell he was so proud. The money wasn't the big thing, pride in his work and that others appreciated him was. Back then he was the bread winner putting Fernanda through med school. That was, let's see, about thirty years ago. Gradually things changed. At the same time her practice and income grew, his art sold less and less and his income went down. As far back as ten years ago I can remember him slowly changing, becoming resentful and sometimes making bitter remarks. I wasn't bothered much about his reactions at the time. A month ago, we were at the convention in Miami talking about taking this cruise home, and they had a huge blowup about paying for the cruise. Lucio was upset when Fernanda paid for the entire cruise. Even though he had no money to contribute he resented the fact that she did. Somehow she calmed him down and we had a pleasant cruise. Lucio seemed quite happy the whole time. Fernanda was too. She felt no hint of any problem until today. Lucio is really a decent person, or was until the situation finally got to him. I feel so terribly sorry for him. He has become his own worst enemy. I haven't the slightest idea what to do or say. I feel helpless."

"I think the man needs good psychiatric help right now, before he is much worse. I'm sure he's salvageable. Why don't you try to arrange help for him, find a good psychiatrist? Fernanda could help. I'm sure the hospital where she practices has one, if not on staff, then by referral. That might even salvage their marriage. Fernanda's furious now, but with the right help, they might be able to patch things up. My God, how many good years did they enjoy each other? Reconciliation is certainly worth a try."

"I'll talk with Adriana. I'm sure we could do something. Nothing ventured, nothing gained."

FORTY-EIGHT

Ragan decided to bite the bullet and call Reese about Marci. After several calls to track him down, a secretary said finally, "Mr. Reese will be with you in a moment."

"Well, Yoder, this is quite a surprise. I suppose you are calling to inquire about your wife."

"Where is she, Reese? I complied with all of your requests but still heard nothing. Where is she?"

"Right now she is about a hundred miles upriver from Manaus in an Indian village. She's quite well."

"How in hell can you say that? Those villages possess no system of communication other than by river boat."

"That's not so. They communicate village to village by voice messages. Here in Manaus we often receive messages from remote villages that way in two or three days. Don't worry, she's fine."

"Pardon me if I don't believe you. You said you would bring her back to Manaus right away. That was four days ago."

"Things move slowly here on the Amazon. Arrangements to bring her to Manaus could take a month or more ."

"You're stalling. Give me the name of the village, and someone will come to pick her up in one day."

"Things are not that simple. I made a deal with the village elders to deliver certain products in exchange for their taking care of your wife. Once those items are delivered, she will be free to go."

"What products are those?"

"I am not free to divulge that information. You'll have to trust me."

"No way I would ever trust you about anything. Call me and tell me as soon as you decide to free her."

"Where are you exactly? My phone magic does not indicate a location. Why is that."

"You know damned well why. Satellite phones never show a location. It's impossible for them to do so."

"In other words, you could be right across the street from me and I would never know. True or false?"

"True. So what?"

"That means I do not have any idea if you followed my directions and left Manaus or not. Call me on a land line or cell phone, and I'll believe you. Otherwise I won't."

"Okay, you bastard. I'll do that."

Ragan hung up and immediately called the sheriff's office in Warsaw. Ellen answered. "Ellen, do we still run that piggy back phone system?"

"Sure do, what do you want?"

"Dial this number for me and patch this call through."

Within a minute the phone was ringing. Once more after several requests a secretary said, "Mr. Reese will be with you in a moment."

"That must be you. Yoder, you are calling from the KC sheriff's office. How come?"

"That's where I work, stupid. You should have that information."

"Okay. Now I can start the ball rolling to release your wife. She should be in Manaus in two or three weeks."

"I want her sooner than that. I'll fly down for her."

"You'll do no such thing. Your friends here can arrange for her flight and take her to the airport. You can meet her in Miami or Chicago or wherever."

"Tell me where and when."

"Of course."

After Ragan hung up he said to himself, *You miserable bastard. A big surprise is still in store for you.*

"Ragan! Fernanda is on the phone. She wants to talk to you. This time she is excited and happy."

"Wonderful, I'll be right down."

"Okay, Fernanda, what is it?"

"I found Marci. She's in one of my Desanna villages about a hundred miles up river. She's Okay."

"Wonderful! How do we rescue her?"

"The fastest way is to charter a speedboat. That would take us to the village in about four hours up and four hours back. I must go with you."

"How do I charter this speedboat?"

"Call Amazon Speedboat Charters. Here's their number. Advance payment will be required."

"No problem. I'll let you know as soon as things are arranged."

✳ 1:00 pm ✳

They were on the river headed east, upriver by one o'clock. The captain said that as long as he still has light when we leave the village he can take the boat to Manaus. We can see the river by the light of a full moon and the lights of Manaus will guide us into the marina.

✳ 3:45 pm ✳

After flying up the river, they pulled into the dock at the village at quarter to four. No one was near the shore. They got out and Fernanda led them up to the village. When they arrived, they could not believe their eyes. There was Marci in her flower dress and bare feet leading the entire village in a line dance. She saw Fernanda first and ran to her. Then she saw Ragan. In a minute they were wrapped in each other's arms. They stayed that way for a long time, tears of joy running down their faces. The villagers stood around smiling. Fernanda conferred with the chief for some time, then came over to the still entwined couple.

"I thought you'd like to know," Fernanda said. "The chief said the entire village is overjoyed at your happy reunion. They fully understand both the tears and the joy. He also told me that the entire village is in love with you, Marci. You made quite an impression, a fine impression on the villagers. The chief calls you strong white woman and said you are the strongest woman he has ever met. He would like you as one of his wives but understands you belong to Ragan. He also says Ragan must be a powerful chief to have such a woman."

Marci said, "You tell the chief and the entire village that I thank them for their kindness and love them for their friendship. Tell them I will never forget them and the love they showed me. We may speak different languages but managed to communicate extremely well. They are a wonderful, loving people, and I will miss them all. Ragan, that was one of the most wonderful memorable experiences of my entire life. When I first walked into their village, I had no idea the experience would turn out so wonderfully."

Marci ran back to one of the huts to retrieve several gifts the children had made for her. She also removed the Glock in its plastic bag from beneath her sleeping mat and stuck the gun into one of the gift baskets. She joined the entire village as they walked down to the dock. Before they boarded, the chief walked up to Marci and offered her his ceremonial shield. She looked at Fernanda not knowing what to do.

"That, my dear, is the highest honor a chief can bestow on any person. Many hours of hard work with expensive material was required to make that shield. Please accept the gift graciously. He will be crushed if you do not."

She handed the shield to Fernanda, took the chief's shoulders in her hands and pressed both cheeks to his. There were tears in both of their eyes. The villagers stood watching for a long time as their boat went down river. The entire village would remember the "strong white woman" for a long time.

✳ 11:45 pm ✳

They pulled into the Fittipaldi's garage a little before midnight after dropping Fernanda at her home. They had a wonderful reunion with Adriana and Bráulio and stayed up until almost two telling them about the entire episode. They decided to invite Fernanda for dinner on Friday to gather her input from the story.

FORTY-NINE
✳ Friday, February 1, 2013, 9.45 am ✳

Ragan received a satellite call from the KC sheriff's office.

"Ragan. This is Gordy. You're gonna like this important information."

"Shoot, Gordy."

As per your request, we monitored several credit card accounts for unusual activity. We finally hit the jackpot."

"Reese's account?"

"No, Beth McIlheney's. Reese probably used that account thinking it unlikely to be monitored. Two tickets to Dominica for Tuesday were purchased using her credit card. The flight stops in Panama for a couple of hours and arrives in San Juan late afternoon. The flight to Dominica is a puddle jumper that leaves San Juan at six- thirty. The reservations are for Jerome Rumsford and Beth McIlheney."

"Hallelujah and amen. A gift from heaven. I'll be in San Juan right away to prepare a welcome."

"We already contacted the San Juan Police and the Federal Marshall's office in San Juan. We sent copies of the warrants and extradition order just in case. We also told them you would be taking the prisoner back to Indiana."

"We'll wrap things up here quickly, pack up and head out. I want to be in San Juan on Monday at the latest. I'm going to try for Sunday. I made some wonderful and helpful friends here in Manaus. Their connections made this a lot easier. I'll keep you aware of what's going on. Thanks a lot. That's terrific information. Now perhaps we can nail that SOB."

"The entire department is following this and wishes you luck."

"I'll take all the luck I can, good luck that is. We will be back soon. Bye."

Marci was sitting next to Ragan and heard one side of the conversation.

"That was Gordy from Warsaw and I heard we're headed for San Juan and then home after arresting Reese?"

"Yep! We'll pack up, get ready to leave, and say goodbye to our friends here as quickly as we can. First I must call Adriana to discover if she has any way we can be certain that it's Reese on the plane. He could be sending one of his men as a test to see if it's safe for him, and come later. If he does that and we try to arrest him, he will be alerted and our plans will be foiled. I'm calling her right now."

Ragan called Adriana, told her about Reese and asked for her help.

"I'll find out what can be done and call you back. There must be some way to be sure it's him on the plane. All I need to find out is how."

Half an hour later she called back. "Good news. Security takes a photo of each passenger as they board to check against their IDs. At my request, they will send a copy of that photo of Reese to the Marshal's office in San Juan with your name attached. That's a twelve hour flight with one stop in Panama. They arrive in San Juan shortly after four in the afternoon and change planes for Dominica. He must get off the plane and enter the terminal. With almost three hours between his flights, you will have plenty of time to catch him."

"Terrific! You're an angel. How can we thank you, Bráulio, and Fernanda for all the wonderful things you did for us? You are all truly exceptional friends. We'd like to take you all out for dinner this evening. Can you go?"

"We would be delighted. Fernanda is planning to come here for dinner this evening anyway so that will work out well. See you later."

✳ 6:45 pm ✳

They decided to go to the Soho Lounge, a Japanese restaurant with a fabulous reputation not far from the hotel where they first stayed. They had a wonderful evening recalling and recounting many of the adventures and significant happenings they experienced together. Several fabulous toasts were made over the evening. They had a long discussion of where they might meet again. Several suggestions were made before they agreed to keep in touch and try to be together once every couple of years. At midnight they returned to the Fittipaldi's house.

They stayed up talking till nearly three in the morning.

"In twenty four hours our flight leaves for San Juan," Ragan said. "We have a lot to do in the next twenty-four hours so I think we should go to bed."

"It's Saturday," Adriana said. I'm sure we can take care of many things for you after you leave. The packages you are shipping for instance, we can do that for you. All you need do is provide the address."

"We can pack everything we will need in our one big suitcase and the carry on," Marci said. Everything else we can ship, right, Ragan?"

"Right. We'd better head for bed so good night. See you all in the morning."

FIFTY

Marci shook Ragan awake. "Let's move! We've a big day today. Lots to do."

Ragan moaned. "We stayed up way too late last night. You're right though, we had better start moving. You shower first and I'll start packing the first box."

After a knock on the door. Bráulio said, "Okay you two, Adriana says breakfast in fifteen minutes. Can you come down?"

"We'll be right down," Marci said. "We showered and dressed already and are now packing things."

✳   ✳   ✳

A number of sleepy faces sat at the breakfast tale, but soon lively conversation woke everyone.

"How are you going to handle your rental car?" Bráulio asked. "It's not from a normal rental company so you probably cannot use the rental return at the airport."

"Already arranged for, "Ragan said. "The shop that owns it will send a man to the airport to pick it up when we are at the terminal. Fortunately I didn't need the special handling qualities it provided. I did benefit from the special appearance qualities I wanted. Noone would ever think the car was a rental or a vehicle that would attract notice."

By five they had everything packed and ready to go. They could finally relax. They had dinner and sat in the living room talking until after midnight when they had to leave. Another warm and teary session of goodbyes took some time. With the shipping boxes completely full, he decided to check the film case as luggage so he would have no problems with security. He planned to use his law officer badge and papers to take it through. Once he reached San Juan the case would no longer pose a problem.

When security balked at letting the film box through as checked luggage, he unlocked and opened it, showing the empty insides. He told them to call the KC sheriff's office if they doubted his word. Soon the shift supervisor came over and after a short discussion, let the box through as long as it was checked. They slept most of the long flight to Panama, but were awake on the leg to San Juan.

✳ Sunday, February 3, 2013, 4:35 pm ✳

They picked up their rental car and headed for the airport hotel. Ragan called the US Marshal's office and found that the warrants had been received and authenticated. So far everything was moving along smoothly. They had nothing to do until Tuesday morning when they would go to the Marshal's office in Hato Rey and look at the photo of the man who boarded the flight in Manaus. Monday they spent the day being tourists. They drove around San Juan sight seeing. They visited the old fort and did some tourist shopping. Late in the day they found a small restaurant and had dinner. They were back at their hotel by nine.

"We've a big day tomorrow," Ragan said. "I'm going to crash and get a good night's sleep. We can eat a leisurely breakfast in the morning and check out. I'll call Gordy to find out if he has anything new

✳ Tuesday, February 5, 2013, 9:00 am ✳

As they drove up to the Marshal's office, Ragan said, "Well, we approach another moment of truth. Would you bet whether this photo is our man or not?"

Marci smiled. "To quote an old, old saying, I am not a betting man."

"Okay. I guess we'll look and see."

They examined the photo which was definitely of Jerry Reese or Jake Ramsey. Then his satellite phone rang. Gordy was calling.

"Ragan, we've been monitoring the passenger lists from the flight your man was on. Jerome Rumsford got off the plane in Panama along with seven others. Nine passengers boarded the plane for San Juan. He was not one of those passengers. He appears to have stayed in Panama."

"Damn. Wait, can you give me the names of those nine new passengers? ID photos would be helpful also."

"I the names I can give you, but no ID photos. I already asked."

"How many were men?"

"Five."

"Can you tell if any were traveling together? Oh, and can you try to run down any information on the five men?"

"I'll give you the names of those traveling together in a moment. Any run down on the passengers will take awhile. Here, two of the women are traveling together, so too are two of the men. One man is traveling with one of the other women. Does that help?"

"Text me all of that information please. I'll get back to you if I come up with any more questions."

They sat at a small table and Ragan produced a pad of paper.

"First I'll study this information. I'm quite sure one of those new passengers is our man in disguise. Now we must figure out which one by process of elimination. I should be receiving a text with the names in a minute or two."

Marci said, "I got most of that hearing only your conversation over the phone. So our man got off of the plane in Panama and did not get back on as Jerome Rumsford. You will be getting a list of all the new passengers, right?"

"Right. I'm going to need your fine instincts to classify those new passengers from the most likely to the least. Wait, my phone's buzzing with the text . . . I'm listing those traveling alone first, second the guys traveling together, then the rest . . . now, all of them are listed."

Marci said, "You didn't list the women. I think that's a mistake. That's the same flight we took yesterday and we had almost a two-hour layover. That's plenty of time for a man to change into a disguise as a woman."

"Good point."

"Only one woman is traveling alone. Her name is June Rice. Notice the initials? I'll bet that's your man."

"I thought you weren't a betting man."

"No, but I could be a betting woman," Marci said with a huge grin.

Ragan was immediately on the phone with Gordy. "Try to find out anything you can about a passenger named June Rice who boarded in Panama. Oh and find out how she paid for her ticket. Call me as soon as you learn anything."

His phone rang almost immediately. Gordy again. "Well you are on the right track. Beth McIlheney paid for her tickets. So far we've found no records of a June Rice in anything related. We'll keep checking."

"I'll tell you what happens after we figure out how to penetrate that disguise. Bye."

Ragan looked at Marci and said, "We have almost six hours to come up with a way to figure out which female passenger is June Rice and find any other likely suspects and figure out whom they are. Again we'll use a process of elimination. We should speak to the Marshals and find out if they can provide any manpower to help. The warrants are in their possession you know."

Ragan went to the desk and was soon talking with Marshal Gregory Zim. The marshal was already on the case because of the warrants and was glad to meet Ragan. He told Zim about June Rice and his suspicion that she is actually Jerry Reese, the man named in the warrants.

"You know they all go through customs, don't you?" Zim said.

"Even if they are not staying here? I thought anyone who is proceeding to another country and not staying in Puerto Rico could wait in the International zone and not go through customs."

"Not so in Puerto Rico. If you change planes here, you must go through customs and immigration. Only those who stay on their plane can skip customs inspection. They must provide identification. If we flag a name, they will hold that individual for us to make a closer examination. If you provide me with a list of names, we will check each one of them out.

Sometimes with a dangerous criminal, we place a blue tag on their papers or luggage. We apprehend them in the passage way outside where a lot less people are present."

"Sounds effective," Marci said. "Does this happen often?"

"More often than we would like. You wouldn't believe how stupid some of these criminals or fugitives are and what they try to pull. I've seen IDs that were so bad they look like they were made with a kid's crayon set. Then we find the truly clever ones with authentic appearing IDs. Some of those slip through. With the information you provided on Reese, I doubt he will slip through. Still, he could."

"How is that possible?" Marci asked.

"They sometimes pull what we refer to as a double switch. Like in this case, we are fairly sure June Rice is our man. Suppose she is a fake and Reese is actually taking another plane under still another name? While we are occupied with Rice, he comes through with authentic looking papers under another name unknown to us. We've seen that several times."

"Great. Do you have any suggestions as to how we can give it our best shot?"

"Yes, take the list you have, prioritize it, and give it to us. We'll stop each of those and will probably pass them in less than a minute unless something is fishy. If that happens we will do a thorough investigation. We miss few at that point. Does he know what either of you look like?"

"He probably does," Ragan said. "My guess is his people have photographs. They abducted Marci in Manaus."

"Please stay out of sight from those coming through customs. If he sees you he could be spooked. This could make our job much more difficult. Near customs is a small waiting room where you will not be observed until they pass completely through. By then the guilty party or parties will be under arrest."

"Thanks, Marshal Zim. I hope all goes well this afternoon."

"We're quite well prepared so I am confident things will go as planned."

"Hopefully Murphy's law will not prevail. See you later at customs."

They walked out of the Marshals' office and drove back toward the airport searching for a restaurant for lunch. They found the White Lotus Asian Bistro and relaxed for a leisurely lunch.

Ragan leaned back. "Well sweetie, with any luck we should be on our way home tomorrow, if all goes well today. I listed us on the earliest flight I could find, a United non-stop at 2:10 tomorrow afternoon. We arrive at O'Hare at quarter after six."

"How are we taking our prisoner to Warsaw?"

"Gordy will meet us at O'Hare with a police wagon. Your son will pick us up in our truck, and we can head for home. With good luck we will be home by nine-thirty, ten at the latest."

"We could stay at Bruce and Miriam's for a visit of a day or two. I don't visit them often enough."

"Sure, if you want to. Why don't you ask them when you call to arrange our being picked up? Of course, none of this is a done deal until Reese is in custody. I hope nothing goes wrong."

"You can say that again."

✳ 2:40 pm ✳

They drove to the airport, parked, and headed for Customs where they met Marshal Zim and several others.

"You are here in force. That's encouraging," Ragan said

Zim smiled. "Ragan, I did a bit of checking on you, you know, routine checks of your history. We always do so to make sure. You have quite a reputation in Chicago. Voted 'Top Cop' by your fellow officers, that's quite an honor. How come you are now part of the sheriff's office in a small town in Indiana? That's quite a switch."

Ragan laughed. "I retired a few years ago to where I grew up and went to high school. I love the place, that's why. A good friend got me to help the locals with a couple of cases and before long, well, here I am. I work at my own pace, don't take on a full load of cases, and thoroughly enjoy the work."

"I definitely won't ask how you came to be chasing a thief in South America with your lovely wife along. I'm afraid that would take far too long to tell."

Ragan laughed heartily. "You're right. It's quite complicated and would take a long time to explain. Let's say I'm mixing business with pleasure."

"Good answer," Zim said with a wide grin. "Now I'd better check my men and make sure they're ready. Sometimes these flights come in half an hour or more early. We are ready for that. Oh yes, we do use a cover story for those we take aside. The story is we are making random special checks of about one passenger in every ten."

✳ 3:40 pm ✳

The plane was indeed twenty minutes early. Everyone was in place. Ragan and Marci were in the little room and passengers began streaming into the area after getting their luggage. The Embraer aircraft holds only 74 passengers so for them to go through customs won't take long. Almost immediately as they began coming through the customs check, one of the marshals took a man aside. After talking to him and examining his ID, he was let go.

A ruckus erupted in the hallway. A woman was struggling with two marshals

"I'll bet that's our man," Ragan said. "Look, they're putting him or her in handcuffs. Now they've pulled off his wig. It's Reese for sure. Wait, now they are holding another woman in handcuffs. That one is obviously a woman, no doubt. I'll bet that's Beth McIlheney."

Marshal Zim motioned for Ragan to come over. Marci stepped out of the room and waited nearby. As soon as he got close enough, he recognized Reese from photos he had seen.

"I think this is your man, Ragan," Zim said.

"That's him for sure, Zim. No doubt."

Reese sneered at Ragan, "Now your wife will never come out of the jungle you damned fool."

Ragan laughed in his face and pointed. "Notice the lovely lady over there in the green dress? that's my wife, Marci. Not only did she enjoy her stay in the village, but they adored her. If any of your people ever go back to the village they will find Marci is a legend among the natives. They even named her, Strong White Woman. Soon you'll be facing a judge in court in Warsaw. I will guarantee you he will not refer to you as Strong White Man."

Ragan turned to Zim. "We made reservations on a United flight to Chicago tomorrow afternoon. Will all the paperwork be ready for me to take him?"

"Most is all set. The warrants from Indiana are okay and we both need to sign the transfer papers which are with me in my briefcase. He'll sit in our holding cell until you come for him tomorrow. Good luck, by the way. You've transported prisoners before, and Reese doesn't seem to me to be a violent man, but I'd still keep him cuffed."

"I will, thanks. What about the woman? We have no interest in her. She's just a name to us."

"We'll find out if she has any outstanding warrants and if not, we'll release her."

"Marci and I are going to do a bit more sight seeing. We'll pick him up by noon. Bye."

FIFTY-ONE

Ragan and Reese, cuffed together were seated in the boarding area. Marci was seated across from them.

Reese leaned over and whispered to Ragan, "You know, I have scads of money. I could pay you plenty to slip those handcuffs off and let me escape. This could happen in the men's room and nobody would know."

Ragan almost doubled over in laughter. "And what ever made you think you could bribe me successfully?"

"Policemen do not make much money, I know. Half a million in a Swiss bank account could be yours if you let me escape."

Again Ragan laughed. "Reese, your total net worth is between three and four million. Few people ever learn how much I'm worth because I don't tell anyone. In your case I'll make an exception. If I wanted to, I could buy and sell you, your houses and companies and hardly miss a step. My net worth is more than ten times yours, all honestly gained. Now shut up and think about where you'll be for the next eight or ten years. Will any of your property still be yours when you are released?"

Completely beaten, Reese slumped back in his seat. Across the aisle, Marci was talking to her son, Bruce on her cell phone. When she hung up, she turned toward Ragan.

"Bruce will pick us up. He says the weather is quite cold and snowy and they will bring our winter things and meet us inside the terminal. They would love for us to stay a few days."

"There's no reason why we couldn't. Once I turn moron here over to Gordy, I won't be needed until the trial. Now I'm going to call one of my friends on the Chicago Police. They will send an officer to meet us and accompany Reese to our prisoner transport vehicle. Gordy said it would be their SUV if available."

✳ 6:30 pm ✳

When they walked off the plane, Gordy was waiting with two Chicago policemen. After introductions, Ragan transferred the cuffs from his wrist to Gordy's. Both officers were known by Ragan when he was on the force. They talked over old times as they walked through the terminal. After Gordy left with Reese, they climbed into Bruce's car and were off to his home.

The visit with Bruce, Miriam, and their two girls stretched into Sunday. When they finally walked into Marci's house late Sunday afternoon, they were greeted with their shipping boxes on the back porch. While in Puerto Rico they arranged for their luggage in Miami to be sent to them the end of the week. They were both tired of travel and happy to be able to relax at home.

"Let's not tell anyone we're home for a day or two," Marci said. "I'd like to unpack and put our things away before I tackle everything that piled up while we were gone. I must go to the hospital in the morning. I phoned Doris when we were in Puerto Rico but couldn't tell her exactly when we would be back. She's the one person I'll call right now."

Ragan waited, grinning. "Is that everything? If so, I'll go take the rest of the things out of the truck and bring them in while you talk to Doris. Unless I miss my guess you'll be on the phone for an hour or more. By that time, I'll unpack all the boxes and our suitcases. The dirty clothes will go in the laundry room, and everything else will be ready to put away. Tomorrow, when you go to the hospital, I'll go to the sheriff's to learn what's happening. I'll also be bogged down with one huge report to write and file."

✳ August ✳

Over the next few months a lot of changes were made. Ragan's house was completed and they moved in. They decided to marry in September and began planning the wedding. With the merging of two households they gave quite a bit of furniture and household items away, putting those things they did not want to part with in storage. They decided to have a house warming party in August which was a huge success. After the party Ragan and Marci were relaxing on the couch looking out over the lake.

Macri turned and looked directly at Ragan. "Dear man, are you ready for a real shock?"

Ragan immediately sat bolt upright. "You sound serious. What is it?"

"I hope it isn't too much of a shock?"

"For God's sake, Marci what is it? Tell me."

"I had my annual physical last week at the hospital. When the doctor spoke to me about it after, I received a real shock. I hardly know how to tell you.'"

"Oh, my God! What's wrong? Is it serious?"

"Nothing's really wrong, but it is serious, unlikely and almost impossible."

Ragan was visibly shaken. "Before I have a heart attack, tell me, please."

"Ragan, I'm 52, soon to be 53, and . . . I'm pregnant!"

SOME PHOTOS OF PLACES AND THINGS IN THE STORY

Ragan's quiet-looking fire-breathing S10 pickup

Ragan's house on Kalorama Road from the lake. It faces southwest by west. The Hobie 16 sailboat sits on its rack on the beach.

Top photo - detail of Willow bend

Bottom photo - Tippy narrows at Willow Bend

❶ Ragan's house on Kalorama Road.

❷ The sailboat accident occurred here.